For David,
for Abigail and for Jamie

Excerpt from *The Guardian Stage News*
Macbeth review – stunning discovery in Nazari

"This controversial and stylised production of 'Macbeth' by the theatre world's most iconoclastic director relies on bizarre effects to portray the darkness of the play. Dressed in black, for these are the spirits of the night, the Weird Sisters are more subhuman than supernatural. And a number of the younger actors disappoint. But there is one glorious exception to the indifferent acting. Alice Nazari, though herself fresh from drama school, is magnificent as Lady Macbeth. The decision to cast an actress of African-Iranian heritage as Lady M. defied convention. And yet Alice Nazari commands the stage as Shakespeare's most dauntless and strong-willed female character; decidedly malevolent and convincingly paranoid, she truly embodies the spirit of the play, and takes on a heart of darkness. Remember the name, for, if her talent is properly managed, she has a glittering future ahead of her."

# CHAPTER ONE

Zoe ran through the wood in gathering dusk, her heart racing. She clutched the child's hand, which kept slipping out of hers.

Sweat drenched her blouse, sticking it to her jacket, despite the dank chill in the air. They pounded along a narrow bramble-choked path. Zoe winced and the child sobbed, as spiky stems tore at their clothes and flesh, drawing blood.

Their breathing came fast and jagged. They had miles ahead of them with no prospect of rest, running for their lives.

They came out into a field. Her chest burning, and tears stinging her eyes, Zoe paused to wipe sweat and hair away, both from her face and from the child's. Before them was a ditch, filled with mud, half-hidden by low-hanging field maples. She twisted round and saw their pursuer burst out from among the trees on the opposite side of the field. Zoe seized the child in her arms, and plunged into the ditch, fighting her way through the twigs and branches of the trees beyond it. The child screamed and clung to her, soaked in mud, scratched and bruised...

Zoe sat up in bed with a shriek. Theo woke, rolled over and held her close.

"Zoe, Zoe," he moaned, "not another nightmare, surely?"

"Yes," she whispered. "The child... we were running through a wood... someone was trying to kill us."

Theo's heart beat fast against hers. He looked at her, perplexed, stroking her hair and face.

"Calmer now?" he said after a couple of minutes.

She nodded.

"You're safe. I love you," he said.

They both lay down and Theo went back to sleep. But Zoe lay awake for a long while, thinking about the dream.

It was still only three in the morning.

"What's the matter, Alice?" asked Zoe in the reception office later, gazing at her colleague, seated diagonally across from her.

Alice's milk-chocolate-coloured skin gleamed in the light from the window, as did her thick black hair, tied in a high ponytail. Her forehead creased into a look of concern.

"Sorry," she said, "that dream of yours gives me the creeps. I don't mean to scare you any more, Zoe, but… well, I've had a few weird things happen to *me* lately…" She stopped as the reception door opened, and two guests came in carrying their luggage.

Zoe jumped up.

"Brian and Jasper," she cried, "ready to leave? It's been so good getting to know you both this week."

"Thanks, Zoe," said Brian. "It's been an amazing week."

"We've both found so much here," said Jasper.

"Even though I made a mess of my marbling technique," remarked Brian, "and Jasper's pot broke in the kiln."

"We got something far more important out of it though," added Jasper. "Peace, tranquility, soul…"

Zoe smiled warmly at them both.

"I'm so pleased," she said.

"Before we go," said Brian, "we need to tell you something. As we crossed the courtyard we saw a seriously scruffy guy stumbling along the path, past the barn."

"Didn't look like a guest," added Jasper.

Brian laughed.

Zoe pursed her lips. "Scruffy, you say?"

"Yeah, looked a bit like a tramp."

Zoe glanced at Alice, who'd raised her eyebrows.

"Which direction was he heading?" she asked.

"Away from us, towards the lawn, as if he'd already crossed the courtyard. But you'd have seen him if he'd gone past your office window."

"Ok," said Zoe. "Thanks for telling us. I'll go and check him out."

She saw him as soon as she walked out of reception. He'd now reached the lawn. That day they had three guests on the property; those who'd chosen to stay on from the previous week. Apart from them, there should only be staff around. The new guests for next week's creative arts course were not due to arrive until the following day.

And he looked nothing like any of their three remaining guests.

A twig cracked beneath his feet as he trod on it. She hurried after him, calling out, "Excuse me."

He turned and glared at her.

In the past, Zoe had preferred to keep her experience of vagrants safely behind the doors of a drop-in centre. She'd helped out in one during her university vacation, five years before, in south London.

But here in this beautiful Gloucestershire valley he seemed strangely out of place. Zoe guessed he'd made his way along the lane from the nearest village, a mile away, where perhaps he'd have been hoping for a food handout. She imagined he was now trying his luck here too.

He wore a long, filthy raincoat. Bloodshot eyes held her in scrutiny; thick beard and matted hair; half-full bottle of wine in his hand.

She was determined to be kind and helpful.

"Hello," she said. "Can I help you?"

He grunted. A stench of sweat came to her nostrils.

"What do you want?" she asked softly.

The tramp moved close, and opened his mouth as if to speak. She smelt his foul breath. Then he spat on the ground, in front of her feet. She recoiled.

"Don't do that," she said. "I just want to help you."

He threw her a look of contempt, and slunk away, this time towards the south, disappearing along the path which led past the converted goose house, in the direction of the car park. She drew in her breath. If he'd been less aggressive she'd have been only too happy to give him some food. And now she was worried that he might be tempted to break into one of the cars.

She'd need to find Bernie, their veteran house manager, and ask for help. She turned quickly towards the courtyard. She'd seen Bernie earlier, going to do some work in one of the cabins.

Then she saw a child in front of her. She stopped dead. A little girl: long fair hair, wearing a green dress. She seemed to be four or five years old, and Zoe saw no adult with her. As centre administrator Zoe knew the name of each guest. There was no child among them.

"Hello," said Zoe. She smiled. "Are you lost?"

"Where's my daddy?" asked the little girl.

"Your daddy?" repeated Zoe. "I don't know. What's his name? What does he look like?"

The child made no reply. Instead, she looked through Zoe.

Confused, Zoe swung round, expecting to see the child's father. But there was no one. Then Vito barked. Distracted, Zoe glanced away towards the east. Perhaps their golden labrador had found the tramp. But no, he bounded alone amongst the lower branches of the conifer trees.

Zoe turned back again to the little girl. She'd gone. Zoe's

mouth went dry. She rubbed her eyes, but when she put her hands down again, there was still no sign of the child. Zoe hadn't expected her to move so fast.

She looked around her, perplexed. Then her stomach tightened.

"Oh my God! Where's she gone? Suppose she went in the same direction as the tramp?"

Terrified the child might meet up with the vagrant and get into some kind of trouble, she was about to run up the path to the car park when she heard a familiar voice behind her.

"Hi there, Zoe."

She whirled. A silver-haired man appraised her, with an amused light in his eye.

"Bernie," she said. "Thank God." She always felt safe with Bernie around – he had already spent three decades working as a house manager with a much bigger conference centre in Yorkshire, before he took this job down in the Cotswolds. For Zoe, he was almost like a grandfather-figure. "I've just seen a little girl who was asking for her father. I looked away for one moment and when I turned back she'd gone."

"I've not seen anyone here with a child," he said.

"That's not all. Just a few moments before, I saw this foul-looking tramp with a bottle. He went up the path to the car park. I thought he might break into one of the cars. But what worries me now is what's happened to that child. Suppose she's still wandering around lost and she gets tangled up with him."

"Ok, Zoe. Calm down. I'll deal with it," Bernie said. "I'll go myself right now, and look for them."

He whistled, and their golden labrador bounded up to him.

"Good boy, Vito. Come on. We're on a hunt," he said. Man and dog then hurried up the path.

"Thanks, Bernie," she called.

Zoe returned to the office, nervous and jittery. She felt a certain sense of relief that Bernie was on the track of the tramp and child, but she still wouldn't be settled in her mind till he'd reported back. Meanwhile, hopefully she could have a chat with Alice about those 'weird' experiences she'd mentioned earlier, and find out why she'd reacted like that to Zoe's account of her dream.

But as she entered, the phone rang. Alice took the call.

"Good morning. Celtic Knot Creative Arts Centre." She listened then looked up at Zoe. "Zoe, do you know anyone called James Willoughby?"

"James Willoughby?" Zoe said. "Well, if it's the one I'm thinking of, yes, I do know him, from a few years back. Why?"

Alice tucked the phone under her chin and typed another few words on her keyboard. "Yes, Zoe remembers you. No, that's fine. You'll see a marked route round the front of the building to the reception at the back. There's a notice on the door. Come straight in."

She put the phone down.

"So, you knew him before. Ex-lover?"

"No way – not *him*!" said Zoe. Then she became reflective. "James Willoughby," she mused, drumming her fingers on the desk. "Wonder why *he's* turned up? *You'll* find something in common with him, Alice. He's an actor."

"Is he?" said Alice. "Ought I to have heard of him?"

Zoe laughed. "Do I detect some professional rivalry there?"

"Not at all," protested Alice. "Go on, jog my memory."

"*Journey to the Scaffold*. Seen it? 18 certificate; he played the priest."

"Oh God, I do know it, yes. The critics slated it, didn't they?"

Zoe smiled. "He may not like to be reminded."

"I promise to be the soul of tact," said Alice. She turned back to her computer and continued clattering at the keyboard. Zoe remained standing, ready to greet the new arrival.

A few minutes later, the office door opened, and two people stepped in: a man and a woman.

The man scrutinised Zoe, his expression keen and intelligent, while his companion fell back behind him. He wore a classic charcoal slim-fit suit with a blue check shirt. A wave of cologne assaulted her senses. Armani Code, she guessed, pleased at the sharpness of her own recall. She'd sniffed some in House of Fraser on the Promenade in Cheltenham just the Saturday before. He radiated style and confidence.

Then he strode forward and grasped Zoe's hand.

"Zoe," he said. "What a delight to catch up with old friends; and to find you as gorgeous as ever." His tone was clear-cut. "How could anyone forget your red-gold hair and those wild green eyes?"

"Thank you, James," she said, freeing her hand as quickly as she could, and taking two or three steps backwards. When she'd known James before she'd preferred to keep her distance. If he came too close, she felt smothered. "Not so wild these days, I hope. Well, this is a… nice surprise to see you here."

"I should have called in on you much sooner. I've been planning to, ever since I first came across your website. What a lot of changes in only three years. I expect the Reverend Theo is the moving force behind that. Is he around?"

"No, he's at a meeting in Birmingham. And you need only call him Theo."

"Of course. I look forward to seeing him when he gets back, and catching up with him again. I must admit it came as rather a shock when I first discovered you two had got married. I simply hadn't picked you out as at all likely to marry a priest. And that would have been not long after you and I last saw each other."

"Yes," she said.

"Just a few months later, in fact," he remarked. "I found out from your homepage."

Zoe nodded. She turned to indicate Alice, who sat with elbow on desk, chin resting on her thumb, index finger pointing up towards her face. "And here's our bookings secretary, Alice Nazari."

"Pleased to meet you," said Alice, removing her elbow from the desk.

James gave a small bow. "The pleasure's all mine."

Then he indicated his companion, who'd just moved to stand beside him, drawing Zoe's eye as she did so.

"Natasha – let me introduce you to these two ladies." Natasha nodded, a sweet, solemn expression on her face.

Zoe caught her breath.

"Natasha Morrigan," said James.

Natasha stood a few centimetres higher than James; and Zoe knew *him* to be well above average height himself, being six-feet tall. Natasha's pale skin seemed translucent. Her eyes were a startling sapphire blue, and her ash-blonde hair fell loose to her waist, with several braids plaited into it. The soft folds of her long white silk dress floated around her with every movement. She was the loveliest woman Zoe had ever met; though she did think Natasha's silk dress a strange choice for cool autumn weather in the countryside.

Regarding Zoe with a calm expression, Natasha gave Zoe her hand. Natasha's hold was firm, but not too much so, and she released it at just the right moment, before she turned her attention to Alice, and shook her hand too.

James's gaze had been fixed on Natasha all this while, his lips slightly parted, eyes wide open.

Then, seeming to recollect himself, he swung to face Zoe once more. "You may have noticed me on the big screen since we last met."

"Yes," she said.

"What did you think?" he asked.

"Strong story," she said, "but your fate was a bit too graphic for me."

James sighed. "Yes. And I went largely unnoticed by the critics."

Zoe cleared her throat, ready to say something appropriate, but Alice broke in.

"I was offered work as an extra on that film," she said, "but I passed on it."

"Oh?" James turned his gaze on her.

"Alice is an actor too, James," said Zoe.

"I trained at Bristol," said Alice. "I'm waiting to hear from my agent about new work. I help out here part-time."

James raised his eyebrows. "So what are you doing here in the Cotswolds, Alice? All your big opportunities will be in London. Shouldn't you be on the spot?"

"A lot of people think that," said Alice coolly. "Some of my friends from drama school went to London hoping for an acting job; and they're having a really tough time. I'm glad I've stayed in Cirencester with my mum for the time being, and that I've got this job. It suits me fine while I'm waiting for a part. And Zoe and Theo understand my situation. I can be on a train to London in half an hour if my agent calls with an audition."

"Fair enough," said James, his eyes trained on her.

Zoe had heard a lot about this from Alice, ever since she'd persuaded Theo and their chair of trustees, Jessica, to appoint Alice to the job six weeks before. They'd all known it was a risk. Alice could be up and off as soon as she won a part. But it was a risk Zoe was happy to take because she liked Alice so much and believed she was exactly right for this centre. And – though she didn't dare admit it to Jessica – she felt something special, too, for Alice, because she herself had as a child dreamed of becoming a film actress.

"I've been based in London myself since I saw you last, Zoe," said James. "Should still have some of my cards left; do take one." He drew a card from his pocket and handed it to her.

She studied it then passed it to Alice to read.

James Willoughby, PhD, Actor

Equity member

For casting enquiries, contact my agent

And there followed a London address.

"So you no longer hold your academic post at Edinburgh University?" enquired Zoe. "I thought you were a research fellow there?"

"Used to be," said James.

Before he could expand on the subject, Natasha gave a light laugh. "James is far too busy now to continue his academic career."

"Busy with acting?" asked Zoe.

Natasha shook her head, smiling, but gave no further details.

"So, James," said Zoe, "what brings you and Natasha to visit us today?"

James thrust his hands into both pockets. "A great discovery."

"That sounds exciting," she replied.

"Yes. Recently I've been interested in looking up my family and researching my history; and I've traced my father's line back to the sixteenth century."

"Fantastic."

"So imagine how thrilled I was," said James, "when I learned my fifteen-times great-grandfather was the very yeoman farmer who built this house."

Zoe's eyes opened wide. "Wow. You sure?"

"Oh, it was a long process," said James. "Sometimes, of course, it's impossible to get hold of birth, marriage and death certificates. They weren't issued prior to the nineteenth century. Churches recorded births and deaths but not all records survive. But good evidence links me through to one Thomas Willoughby, 1503-1562, a *'man well at ease and having honestlie to live, and yet not a gentleman'*. He acquired the lands around here, and in 1532 he built this house, then called *Owlecotes*."

"And did the house pass down through his descendants for the next few generations?" enquired Zoe.

"Yes. But during the late 1600s, one of them must have sold it on, for it passed out of the family."

"Fascinating," said Zoe. "This house is, of course, full of stories."

"Yes," broke in Alice, "because spirits lie hidden in the timbers."

James chuckled. "Well put, Alice," he said. He turned back to Zoe. "As fellow actors, we understand each other."

James snapped into a brisk tone of voice. "So, Zoe," he said, "you and Theo have added a reception office here, and carried out other building work. Listed planning consent must have taken a long time."

"Several months," said Zoe. "Theo and I are employed by the Trust. They make the decisions."

Meanwhile, she noted, Natasha began to walk around the office, looking at things – books, labels on files, pictures on the wall.

"Yes, noticed a section on your website about the trustees.

Didn't get into it though," said James. "Great design, by the way. And this set-up – creative arts centre – wonderful idea."

Zoe wondered what James's relationship with Natasha was. She'd rather expected him to volunteer this information. Natasha had no ring on her finger. But from the expression in James's eye whenever he looked at her, she deduced that they were lovers.

James continued speaking. "I enjoyed reading Theo's vision statement on the homepage."

"Thank you." Zoe looked back at James again. He was – on the surface – charming, just as he had been before. But even so, there was, for her, still that disturbing note. She decided to have a word with Alice about it later, when James and Natasha had gone. For Alice had a special 'sensitivity' about people, Zoe understood. Alice described it as a 'sixth sense'. It was a gift she'd been born with. She saw pictures in her mind's eye, and then read those pictures as energy that told a story.

"Any chance we can book in for a course?" said James.

Zoe started.

"Sure we're right for you?" she asked. She caught Alice's glance, but couldn't interpret the message in it.

"Oh, yes," said James. "We'd love it. Do please tell me if you have any vacancies this week."

"This week? That's very short notice." But Zoe knew they had some spare places.

Alice reached for the diary, which was open at the current week. James came and glanced at it with her.

Zoe felt a sense of disdain. She joined Alice herself, and saw the vacancies in the schedule.

"Double room?" she said between gritted teeth.

"Oh no. Separate." Natasha had finished her survey of the office, and was seated on one of the easy chairs.

Zoe stared at her. Then she pulled her gaze away.

James cleared his throat. "Is the goose house still available as ensuite accommodation?" he asked.

"Yes it is," said Alice.

"Then it's ideal for Natasha," James said. "Is there another room available for me?"

"Well," said Alice, "there *is* one free room on the first floor, right next to the inglenook chimney stack."

"Perfect," said James. "I'm thrilled. What a stroke of luck, us calling in like this, with a free week ahead of us; though we had hoped that, as it's autumn, you might have some spare places."

Zoe wondered what Theo would make of the new arrivals.

"What strange twists and turns life takes," James observed, studying Zoe's face.

"Any plans to start a family, Zoe?" Natasha enquired.

"No, not right now. We're both so busy with the centre."

Natasha's eyes seemed to penetrate Zoe's.

"Don't leave it too long, will you?" she said.

With an intense effort, Zoe tore her gaze away. She and Theo had been trying for a baby all this year. That was information they'd shared only with Alice.

She turned to a pile of paperwork on the desk and picked up a couple of A4 sheets.

"We need each of you to fill out a booking form," she said.

"Of course." Natasha got up and came to stand beside James. They both completed their forms. Zoe saw that Natasha gave a different London address to his.

"We'll collect our luggage and bring it into the entrance hall," said James. "Then I should love to show Natasha through the house."

"When you're ready," said Zoe, "come back, and I'll take you both through the ground-floor rooms."

James nodded, and they left the office, nearly bumping into Bernie.

He acknowledged them courteously then came into the office.

"Bernie!" said Zoe. "Did you find the little girl?"

"No. Sorry. No sign of her," replied Bernie. "Nor the tramp either. I combed the grounds. Vito would have sniffed them out, I'm sure."

"Oh dear," said Zoe. She bit her lip. Then she noticed the look on Alice's face.

"What little girl?" Alice asked.

"Have to get on. See you later," said Bernie, disappearing out through the doorway.

As soon as the door closed, Zoe shared with Alice the story of her two encounters near the barn earlier that morning.

Alice stared at her. Zoe felt uncomfortable.

"Did you say the child looked *through* you?" asked Alice.

"Yes. Alice, what's the problem? You've been a bit down in the last couple of days. I couldn't help noticing. And earlier you said something about *weird experiences*."

Alice nodded. "I'd love to tell you. But I feel I'd sooner share it with both you and Theo. Can I wait until he's free to hear as well?"

"Well yes, of course, if you don't mind coming back here this evening at about six."

"That's fine."

"Now, Alice, tell me what you think of James and Natasha."

Alice shook her head. "Only this," she said. "When I looked at them both I saw one of my mental pictures. It was of a tarantula on a jewelled mask."

When Zoe spoke again there was a tremor in her voice. "What on earth do you mean by that?"

"Sixth sense," said Alice. "How did you know James before?"

"About four years ago, I came to this house when it was in

14

the hands of the previous owner," said Zoe. "I was a different person then, Alice. A New Age group occupied the house, and I was attracted here."

"You've kept that dark!" said Alice. "Why didn't you tell me before?"

"Didn't want to," admitted Zoe. "Preferred to put all that behind me."

Alice considered this. "Tell me more."

"Theo arrived a few days after I did. You know him; he's all about people on spiritual journeys. And not long afterwards, he and I fell in love. But to make the rest of it brief – James was a member of the group. The leader had been his PhD student at Edinburgh University. So, that's how I met him."

"Hmm," said Alice, resting her chin on her hands. "I'll save what I think about James and Natasha till our meeting later. But meanwhile I feel I have to tell you this: your dream and the little girl you saw…"

"Yes?"

Alice's eyes opened wide.

"They're not just a coincidence. They're serious. I'll tell both you and Theo why later."

With this ominous remark, Zoe had to be satisfied.

The library door opened at six o'clock and Theo stepped in from the entrance hall. The library was a warm, inviting room, furnished with a large, round table and a group of armchairs, and lined with well-filled bookshelves.

Theo closed the door behind him, went straight to Zoe where she stood beside the lamp which she'd just switched on, took her face in both hands, and kissed her. Then, letting go of her, he brushed his fair hair off his forehead whilst holding her in a tender gaze.

"What's up, Zoe? You look flushed."

Zoe caught a glimpse of their reflection in the oak-framed mirror to the left of the door: a loving couple, who appeared in the glowing lamplight to be surrounded by a golden aura.

"Yes, a bit jumpy," she admitted, "with all that's happened today."

He squeezed her hand. The door opened again.

"Alice," Theo said. "Come and join us."

"Thanks."

He drew out a chair for her from the round oak table and they all seated themselves.

"Ok, Alice," began Theo. "You've come back in again today, because you wanted to tell us something. Go ahead."

"Call me supersensitive if you wish," said Alice, "but I knew I couldn't keep this to myself any longer, when Zoe first told me about the dream she had last night: running with a child through a wood, both in fear for their lives. Then when she saw a little girl near the barn this morning who asked for her daddy, then disappeared; I knew this was serious."

"We're intrigued," said Theo. "Tell us more."

"Before Zoe's dream, I'd decided to keep quiet about this. But that's changed now. You see, I've had three weird experiences in the past few weeks; all to do with a young child."

Zoe's mouth went dry. She sat forward with her elbows on the table.

"*Three weird experiences*?" she said.

"Yes. And even now I still wonder whether I should tell you. They're quite unsettling. Might even make things worse." She reached for her bag, almost as if planning to leave.

Theo put a hand on her arm. "Stay. We want to hear your stories."

"Are you sure? They're about ghosts," said Alice.

# CHAPTER TWO

Zoe gave a start. Both she and Theo refocused on Alice.

"Do you believe in ghosts?" asked Alice.

"Yes, I do, as it happens," said Theo. "I've seen them myself."

Zoe glanced at the door. She'd felt a cold draught.

She saw the door was ajar. She got up straightaway and went over, first checking out in the entrance hall to see if the front door was open. It was closed. She walked back into the library and shut the door behind her. She'd sooner they had this conversation with nobody else overhearing.

"And you, Zoe?" enquired Alice.

"Yes, I believe too," said Zoe. "But Theo – you've seen them? When? Where?"

"My story will wait," replied Theo. "It concerns ghostly monks. Let's hear Alice's story right now."

Zoe wriggled into a more comfortable position on her chair.

"Go on, Alice," she said.

"OK. I babysit now and again for families on holiday in the area. I sat for a family not far from here, one Saturday, six weeks ago.

"The house is built down the side of a steep slope, with three levels. The front door leads to a hallway on the ground floor. Downstairs on the mid-level, are the bedrooms. The sitting room's on the lowest level.

"On this Saturday evening, we chatted for a few minutes. The parents had put the children to bed before I arrived and said they should be asleep very soon. Then they left, locking the front door behind them and taking the key. They'd given me a key which I could use to open the door, should there be any need.

"I began to walk downstairs to the bedrooms. As I did so, the temperature dropped.

"I couldn't work it out. After all, it was August. I went down to the sitting room to watch TV. After ten minutes, the cold sensation passed.

"A few hours later, I turned the TV off and began to read a book.

"A thud hit the ceiling above my head. Footsteps crossed the ceiling. The top-level front door opened, and slammed shut. I jumped up at once, to go and check on the children. As I ran upstairs, I glanced at my watch. It was twenty-past midnight. I thought the parents must be back though I wasn't expecting them until about one o'clock.

"As I got to the bedroom door there was complete silence. I'd heard no sound of gravel crunching outside the front door or of footsteps on the stairs to the mid-level.

"Poppy, aged four, sat up in bed, and seemed uneasy. Her older brother, Tom, lay curled up. But he too was awake. There was no sign of the parents.

"'Anything wrong?' I asked.

"'No,' said Poppy.

"'Did you get out of bed?'

"'No,' the little girl replied.

"Neither child could explain further, but Poppy seemed a bit scared by my questions. I comforted her then went upstairs to the entrance, and tried the front door. It was locked. I went back downstairs. Nothing else happened and the parents came back at one thirty. I said nothing about it to them. I said goodbye and drove home. During the next week, I came here every morning and worked as usual, and as you know, didn't mention the incident. However, the couple asked me to babysit again the following Saturday.

"Remembering the incident, I was a bit unnerved. Then I tried to convince myself it had just been my imagination.

"After the parents had left, I made myself a cup of coffee, and sat and watched TV.

"At twenty-past midnight, the same thing happened.

"I froze, as the footsteps crossed the ceiling: heavy, deliberate footsteps; not those of a child. I leapt to my feet and ran upstairs and into the children's bedroom. As I did so, the front door banged. This time the children clung together, staring at their bedroom door. They looked surprised and scared. I went to check on the front door, which was locked. Then I took them both downstairs for a drink, and half an hour later settled them back in bed.

"When the parents returned, I told them the story. Neither could make sense of it. They'd locked the front door when they left. They'd had to unlock it to get in again. They couldn't explain why the front door might have opened and banged closed, on two occasions. But the next day they packed up, and went back home to London.

"On the Monday," said Alice, "I told an actor friend, who I know is open to the paranormal. He asked about the house. Turned out, he knew it. 'People tell funny stories about the house. Doors and windows open or close, with no wind'."

Theo had interlaced his fingers as he listened to Alice. Now a line appeared on his forehead.

Alice moistened her lips. "I learned the previous owner's husband died twelve months ago."

Theo and Zoe looked at each other.

"It must have been him," said Zoe.

Theo turned back to Alice. "A very spooky tale," he said, "but it doesn't seem in any way related to Zoe's dream, or the little girl she met near the barn."

"Then you need to know what happened next," said Alice.

"Go on," said Zoe.

"It was the Friday of the following week," said Alice. "I was driving south, heading for the A417 to Cirencester. It was ten-to-six in the evening. As it happens, I was two minutes up the lane from our main gateway. A very small girl broke out from the edge of the road. She ran in front of my car. I had no time to brake or swerve. But she stopped and looked at me. There was no expression on her face. Then I hit her and she went under the car."

Zoe stared at her. Her fingers had gone numb. She flexed them repeatedly then clasped her hands together under the table.

"What happened then?" Theo asked.

"I stopped and got out. I was trembling all over, my heart was banging against my ribcage, and I felt cold as ice. I expected to find a body. But there was nothing."

Zoe moistened her lips. "Nothing?"

"No. Nobody there."

"How old was the girl?"

"Four or five."

Zoe's stomach flipped. An image flashed across her mind's eye: a little girl; four or five years old; long fair hair, green dress.

Her heart was pumping faster. She looked at Theo. His mouth had fallen open.

Alice spoke on, more quickly now. "I hunted everywhere I thought her body may have gone. I had a torch in the car. I shone it into the ditch at the side of the road, up and down the hedge; I even climbed through a gap in the hedge to see if her body had been thrown over it into the field. I found nothing."

"Did you call the police?" asked Theo.

"Yes. They did a search. Their community support officer rang later and said they found nothing. No Missing Person report with which to match the child. Since there was nothing to go on, there was little they could do."

"I can't believe you didn't tell us this earlier."

"Ah. I was just a little concerned that you wouldn't be very positive about my ghost stories," said Alice, looking at Theo. "I've met some clergy people in the past who'd dismiss these experiences as my imagination."

"Well, have no fears about that," Theo said. "I take your stories seriously."

"Thank you," said Alice. "I'm still jittery every time I drive up that lane. I can't shake off the idea there's a body there somewhere, despite the fact that the police searched the area thoroughly. Every day I look in the papers for news of a missing child. Right now, every instinct tells me she was a ghost."

Theo turned to Zoe.

"You said the child you met *looked through* you."

"Yes," said Zoe. "I was petrified."

"That says it all," insisted Alice. "Your gut instinct was: *This isn't a normal physical child*."

"But why did she appear to us?" asked Zoe.

Theo took her hand. "Alice still has another story to tell."

Both looked at Alice again.

"Yes," said Alice. "It happened a week later, again on the Friday. I was going to London for a meeting. Got on the train at Kemble and found a seat. At the next stop, a small girl came along and sat in the seat opposite. As the train began to move off, I thought, *doesn't she have an adult with her?* She seemed four or five years old. I supposed the adult had perhaps gone to the toilet.

"Ten minutes passed and nobody came along. I looked up. The girl didn't seem at all worried to be left alone. I was about to speak to her, but something prevented me. My heart began to beat faster. My palms sweated. We drew in to the next station. As the train stopped, the child got up, walked to the door, and jumped out onto the platform.

"After the train moved off, I spent several minutes trying to calm down. I was in a cold sweat. I closed my eyes for a few minutes. When I opened them, the train was waiting at the next station. To my horror, I saw the same child seated in front of me.

"I froze with terror. I stared at her. She looked through me. I got up, grabbed my bag and coat, and ran the whole length of the train.

"At Paddington I raced off for fear of seeing her on the platform. But I didn't see her again."

Alice stopped and looked from Theo to Zoe and back again.

Zoe wrapped her arms around herself, instinctively seeking some kind of reassurance.

She turned to Theo. "What d'you make of it?"

Theo rubbed his chin. "I've come across several paranormal tales involving children. And young children also do tend to attract psychic phenomena."

Zoe ran her hands through her hair. "But Theo, do you believe that Alice and I both saw a ghost?"

"Yes," said Theo. "As I said earlier, I've seen ghostly monks myself, in the London church where I served my curacy. And so I've done some soul-searching on the subject. It talks in the scripture about what happens when you die. *We're asleep* is the Bible's picture. But does that mean all beings that have ever been, are 'sleeping', in that sense? Are there some souls that are not resting in peace?"

"Like the little girl?" said Zoe.

"Perhaps. There are some things that God wants us to understand," replied Theo, "and there are other things that are not for us to understand, and which are beyond our imagination. Yes, I believe in ghosts. But we cannot yet know what the appearance of the little girl means."

He looked at Alice. "Remembering the little girl you babysat, Alice; were she and the ghost child one and the same?"

Alice shook her head. Her skin had tightened around her jawline.

It occurred to Zoe that the child could be a doppelgänger, the ghost of a person still alive. She'd heard stories of these out-of-body apparitions.

"Theo, what does it mean?" she asked urgently.

Theo shook his head. "No idea. I'm baffled." He turned to Alice again. "All I can suggest is that you write these incidents down. If anything else strange happens, they'll be important."

"I will," she said. "And there was one other thing I wanted to talk to you about. Well, two actually: James and Natasha."

Zoe held her head up. "What about them?"

"You know your stories of Celtic saints, Theo?" said Alice. She laid her arm across the back of the chair. Her russet-coloured leather jacket creaked. "I love them: Ninian, Columba, Francis… they all believed in entertaining strangers, in case they turned out to be angels; great stuff. But …"

Theo sat with chin cupped in hand. "Yes, go on."

She nodded. "When Zoe and I were with Natasha and James this morning, I had a picture. It was of a tarantula crawling over a jewelled masquerade mask."

Zoe shuddered. She shot a quick glance at Theo. They both knew about Alice's mental pictures: a vision of an apparently ordinary situation, in which she'd see something that told a different story from what lay on the surface. And, as with her finely-tuned instincts about non-verbal messages and body language, she'd mostly been proved right.

"A tarantula and a jewelled mask? In James and Natasha?" asked Theo.

"Yes," said Alice.

"That's a vivid image," said Theo. "Why should they give you that impression? James does have a rather haughty manner, I agree. But, to see him and Natasha in those terms…"

"Sorry. It's how I feel."

"Alice, I respect your feelings," said Theo, "but we've offered them our hospitality. We can't judge them on the basis of one of your mental pictures."

Zoe fiddled with the gold cross hanging on a chain round her neck then moved her hand to her left shoulder, clasping her arm across her body.

"Natasha asked if we planned to start a family," she said.

Theo smiled and put his arm round her. "We do. It's a natural question to ask."

She nodded.

Theo looked at Alice. "Despite your feelings, we must accept James and Natasha. They have a right to be here. We're open to all, as long as people respect our guidelines."

"Sorry Theo. I don't trust James – or Natasha," said Alice. "She has some kind of spiritual aura around her. But I don't feel good about it."

"What do you mean by that, Alice?" asked Theo, removing his arm from Zoe's shoulder and sitting forward with a frown.

Zoe chewed her lip. Her spine prickled.

"Can't be more specific," said Alice. "Just trying to be honest with you about how I feel; and Natasha's words about starting a family… Of course it seems perfectly innocuous. But I believe there's more to *that* too."

"Let's leave the subject for the time being," said Theo.

"Right." Alice got up, picked up her handbag, and pulled her car keys out of her pocket. "Thanks for listening to me. Bye."

"Alice…" began Zoe.

But Alice had already walked out into the entrance hall. They heard the front door open, then close.

Silence followed. They heard no sound of gravel crunching beneath her feet.

Zoe looked at Theo. They both got up and went out of the house to see if Alice was still there and needed anything else. But she was nowhere to be seen. Zoe looked to the right, across to the conifers where Alice could have gone, choosing the woodland walk to the back of the car park. But there was no sign of her.

She might have gone up the drive which was more open and a route Zoe herself often preferred, when the light was fading, or in the dark. She looked straight ahead up the hill, and again saw no-one.

A curious silence hung over the scene. She shivered. They both turned and went back into the house.

"Where's she gone?" asked Zoe.

Their eyes met. Theo's face was white.

# CHAPTER THREE

A quarter of an hour later, Zoe was in the sitting room doing her usual check. There wouldn't be many of them that evening for dinner, which was just as well, as Zoe felt nervy from the day's odd events. It wasn't until the following afternoon that she and Theo would be welcoming their new intake of guests for next week. In addition to James and Natasha, there were just three more guests that evening, those who'd stayed on from last week's painting, marbling and ceramics course, Cynthia, Gareth and Heidi.

Gareth was a successful artist who lived on the earnings from his work, painted the subjects he knew to be most popular, and always had an eye to the best cash return. Heidi was married to a university professor and had arrived feeling jaded and stressed with her role in supporting him and interminably entertaining all his colleagues, research students and professional contacts; she'd come to the centre to 'find herself' so she'd told Zoe. And Cynthia had just gone through a hurtful divorce and was cynical about life and men in general, but had been persuaded by her therapist to try a creative arts retreat to refresh herself; mind, body and soul.

Zoe knew people came here with high expectations, and she and Theo did everything possible to fulfil the hopes of their guests. Most of those who came regarded themselves as 'spiritual but not religious'; though Theo was a priest, and the inspiration for the centre came from Celtic Christian spirituality, they were open to all, of any faith or none.

Right now, Theo had gone to sort out a menu issue with Miles, the chef, and Zoe had come to check the sitting room; the guests usually gathered in here for coffee after dinner and she liked to make sure it was as comfortable as possible for them. She walked around checking the bowls were full of chocolate mints, the flower arrangements fresh and none of the candles needed replenishing.

All was as it should be and Zoe sank into one of the emerald-green armchairs to relax for five minutes. It was a luxury to be alone in here; on the way through the entrance hall she'd passed Heidi and Cynthia, who were just going upstairs, and she'd also greeted Gareth as he headed into the library for a quiet half an hour's read before dinner.

A book lying open on a chair in the corner caught Zoe's eye.

She picked it up and began to read:

On the morning of September 8th, 1560, at the isolated manor of Cumnor Place, the body of a young woman was found at the bottom of a staircase, her neck broken. But this was no ordinary death. Amy Robsart was the wife of Elizabeth I's great favourite, Robert Dudley, the man who many believed she would marry, were he free…

Ah, she thought, looking at the cover. *Death and the Virgin: Elizabeth, Dudley and the Mysterious Fate of Amy Robsart* by Chris Skidmore. One of the guests had clearly chosen reading matter to match their location, in a sixteenth-century manor house.

The subject of first wives pulled Zoe's mind off on a tangent. Theo's first wife had divorced him nine years before.

27

He'd told Zoe the circumstances, and she felt confident he'd shared everything with her.

It seemed to Zoe, though, that even with his first wife, Theo was too ready to place his confidence in the goodness of others; because it did sting a little sometimes, when he spent more time making himself available to other people, than listening to her.

And although she loved him, Zoe couldn't shift off one particular doubt about her husband; the question of whether he'd stay free of the depression that had stalked him at various points in his life. Before they married, Theo had told her he'd suffered from this in the past.

Sighing, she replaced the book as she'd found it, open at the account of the story of the ill-fated Amy. Suddenly she was electrified by screams outside on the staircase from the first floor. She heard something – or somebody – tumble down the stairs.

Vito leapt up. Zoe dashed across to the door. Vito was already there, standing on his hind legs, pawing at the timber panels. Zoe opened the door. Vito hurtled into the entrance hall ahead of her. The first thing Zoe saw was Cynthia lying on the floor in a heap at the foot of the staircase. One leg was bent under the other. Her long brown hair had escaped from its pins, and fanned over her face. Vito was by Cynthia's side, sniffing at her hair, nosing at her forehead, his tail drooping.

Before Zoe could say anything, the library door opened and Gareth put his head out. Heidi and Alice had appeared on the first-floor landing and were hurrying down to join them. Zoe hardly had time to quiz Alice on what she was still doing in the house, though it made sense of why she hadn't heard her footsteps crossing the gravel.

"Cynthia! What's happened?" she gasped.

Bewildered, she hurried across and fell on her knees beside Cynthia. Gareth, Heidi and Alice were close behind Zoe, leaning over her.

"Keep her immobile," said Alice. "You don't know what injuries she has. I'll call an ambulance." She pulled her mobile from her pocket and began to tap.

Meanwhile, Heidi pushed the hair off Cynthia's face so they could see her better, and Zoe was bending low, ear to Cynthia's chest.

Having finished her call, Alice rejoined the group clustered round the patient. "Cynthia!" she said. "Hello? Can you hear me?"

No reply. Zoe's heart pounded. She took Cynthia's wrist and checked her pulse. Then she put her ear to Cynthia's mouth.

"She's breathing all right."

"Any obvious signs of injury?" asked Gareth.

Zoe gently parted Cynthia's hair in several places over her scalp for signs of wounds or blood. She found none. Alice was checking Cynthia's ears, nose and her eyes.

"Can't see any bleeding," she said. "But she's unconscious. That's bad. Could be an internal head injury."

"Do we need to cover her?" asked Heidi, her voice trembling.

"Good idea. I'll go and get a blanket." Gareth stepped over Cynthia's body onto the first stair. As he bounded up the stairs, Zoe continued searching Cynthia's face and head for any signs of injury they might have missed.

Then she noticed Cynthia's eyelids flicker. Her eyes opened wide with a terrified expression. She shook her head, and kicked out – including, Zoe noticed with horror, the leg that had been bent at an awkward angle. If it hadn't been broken before, Zoe feared it would be now. She shifted aside to avoid being kicked.

"Cynthia!" she cried. "Calm down! But thank God you're awake."

Cynthia struggled to sit up.

"Where am I?" she cried. "What happened? What's going on?"

"You fell downstairs. You were unconscious. We've called an ambulance."

Now Cynthia was sitting, Zoe put her arm under her shoulders and guided her to lean against her. She wiped some more of Cynthia's hair away from her face.

Alice pressed in close to Zoe, eyes fixed on Cynthia. "How do you feel? Does your head hurt? Can you feel your arms and legs? Do you feel sick?"

Gareth reappeared at the bend of the staircase holding a blanket and came down to them. He edged round Cynthia, holding the blanket out wide.

Zoe took the blanket and put it around Cynthia's shoulders.

Cynthia ignored the questions, but gasped, "Why…? What…? Who…?"

At least her speech didn't sound slurred.

"What's going on here?"

Zoe looked up. Another figure had appeared at the bend of the staircase. "James!"

"Cynthia has been hurt," cried Heidi.

James descended to the hall at a leisurely pace.

"She fell downstairs. An ambulance is on its way," said Zoe. Then she noticed Natasha following behind James.

"Can I help?" Natasha asked. "Let me have a look at her." Gareth had moved back several paces, gazing at Natasha. Alice rose to her feet and joined him. Zoe stayed where she was. Heidi had remained a little apart from the others for the past few minutes, looking helpless and scared. Natasha, meanwhile, crouched down beside Cynthia. But instead of examining her face and head in the way Zoe had, she began whispering words Zoe couldn't catch.

Then she placed one hand on Cynthia's head and another over her heart.

"There are injuries," said Natasha. "I sense them. But I can heal you, Cynthia, if you wish. Would you like me to?"

Zoe couldn't tell whether Cynthia had moved her lips or not. Something made her look up from her kneeling position and she caught Alice's eye. Then she saw the expression on Heidi's and Gareth's faces. Both had changed colour. Their mouths had fallen open, and their eyes were focused on Natasha.

Zoe looked back at Natasha who was murmuring words Zoe didn't recognise. Her voice had the same effect upon Zoe as a glowing log fire might have. Warmth and peace stole through her body, starting with her fingers and moving up her arms.

Cynthia's hands fell to her sides, her fingers relaxed. She lifted her head and looked around with a quizzical expression then smiled at them all.

"So sorry," she said. "What happened? I was at the top of the stairs, and then it's a blank. Before that, I was chatting to Alice. She'd given me my change for some cards I bought earlier in reception…"

"Did you see what happened, Alice?" asked Zoe.

"No. I was just about to go downstairs myself, when Cynthia flew past me. I had no idea why. The floorboards aren't slippery and there was no obstacle."

Cynthia looked puzzled.

"I've no memory of that at all. It seems I must have lost my footing at the top of the stairs."

Natasha leaned her head in towards her and said something in a soft voice. Zoe couldn't catch the words.

"Thank you, Natasha," said Cynthia. "I don't know what you did, or how – but I feel perfectly all right."

"You're welcome," said Natasha, standing up again.

Zoe stared at Cynthia, incredulous. She'd hit her head. She'd been unconscious for a few minutes. She could have internal bleeding. If Natasha had given her a sense of peace, fine. But there would be no way Natasha could have affected whatever injuries Cynthia might have, internal or external.

Outside, a vehicle raced down the drive towards the house.

"Ambulance," said Zoe, jumping back up again and running to the front door. As she pulled it back, the ambulance drew to a halt in the gravel forecourt a few metres away and the doors burst open.

Two paramedics sprang from the ambulance and hurried over the threshold.

"Where's the patient?" said one of them.

Zoe indicated Cynthia.

"How long was she unconscious?" asked the other.

"A couple of minutes," said Zoe.

The two paramedics looked into Cynthia's eyes with a torch, examined behind her ears, and began probing her arms and legs and asking if she could feel it. They questioned her as Alice had done earlier, looking for pain or sickness or numbness.

"Tell me if this hurts," said one paramedic, feeling her calf muscles. His colleague rolled up her long sleeves and felt Cynthia's arms from armpit to wrist, then tested her blood pressure. Finally the two of them conferred together for a few seconds. Then one turned and met Zoe's eyes. "No obvious signs of injury, she says she's not in pain, her speech is clear, she has full sensation in her limbs, blood pressure's fine, she answers questions as I'd expect…"

"But we'll take her in," said his colleague. "Any possibility of internal injury, she needs to be checked out, and under observation for four hours."

"Look, I'm all right," said Cynthia.

"But Cynthia, you can't be," said Zoe. Natasha gave her a strange look. Zoe felt as if she was being studied; coldly, dispassionately, as if her thoughts and ideas were being extracted and laid out on a laboratory bench to be examined.

"Natasha healed her," whispered Heidi, who was standing just behind Zoe.

"No she didn't," insisted Zoe, fighting against the bizarre impression Natasha had made upon her. "She just helped Cynthia feel calmer."

"We must take you in," said the first paramedic.

"And if I refuse?" queried Cynthia.

"We'd need you to sign a disclaimer."

"All right," she sighed. "I'll go in."

After the ambulance had gone, with Cynthia on board, Gareth stepped forward. His usually red face had increased in colour, if that was possible, and his eyes glowed with excitement.

"Never seen anything like this before," he said. "I'd have been the first to laugh if you'd told me the story. But I've seen it with my own eyes. Looks as if Natasha healed her."

Zoe bit her lip. "She can't have."

She caught James and Natasha exchanging a glance.

Alice was first to break the silence. "Have you ever done anything like this before, Natasha?" she asked.

"Several times," replied Natasha.

Zoe saw Heidi's eyes light up. She felt a powerful urge to get away from the scene. Instead of sharing Heidi's and Gareth's amazement and wonder, she had strong doubts. For if observation and a scan proved Cynthia entirely free from any injury, then Zoe had never seen anyone healed so fast.

CHAPTER FOUR

Zoe met Theo in the courtyard as they stood aside to let the guests move to the dining area ahead of them.

"We don't yet understand what happened to Cynthia," said Theo quietly to her, "so let's not jump to any conclusions."

He rubbed his chin. He seemed drained. *Perhaps*, thought Zoe, *he's been working too hard*.

"You look tired. What's going on?" she asked, putting her arms round him.

He kissed her on the head.

"Nothing to worry about," he said. "I'll shorten this evening's session a bit and take the chance of an early night. No possibility of that tomorrow, with the new intake of guests arriving."

Zoe gazed at him. In the space of only an hour, he'd changed.

The new guests were due to arrive from three o'clock onwards that afternoon and at midday, Zoe was in the office printing off name badges.

Cynthia had appeared at breakfast, her eyes sparkling, to report that the doctors in A & E had found her in perfect health. Zoe refused to believe Natasha had healed her. She persuaded herself it was a lucky escape. Things like that happened sometimes.

Clearly, though, Gareth, Cynthia and Heidi all thought

otherwise. They could hardly take their eyes off Natasha whenever she was near, and took every opportunity to speak to her and listen enraptured to what she had to say.

On the desk before Zoe, lay a pile of completed registration forms. She looked up at Theo, who'd just brought a box of cards and envelopes over to her.

"Cynthia was lucky, wasn't she?"

"'Lucky', you call it?" said Theo.

"Yes, I do. You don't believe this stuff about Natasha healing her, do you?"

"Let's put it like this," he said. "I don't believe in instant 'miracle' healing. As you know, alongside conventional medical help, people do sometimes ask me to pray for their healing. It comforts them. And sometimes, people are healed. At other times, not. Our God is not a push-button God."

"No, of course not," said Zoe. "And it doesn't make sense that Natasha…"

But her sentence was never finished. They'd both heard glass smashing out in the courtyard.

Theo jumped to his feet and headed for the external door. Zoe followed.

The atmosphere closed in around them, humid and oppressive. A mist hung low in tendrils about the trees, over the sculpture fountain and the outbuildings. A yell came to Zoe's ears. "The barn window!"

She ran across the courtyard to the barn then stopped short, staring up at the east-facing window, which had been engraved with a Celtic cross. In its place appeared a gaping hole with jagged edges.

Griff, the creative-writing tutor, rushed out through the central barn doorway, followed by Cynthia and Heidi.

"Heidi's hurt," called Griff as Zoe and Theo ran over to

him. Blood blossomed through the long sleeve of Heidi's cream jumper. Zoe's heart clenched.

"Let me look at that," said Theo, gently rolling her sleeve up. "Thank God it's not a cut wrist! Come on. The first-aid box is in reception."

"No, Theo, don't you worry," said Griff, "I'll help her." He put his arm around Heidi who was trembling.

"What happened, Griff?" asked Zoe before he could go.

"Huge stone," he muttered, "flew through the window."

He shepherded Heidi off to the office.

"What about you, Cynthia?" asked Theo."Are you all right?"

"Yes, I think so," said Cynthia. "It's a miracle nobody else was hurt. The stone came through that window so fast. We were with Griff in the upper room. The stone landed downstairs, but glass flew straight at us. There are bits of it everywhere."

Her face had drained of colour.

"How are you feeling?" asked Theo. "Let me take you into the house and make you a hot drink."

"No, no, I'll be all right," she said, with a grateful glance at him.

Bernie and Miles were now hurrying across the courtyard towards them, having emerged from the dining area. They were joined by Gareth who'd just appeared from the back doorway of the house.

"What happened?" cried Miles. "I was in the kitchen and I heard this almighty crash out here… Oh my God." He stopped short, staring at the barn window.

Once inside the barn, Zoe saw shards of glass scattered all over the floor. Some had flown for several metres. As she passed the east spiral staircase, more jagged fragments glinted on the treads halfway up, beneath the spotlights trained on them from the cross-beams overhead. She ran back out through the barn doorway again.

Despite her assurance to Theo of being all right, Cynthia was shaking. Gareth's mouth hung open as he looked at the damage.

Zoe cast a desperate glance at Bernie beside her, who held Vito by the collar. Vito, she noticed, was silent and still.

"Did you see anything, Bernie?" she asked.

Bernie shook his head. Then James approached from the direction of the goose house. There was no sign of Natasha.

"Who could have thrown it?" said Bernie.

Zoe turned to him urgently. "Bernie, what about that tramp I saw yesterday?"

He chewed his lip. "Possibly. He might have got away through the conifers and could be heading back up the drive now." He encouraged Vito into action and both sped along the path through the trees.

James had joined the group. "What a shock for you all," he said. "Whoever did this, we need to find them at once."

"Yes," murmured Zoe. "We have seen a tramp on the property. Bernie's gone to find him now."

"Or it could have been antisocial youths," remarked James.

"If so, they might have gone into the woods," said Zoe, "or up the slope." She pointed west, "and jumped over the fence; or round the north side of the barn and through the gate."

"She's right," said Gareth.

"OK, Gareth, Miles, over the fence at once," ordered James. "Do a sweep of the woods."

Zoe pursed her lips. She knew James was only trying to be helpful, but she'd have preferred him to leave her to issue the instructions.

Miles and Gareth obeyed James's orders and disappeared into the woodland.

Unexpectedly, tears rolled down Zoe's face. Theo squeezed her hand gently then released it.

"Don't worry about this," he said. "We've got people out hunting for whoever's responsible. But we must take care. We can't accuse anyone without proof."

Cynthia glanced from James, to Zoe and Theo, and back again. She looked faintly perplexed.

James gave Zoe a cool scrutiny. Zoe thrust both hands into her pockets and clenched her fists.

"I'm sure we'll get to the bottom of it soon," said James.

CHAPTER FIVE

Miles, Gareth and Bernie had all returned from a fruitless search of the property and headed off with Cynthia to the dining room for lunch. Griff had gone back into the house to fetch Heidi from the sitting room where he'd left her resting after administering first aid to her arm. James had chosen to stay with Theo and Zoe.

"No-one you can think of who has it in for the Celtic Knot, or for what you do here?" said James.

Zoe bit her lip. She still considered that it was most likely to be the tramp. But if it wasn't him, then she was baffled. She refused to believe it could be a former guest. She said nothing.

Theo's eyes looked dull and his face drawn. Zoe thought he was sickening for something. But both of them were shaken by the attack on the barn window, so she reasoned that it may just have been a reaction to that. She took his hand, ready to reassure him, when James's voice cut in.

"Speculation's futile. No point worrying any more."

"True," said Theo. "We've done all we can."

Zoe glanced towards the goose house, where a raven was circling the roof.

"You go on and join the others for lunch, James," said Theo. "We'll be with you in a minute."

James strolled off across the courtyard.

"Where's Natasha?" asked Zoe.

"No idea," said Theo.

"D'you think *she* threw the stone?"

This drew a smile from Theo. "Seems unlikely," he said in a gentle voice.

Zoe wished she could be that confident. But she kept worrying about Natasha and James. Nothing like this had ever happened here before: not before Natasha and James arrived.

She tried to shake off this irrational association between the previous day's new arrivals, and the strange incidents that had been happening this weekend. Neither of the pair had pushed Cynthia downstairs, or thrown the stone – to her knowledge. But, of course, she reminded herself, she didn't know that for certain.

But one thing she did know; since she and Theo had taken up their posts, she'd regarded their lives here at the Celtic Knot as the Garden of Eden.

She and Theo walked across the courtyard to the dining area together. As they reached the sculpture fountain, she made him pause.

"Theo," she said, "I feel there's more to this than just a spiteful person breaking a window; something much bigger behind it."

"Yes," he murmured. "But we'll work through it. We need to keep strong."

"Strong?" She looked at him. Right now, it seemed a sudden gust of wind might blow him over. She squeezed his hand.

"I used to think this place was like paradise," she said. "But now, in a short space of time, it has all got very 'real' – in a bad sense."

Theo looked bemused. "Come on," he said, "things aren't that bleak."

"You think so? Well, perhaps what's been happening here, then, is just 'stuff'," she replied.

Theo shrugged.

Then Zoe thought of James again, and the uncomfortable impression he'd given her, of trying to take charge. Theo hadn't countered it at all. But there again, he wouldn't have done, if he saw the situation differently.

But quite apart from that, of course, Theo never spoke sharply to anyone. Sometimes Zoe wished he would. Jesus, she knew, overturned the traders' tables in the temple. That was something her Muslim friends had, in the past, dived upon, as evidence that Jesus suffered from a bad temper. But to her mind the story showed it was OK to get angry.

Then she chided herself. Theo was unwell today. He needed a good rest. She'd encourage him to go to bed early.

"Come on, let's go in to lunch," said Theo. "The others will be halfway through by now."

No sooner had they entered the dining room, where lunch was in progress, than they saw Natasha rise from her seat at the nearest table and move towards them. She carried a plastic bag which seemed strangely incongruous with her ethereal silk gown.

It was the first time Zoe had seen Natasha that day. But she had to agree with Theo, it seemed ludicrous to suspect Natasha of having thrown the stone through the window. She looked too delicate.

"You mustn't worry, either of you," said Natasha. "Everything will be all right."

She held up the plastic bag. They gazed at it as she opened it to reveal the contents: a bloody bandage.

"What's this all about?" asked Theo.

"I wondered if you have a sterile waste disposal bin," said Natasha. "I need to get rid of this."

Theo opened his mouth to query her further, when Heidi got up from her seat and came to Natasha's side. She now wore a light-blue blouse with long sleeves, instead of the cream jumper through which they'd seen the blood blossoming.

"Hello Heidi," said Zoe. "How's your arm?"

Then she stared. Heidi's face wore a radiant smile.

"What…?" Theo began.

"Heidi doesn't need that dressing any longer," said Natasha.

Zoe swallowed. "But your arm was cut," she said to Heidi. "There was loads of blood."

"It's fine now," said Heidi. "See for yourself."

She rolled up her sleeve and Zoe studied her arm. The skin was clear, smooth and unbroken.

"Natasha is amazing," enthused Heidi. "She came into the sitting room where I was taking a rest. She asked if I wanted her to heal me. Well, of course, after what I saw last night, I said yes. Natasha took my arm and passed her hand over the bandaged area and spoke a few words. Then she removed the bandage. I couldn't believe it. No sign of any wound at all."

She gazed at Natasha, an awed expression on her face. Natasha smiled, but said nothing. Heidi turned back to Zoe again.

"You see, Zoe?" she said in a hushed and reverent voice. "Natasha is truly a miracle worker."

Zoe's jaw tightened. She thrust her hands behind her back so neither Heidi nor Natasha could see her interwoven clenched fingers.

CHAPTER SIX

Theo had gone off as soon as lunch finished to supervise the clear-up in the barn. Zoe headed for reception feeling anxious and agitated and not at all in the right frame of mind to greet the new guests as they arrived. Once at her desk, she called Alice, desperate to bring her up to date with all that had happened that day, in her absence.

"Don't want to unnerve you even more, Zoe," said Alice, "but… from your description, it seems just one creepy thing after another. *And* you say you saw a raven circling the roof? *'The raven himself is hoarse that croaks the fatal entrance of Duncan under my battlements'*."

"Oh come on, Alice, not Lady Macbeth, not right now…" pleaded Zoe, almost laughing despite herself.

"Sorry, couldn't resist. Just be glad I didn't play any of the Weird Sisters. Shakespeare's knowledge of demonology was accurate. All those spells were genuine."

"Yeah, Theo already knew that," said Zoe. "He told me, just after we gave you the job."

"Did he?" responded Alice, her interest piqued. "So you two had doubts about me, even at that stage?"

"He and Jessica might have, but I didn't," said Zoe. "And in fact, I'm incredibly grateful we've got you, Alice. I'm relying on you to make sense of what's going on round here…"

"Are you? No pressure, then," said Alice, laughing.

"… but right at this moment I could do without you

bringing Macbeth into this, and making me feel bad about the raven as well."

"Sorry, Zoe. No more raven references, or Lady Macbeth quotes. I promise."

When her call to Alice was over, Zoe looked at her watch: at least half an hour before the first guest could be expected to arrive. The tramp was still preying on her mind. She knew Bernie and Vito had failed to find him, but she couldn't get rid of the idea he might still be around, and they'd just missed him.

She could spare a few minutes before returning to the office. So she hurried out, locking the door behind her, and whistled Vito to her side. Passing Bernie and Theo outside the barn door, clearing up, she went round the house through the conifers and up the drive towards the brow of the hill, heading towards the place she'd last seen him.

As she walked, Zoe felt sticky: the atmosphere closed in. She stopped to pull off her smart jacket and slung it over her shoulder. The long-sleeved light cotton blouse she wore underneath was enough in this weather.

She looked in vain for the tramp for several minutes. Perhaps he'd disappeared. Then, as she was about to give up, she spotted movement beneath the maples to the east, where the land sloped upwards. Vito tensed at her side. She turned and sharpened her focus. Yes. It was him all right. The long, tatty overcoat hung from his shoulders. It had probably been donated to him twenty years before. Beside her, a low rumble formed in Vito's throat. She glanced down at him. His body was on full alert, his eyes fixed on the tramp.

She and the man moved towards each other. His face was swarthy, or covered with dirt.

"Hello again," she said. There was no point in evading the issue. "Someone just threw a stone through our barn window. Do you know anything about it?"

He stuck out his face, arched his neck and hissed at her. She took two paces back from him.

"Please," she said, "I'm not accusing you. Just wondered if you saw anything."

He gave a low, throaty growl. She tensed.

"You won't do yourself any good hanging around here. Why not come down to the house and let us help you instead? We'll give you some food; and a shower; and some clean clothes."

The vagrant threw her a look of contempt.

Summoning all her self-restraint, she tried again. "Haven't got any sandwiches, or I'd give them to you."

She felt in her pocket, thinking she might have something to offer him, to make him trust her. She found an unopened tube of mints and held them out to him. Then Vito snarled. At once, the man spun round and plunged back into the thicket.

"Oh, Vito," she said. "I was trying to make him trust me. If he *did* throw the stone through the window, it would at least be good to know who did it. Come on. Let's go back. We need to greet the new guests." She headed down the drive at a brisk pace.

But as she walked, she speculated about the vagrant. Her fingers curled. It seemed likely that he spent his nights under the cover of the trees. Perhaps he had a bush bivouac there. But if he did, there'd be a campfire. They'd see smoke rising. And anyway, Bernie would surely have found it.

Casting aside all thoughts of the vagrant for the time being, she focused instead on meeting the new guests.

Taking out her keys at eight o'clock on Monday morning, Zoe was about to unlock the reception door, when she saw Alice hurrying across the courtyard towards her from the north.

The first thing she noticed about her was the expression on her face; flared nostrils and clenched teeth.

Zoe felt an uneasy stirring in her stomach.

"You OK, Alice?" she asked as Alice drew near.

"Hi, yes." Alice gave a nervous laugh. "Sorry. Did I look as if I've seen another ghost? Not quite. No, it was Natasha. Just had a weird conversation with her."

Zoe frowned. "What about?"

"I'd sooner not say," replied Alice, as they both went into the office. "It was bad enough me putting the frighteners on you yesterday afternoon, with my talk of ravens and the Bard's play."

Zoe threw her a quizzical glance.

"On the subject of Natasha," she said, "at breakfast I overheard James chatting to Heidi. She was full of Natasha and her healing power. What a perfect introduction to this week's course for our new guests. It's billed as 'icon painting, calligraphy and poetry'. I'm worried about what our three guests from last week will be telling them. The new lot could get the idea that we've laid on a miracle healer for them as well."

"And what about you, Zoe?" said Alice, dumping her bag down by her desk, taking her jacket off, and hanging it on the back of her chair. "What do *you* believe?"

"I don't know," said Zoe.

Their gaze met.

"OK," said Alice. "What if she *is* actually healing people?"

"Then I want to know by what power she's doing it," Zoe said. Her muscles tensed.

Alice sat down at her desk and fired up her computer. But Zoe still remained standing.

"What I feel", began Alice, "is that those guests were too willing to believe Natasha is good."

The door opened and James came in.

"Good morning, ladies," he said. "Lovely fresh morning, isn't it?"

Zoe gave him a tight-lipped smile.

"And what a delightful group of new guests you have," he remarked.

"Yes, James," she replied.

He turned to Alice.

"I understand from Natasha that you played the Scottish Lady not long ago," he remarked.

Alice nodded.

"Hmmm," said James. "Why *are* you out of work, Alice? Did someone say the name of 'that play' inside the theatre?"

"It was in a deconsecrated church, not a theatre, James," she replied. "And anyway, the curse only operates during the play's run."

"Don't be too sure of that," he smiled.

Alice wore a closed expression and didn't respond.

James swung back to Zoe again.

"Got a bit of a surprise last night," he added. "I was going through your brochure in detail and saw that your chair of trustees is Jessica Leroy. Curious coincidence, but I believe I've met her before, in the past."

"You sure?"

"Pretty sure. Years ago, it was; in Edinburgh; if she's the same person, of course."

"Might be," said Zoe. "Jessica was born and brought up in Northumberland."

"Then she may well have regularly visited Edinburgh. She could be the same person."

"You'll have the chance to find out later, if you're lucky," replied Zoe, seating herself at her desk. "Jessica plans to visit us today. However, she's coming to talk to the staff, not to go into any workshops."

James shot her a glance. She guessed that he planned to lay claim to Jessica's attention at the first opportunity. She pursed her lips as she remembered his version of 'being helpful' at the accident the day before.

"I was in rep," continued James. "We met at a party; brilliant young woman; only seventeen at the time – doing her A levels."

Zoe wondered whether the young Jessica had had a crush on him. She felt sick thinking about it.

"That's fascinating, James," she said. "I expect you'll manage a quick chat with her."

She waited. So did he.

"Anything further you wanted help with?" she asked.

"Ah," he said, perching himself on a corner of Zoe's desk, "perhaps it's not so much a question of you helping me, as me helping you. After yesterday's upsetting events, I felt a strong urge to lend my support."

He crossed one leg over the other and adjusted the knees of his trousers. Zoe noticed the rich burnished leather of his high-quality shoes. She'd grown to loathe his smooth style and sharp dress sense; to her, it merely provided him with the superficial gloss that covered up the undercurrent of manipulation and arrogance.

"As you know," he continued, "I'm a professional actor. So I've got what it takes to deal with people – I'm gregarious, sociable… I can look after your guests, handle their queries, help with workshops and so on."

"No need," said Zoe. "We have Alice with all those skills too."

"Oh, of course," he said with a small, deprecating cough. He fixed his eye upon the bookings secretary.

"Zoe and I manage very well," said Alice. "Why not take a stroll around the grounds and read all the poetry that's carved onto plaques hanging from the trees?"

James laughed. "I've already done that, Alice." He turned back to Zoe. "Do allow me to help in the office this morning."

Zoe decided to call his bluff.

"Very well, then. You can go and do the washing-up."

James chuckled. "A smart reply," he smiled.

Zoe changed the subject.

"How long have you and Natasha known each other? How did you first meet?"

"She and her sister have been friends of mine for a few years now." He levelled his gaze upon her. Then he leaned forward, bringing his face much closer to hers. As he did so, the door opened and Theo walked in. James slipped off the corner of Zoe's desk.

"Hello, James," said Theo.

"Good to see you, Theo. Just having a little chat about Natasha," said James.

"It seems she's on everyone's mind at the moment," said Theo.

James abruptly shifted the topic. "You've got an impressive list of trustees. Seven of them, I see. I look forward to meeting your chairperson, Jessica Leroy. I believe we've met before in the past."

Theo inclined his head in acknowledgement of this. Zoe looked down at her interlaced clenched fingers. James reached into his pocket, brought out his keyring, a silver pentagram holding an assortment of keys, and began weighing it in his palm.

Zoe relaxed. It looked to her as if he planned to take himself off for a scenic drive – perhaps with Natasha – and give them a brief respite from his company. Outside, the first drops of rain began to fall.

"Ah, the rain," said James. "It promised so bright and fair just half an hour ago. Not to be deterred, of course. We're English."

He got up and went over to the door.

"So enjoyed my chat with you. I'll go and see what Natasha's doing. Catch up with you later." And he opened the door and stepped out into the shower of rain.

His last words reminded Zoe she hadn't yet had a chance to probe his relationship with Natasha. But as she turned to look at Alice again she was startled by the expression on her face.

"What is it, Alice?"

"Did you see?" asked Alice.

"See what?" said Zoe.

"The way he moved in on you as if about to speak, then shot back as soon as Theo entered."

"Well, yes," said Zoe.

"He's not just a creep. He's dangerous," said Alice.

Zoe and Theo both stared at her.

"What do you mean?" asked Zoe.

"I sense it," Alice replied. "On the surface he's all charm. But you look in those eyes. And they tell a different story: menacing; mocking; insincere. He's building up to something, for sure. And it isn't good."

CHAPTER SEVEN

At eleven o'clock that morning, Zoe went to the art studio. Jessica was due to arrive at midday and Zoe needed to check on the supply of art materials, tidy up, and wipe down all the tables. The routine activity might settle her thoughts; for Alice's warning preyed on her mind.

A damp mist now hung about the trees, lending the scene a dark, fairy-tale appearance. The first character who came into her mind was the Big Bad Wolf. And then she thought of the central message of those dark tales:

Be warned. There are monsters out there. Beware of strangers. Beware the wolves of the wood.

The atmosphere felt moist and oppressive. Zoe glanced up. Sullen clouds hung low. The light shower had stopped, but there'd be a downpour later on. Beyond the east wall of the barn, she saw a few guests taking a stroll among the conifers, punctuated by long pauses to contemplate the lines of poetry carved into wooden plaques on the trees. They'd now be taking the reflective half-hour that Theo incorporated into the morning's workshop. A couple of guests meditated by the sculpture fountain in the centre of the courtyard. Two bronze cupped hands received a stream of water poured from a stoneware jug. Zoe smiled at the guests as she passed by and turned towards the studio door.

As soon as she entered the studio, she saw James in there with Jessica, whom Zoe had not even realised had arrived yet. They sat in the opposite corner together, beside the artists' easels.

Jessica was a Birmingham businesswoman and visited the centre more often than any of the other trustees, always giving at least a day's notice. Zoe had been expecting her to call in at reception on arrival. It seemed, though, just as Zoe had expected, that James had waylaid her, keen to renew his former acquaintance in Edinburgh. Both turned and saw Zoe as she entered.

"Morning, Zoe," said Jessica, rising to her feet. She was a tall, slim woman with glossy dark-brown hair, who favoured French-navy tailored suits. "I meant to call into the office as soon as I arrived but on the way across the courtyard I had a huge surprise – I met James. You know, we've met before?"

"Yes, James did mention it to me," said Zoe, moving forward to join them.

"Well, Jessica," said James, also getting up, "this has been an enormous pleasure."

"Yes, who'd have thought you and I would meet up again after so many years?" said Jessica.

"Yes, incredible. You were still at school, weren't you? And very bright; you impressed me even then. And here you are now, chair of trustees for this centre… and perfectly suited to the role."

"Thank you, James," smiled Jessica.

"I'm a good judge of character. I know my time here's limited, but if there's any way I can help…"

"That's a kind thought, James," said Jessica, "but I assure you there's no need. We have an excellent team. Enjoy your stay. If there's anything you and Natasha need, please don't hesitate to ask." She faced Zoe. "I'll drop in on the office for a chat with you, Zoe, in half an hour. I'd like to have a word with Theo next, and then Bernie."

"Fine," said Zoe. "I'll just do some sorting out and tidying up in here."

"I'll be off," said James. "See you both later." As James was about to pass Zoe, he stopped and locked eyes with her. She felt angry and out of control. With a desperate effort to hold her feelings in check, she walked away from him.

Taking a deep, calming breath, she went to unlock the cupboard where they stored the finished artworks and ceramics, and checked that everything was in good order. Judging that James would at this stage be well out of the way, she went back out again and crossed the courtyard, which was, as she'd anticipated, now empty of people.

Before she reached the office door, however, the musical lilt of a Welsh accent intervened behind her. "Zoe, sorry to hijack you… but you look troubled."

"Griff," said Zoe, twisting to face him. Her heart often lifted, as it did now, when she looked at their in-house Welsh poet, as she fondly thought of him.

"It's out of character for you to look so glum," he said.

"Not so much now I'm chatting to you, Griff," she smiled.

Griff had a playful, fluid personality, sometimes cheerful, sometimes wistful. He didn't have a girlfriend, as far as Zoe knew, though she'd seen him chatting and laughing with Alice more than a few times; which wouldn't be much help to him, Zoe reflected, if Alice's agent rang and said she'd got her an audition in London, and Alice landed the part and had to go off filming at the other end of the country for six months. Still, she persuaded herself, it was no concern of hers, although she liked both Griff and Alice very much.

"You know, Griff," she said, "we're so lucky to have you here."

He held his hands wide. "The pleasure's all mine, Zoe. I love the job. It's fantastic when people come to us, sick and run-down, and whilst here they make some kind of breakthrough and release whatever it was that blocked their healing. It's great that I can be part of that, teaching creative writing."

"Which, as I know from your own accounts," said Zoe, "sometimes involves sitting on beds with tearful authors counselling them about their novels, late into the night."

"True," he said. "I love the chance to work with people who're despondent and discouraged, knowing I can help them believe in themselves again. And I get the chance to write lots of poetry too: paradise!"

"That's awesome, Griff."

"So, why *were* you looking so worried when I met you just now?"

"Sorry Griff. It's just I really don't like James, and I feel bad about it, as he's a guest. And as for Natasha, I don't know what to make of her."

Griff laughed. "Plenty of other people here know what to make of her," he said. "They love her."

"Already?" she said, her eyes widening. "And what do you think?"

"I think she's lovely. When you're talking to her she makes you feel like you're the only other person in the room. And she has such beautiful eyes – that amazing deep blue."

Zoe bit her lip. "Well, it's clear *you*'re a fan." She gave him a wry smile. Doubts began to needle her. Perhaps Natasha had a dual personality. But she herself only saw Natasha differently from Griff and the others because she trusted Alice's instincts. Zoe refused to believe Alice had been wrong about Natasha. But in that case, she couldn't understand how Natasha had managed so easily to deceive Griff and several guests.

"I've seen the way Natasha talks to the others, too," went on Griff. "People open up to her very quickly. Guests have told me they feel they can share all their problems – not just physical but emotional. She has this special way – people believe she heals them by simply talking to them."

"That cannot really happen, though, Griff," said Zoe. She heard a tremor in her voice.

"Already two people claim she's given them physical healing," said Griff. "Cynthia and Heidi."

Zoe's heart started to hammer.

"Griff," she said, "by what power do you think Natasha's doing this?"

Griff stared at her.

"God, of course," he said. "Soon, word will get round and we'll have a flood of course bookings, all from applicants wanting to come and be healed by Natasha."

Zoe was now breathing faster. "I think Theo and I need to have a talk with Natasha before we allow that to happen," she said, trying to sound calm.

Someone came up behind Zoe. Her stomach tightened. She spun round.

"Natasha," she said.

"Did I alarm you?" enquired Natasha with a sweet smile.

"No, not at all."

Once more, Natasha was dressed all in white. And again, it was an ankle-length dress, this time worn beneath a long, lace cardigan with mother-of-pearl buttons. She favoured dazzling white, too. No cream or ivory for her. Her insistence on this made the blue of her eyes more intense and unsettling.

Griff extended his free hand to Natasha and grasped hers. "Everyone's talking about you, Natasha," he said.

"Thank you."

"The other guests believe you have a healing gift," said

Zoe. "I'm curious to know how many times this has happened for you in the past?"

"Oh, I'm happy to talk about it," responded Natasha. "Not right now, though, as I'm sure you've plenty of work to be getting on with."

Zoe lifted her chin.

"No, I'd like to talk about it right now."

"Very well. I've had success with psychological and emotional problems as well as physical," said Natasha. "Sometimes it does seem like I can heal such things by a touch, or a glance. I can certainly give people a sense of peace."

Zoe moistened her lips. In the past, if she felt herself reacting against someone she didn't know well, she'd preferred to give them the benefit of the doubt.

"But of course you cannot guarantee that," she said.

"No? Why not wait and see. Over the next few days, who knows what may happen?"

"You are having us on, aren't you, Natasha?" insisted Zoe.

Natasha smiled, and didn't reply.

"I've never heard of anyone healing by a touch or a glance," Zoe said, "only Jesus."

For a second, Zoe felt sure she saw Natasha stiffen.

"I suggest you reserve judgement," said Natasha. "Have patience. You will, I hope, be willing to believe the evidence of your own eyes."

Zoe nodded. She didn't know what more she could say.

Griff changed the subject. "Will I see you in my workshop after lunch, Natasha?"

"Maybe," she replied.

"You're very mysterious," commented Griff.

"How long have you and James known each other, Natasha?" asked Zoe.

Natasha raised her hand and pushed her hair back. "Days,

months, years," she said. "What does it matter? Time in this world means nothing."

Zoe's eyes widened. "I'd say it means a lot, much more than I'd like it to."

"Not to me," said Natasha.

"Why, do you exist in some eternal realm?" enquired Zoe flippantly.

"Perhaps I do," she replied, and then switched her attention to a point behind them. Zoe turned to see another guest approach.

"Ah, there's Gareth," said Natasha. "Do excuse me. He mentioned a health problem to me. He agreed to tell me more about it later. I may be able to help him."

She walked past them leaving Zoe staring in disbelief.

"Natasha seems quite charming," said Jessica, as Alice made ready to leave the office at twelve thirty. "Nobody I've spoken to since coming in this morning has had anything to say against her. I've heard words like *spiritual, caring, lovely*. She makes people feel valued. Frankly, I'm delighted we have someone like her with us. See you at lunch."

And with that Jessica walked out of the office.

Zoe turned to Alice. "I feel like screaming," she said.

"And if you were at drama school, I'd say go ahead," replied Alice; "it's all part of the training. But right now, I'm afraid, you'll probably be heard across the courtyard and the guests might think you're being murdered in here."

"True," said Zoe. "How much longer, though, can I continue listening to this stuff about Natasha?"

"Until we find out more about her that might prove otherwise," said Alice. "Meanwhile, listen, there's a book I want to borrow from your library before I go."

"Sure. I'll come through with you and help you find it," said Zoe.

Leaving the office by the internal doorway they walked through the house to the library.

"Alice, I'm afraid," said Zoe.

Alice closed the library door behind them and scrutinized her. "Yes. I know. And I think you have every right to be."

"How can I put it? Theo and I aren't safe. That's how I feel."

Alice stood with her hands on her hips. "Zoe, I'm not going to give you false comfort. I agree with you. But I promise to help in every way I can."

"Alice, if you're right about Natasha, why does nobody else see anything in her manner, her eyes, her tone of voice, her words, to give them a clue? Does she consciously intend to deceive?"

"I believe so," said Alice.

"Let me get you your book," said Zoe, going across to the bookshelf opposite and picking out the book Alice wanted. "Here you are."

"Thanks."

Before Zoe could return to the subject of Natasha, they both heard a motor engine approach the house.

Alice went over to the east window which gave a view onto the gravel forecourt and Zoe followed.

The vehicle swept down the drive towards them, whipping up dust and leaves: a black Porsche Cayenne.

As it neared the farmhouse, it slowed then drew to a halt south of where they stood, close to the conifers.

"We're not expecting any new arrivals," said Zoe. "Must be visitors. Let's go out and meet them."

They left the library and went to open the front door. As they stood on the threshold, they saw James getting out of the Cayenne while Natasha emerged from the conifers; neither seemed to notice Alice and Zoe. Natasha had her back to them as she opened the front passenger door and took something out, which looked like a bundle of clothes. Then she and James disappeared from view, back along the path which led through the conifers to the goose house.

Zoe and Alice exchanged a bewildered glance.

CHAPTER EIGHT

Ten minutes later, Zoe put the phone down after a conversation with the Trust's building insurers, and Miles appeared in the office, with drawn face and wrinkled brow. She braced herself.

"Zoe, sorry to hit you with more bad news, but Theo's asked me to let you know that the ceramic communion set has gone missing."

"Missing? The whole set? Is he sure?"

"I see no reason to doubt him, Zoe. As you know, there was the jug, a large plate and two goblets. Theo tells me the set was locked in the cupboard in the studio. But when he went in there just now, and looked in the cupboard, he found those items had gone."

Zoe's face clouded. Theo's communion set had been made by a visiting ceramic artist, and was very beautiful. After several firings in the kiln, each time with a different overlaid glaze, each piece had been engraved with delicate patterns and painted with cobalt oxide. The artist had presented the set personally to Theo as a thank you gift for all the help and counselling she'd received from him.

"I checked myself at eleven o'clock this morning," said Zoe. "And they were all there. So I can't think what would have happened to them since. Apart from Theo and me, only Bernie has a set of keys. I'll call him."

She made the call then looked up at Miles.

"Nothing. Bernie hasn't been near the cupboard since yesterday afternoon."

She chewed her lip.

"There may have been some misunderstanding. I'll ask Bernie to search the place this afternoon. If it still hasn't turned up by tomorrow, we'll ask the guests at lunchtime."

James's face appeared on her mental screen. He'd been in the studio that morning, with Jessica. But she had no reason to suspect him capable of theft. Besides, she'd seen him leave the studio empty-handed.

There was a knock on the door and three guests entered the office. Zoe blanked James out and hoped desperately that they weren't about to report another healing. She almost breathed a sigh of relief when they began to query her, instead, about the details of that day's programme. Then they all went off to the dining area for lunch, and Zoe followed, locking the office door behind her.

After dinner that evening, Zoe went into the first-floor study and chose an easy chair.

She had twenty minutes free before going back on duty at that evening's event. Theo would lead a calligraphy workshop in the studio. Zoe had no idea whether James and Natasha would be there. With most guests either in their rooms, or still chatting over coffee in the sitting room, she trusted she'd be alone for the next few minutes.

She'd brought her iPad in with her. But her purpose was not to catch up on personal emails. She had other intentions.

The first time she'd known James, more than three years before, her own instincts had guided her to keep away from him and she'd avoided any long conversations with him. So, although she knew he'd done some professional acting, and had spent time as an academic, she knew very little else about him. Now was her chance to do a bit of research.

He merited a mention on several academic websites, as well as International Movie Database, Rotten Tomatoes and Wikipedia. Scrolling down the list of websites, she confirmed that he had, in the past, been on the academic staff at Edinburgh University, teaching psychology; he'd played a priest in *Journey to the Scaffold*; he'd been cast as a vampire and a werewolf a number of times and had also done quite a bit of extras work.

She brought up one of her search pages again. No sign of any unsavoury information about him. If he had the 'dangerous' element that Alice had mentioned, it didn't seem to be something he'd acted on yet; unless of course he'd done it under a different name. And it might be he was waiting for the right time – perhaps the best phase of the lunar calendar.

She remained unsatisfied. She still couldn't make sense of why James and Natasha had chosen to come to this centre. She believed the reason they'd given her and Alice was spurious. Neither of them showed any interest in the workshops. But she was powerless to do anything about it.

The next morning Zoe's heart felt even heavier. The missing jug, plate and goblets had still not come to light. And Theo had woken up tired. Far from being refreshed by an early night, he'd seemed worse. She wondered whether he'd been working too hard, or whether he'd caught a virus.

"Go and lie down again," she'd said to him at breakfast.

"I can't. I have to lead the workshop," he'd replied, and they parted.

"Theo's clearly sickening for something, isn't he?" remarked James an hour later, as Zoe hurried across the courtyard with her fleecy collar up around her neck, to protect her from the icy bite of the air.

She walked through into reception and took up her position behind her computer.

"Natasha would be very happy to heal him," said James, following, and standing in front of her desk.

"You have tremendous faith in Natasha," she said.

"Of course," replied James. "And so does everyone else. Surely, as Christians, you and Theo should be the first to celebrate her gift."

Zoe shot a cold glance at him. "A gift? And where do *you* say it comes from, James?"

Before he could answer, the door opened and Alice came in. Zoe relaxed.

"Morning, Alice," she said.

"Morning, Zoe, James," said Alice, going across to her desk.

James continued addressing Zoe as if Alice hadn't entered the room.

"Quite simply, Zoe, you've no idea of Natasha's power. What you've seen so far is nothing. Nothing at all. She has far more to show you."

The door opened and Natasha walked in, followed by Theo. Zoe got up at once and went to join Theo. She searched his face. His skin was taut over his cheekbones. His complexion seemed muted.

"You still don't look well enough to lead the workshop," she murmured.

"Griff said he'd do it for me," he said. "I'll go and lie down. But first Natasha agreed to come and have a few words with us."

Zoe looked back at Natasha and her stomach tightened. Both Natasha and James had taken easy chairs, while Alice remained at her desk.

"Natasha," said Theo, "Gareth tells me you healed him last

night. He shared the story with me and described how the pain had suddenly left him."

Natasha studied him with a gentle, alert expression.

"Yes," she said softly.

"If these people are right about what they believe has happened to them," said Theo, "that means you've healed three of our guests since you came to us. How do you do it, Natasha? Do you pray? Do you command the disease or injury to be gone? Any special words you use?"

Natasha smiled and folded her hands in her lap.

"Nothing special," she said. "If there *is* a command, it's unconscious and unspoken."

Theo continued to press her. "How often have you done this before?"

"Many times; I've lost count."

Zoe swallowed.

"But," said Theo, "in my experience, a good healing ministry isn't about finding cures – it's about people coming to peace with God over stuff; it's about healing and reconciliation. If we're gifted with a miracle, it's for a reason. Jesus did his miracles to prove a point and say something about the kingdom of God."

Natasha made no response. James cleared his throat as if about to speak. But instead he chose to remain silent.

"I was on a healing team years ago," said Theo, "and I saw somebody's cancer disappear – later to return six months down the line, when the patient had sorted their life out and was ready to go. Miracles are few and far between for a reason."

"You may believe that if you wish," said Natasha. "I, on the other hand, believe that many more miracles happen than we ever acknowledge. However, right now, all I know is the power that's been given to me, which I use for the good of others."

Zoe wanted to take hold of Theo's hand and squeeze it to give him courage. But she couldn't move.

"Very well, Natasha," Theo said. "Please call me first, before you do this again, so I can be present as well."

Natasha trained a long, cool glance on Theo.

"I'll try. But I can't promise. I meet people's needs as they arise; and, of course, only if they ask."

She and James exchanged a smile.

"Shall we be off, Natasha?" said James. "Remember we agreed to try out Griff's poetry workshop."

Zoe started. First workshop she'd known them try. Perhaps they planned to target Griff next.

"OK," said Natasha. "See you later." They both got up and walked out.

Zoe stared intently from Alice to Theo and back again.

"*The power*; does that mean psychic power?" she asked.

"Yes," said Alice. "She's using it for the wrong reasons."

Zoe could swear the temperature in the office had dropped a few degrees. She hugged her arms around herself.

"Can't imagine what those reasons might be, though," added Alice.

"Something in her drives her to fix the problems of others," mused Theo.

"If 'fixing problems' is what she's doing," remarked Alice. "The guests and the rest of the staff think she's some kind of higher spiritual being. I believe they'd do anything for her."

She studied Theo.

"And that's why Zoe and I agree there's something very wrong about it," she said. "This power of hers…where does it stop? And she still hasn't been clear about where it comes from."

Zoe, too, spun to Theo. "What shall we do?" she pleaded.

"I'll have to think about it," he said. "I'm not sure yet that I agree with you about this, Alice. James should be able to help us understand more; he knows Natasha far better than any of us. I'll speak to him alone. But perhaps I'll have another word with Natasha first. By the way, have the missing ceramic pieces turned up again yet?"

"No."

He sighed.

"That's it then. If they don't come to light in the next couple of hours, we'll speak to the guests about it at lunchtime. I'm off to lie down. See you later."

Zoe stood looking at the door after he'd walked out and closed it behind him.

Then she swung round to face Alice again.

"He doesn't see this the way I do," she said. "He's falling under her spell himself."

Her face burned with anger and tears rolled down her cheeks.

CHAPTER NINE

By midday there was still no news of the lost ceramics.

"Alice," said Zoe, "will you stay on, and join us for lunch? I'll need to question the guests about the missing communion set and I'd like you there to give me courage."

"Fine," said Alice.

At twelve thirty, Zoe and Alice locked the office door and walked across the courtyard to the dining area.

During group mealtimes Zoe and Theo usually sat in different places, chatting to separate groups of guests, to spread their hospitality as far as they could. The aroma of hot baked potatoes and vegetable chilli drew the guests in from the cold courtyard. Zoe guessed Theo meant to wait until lunch was over to confront the task of asking the guests if they knew of the missing jug, plate and goblets.

Meanwhile, James sat in the far corner chatting to two ladies. No doubt, thought Zoe, they were going over the details of Natasha's healings, and heaping praise upon her. Natasha herself was nowhere to be seen. Zoe had noticed Natasha was a little erratic in turning up for mealtimes. Perhaps she preferred to remain in the goose house acting out a sinister parody of a mediaeval anchoress in her cell, providing spiritual direction and healing to visitors.

James now sat with one arm folded in front of him to provide a shelf for his right elbow. His chin rested on his fingers. Zoe's muscles tensed. She tried to tear her gaze elsewhere and yet it kept being pulled round, as if by an elastic thread, in James's direction.

"Great place, this," said Gareth, shovelling a forkful of potato into his mouth. "I knew last week's course would be up my street, as painting's my thing. But hey, am I glad I stayed on for this week, too."

"Good to hear that, Gareth," said Zoe. "It's given you a chance to try out something different. You haven't done poetry or calligraphy before, have you?"

"Nothing to do with that," he replied. "No, I was thinking about Natasha."

"Oh," said Zoe, her heart sinking.

"Even if she hadn't healed me, and that's mind-blowing enough in itself, she'd still be the most incredible person I've ever met," declared Gareth. His eyes widened as he spoke and his pupils dilated. "What a woman: her voice; her figure; her face!"

Zoe didn't respond.

Gareth continued, undeterred. "And when I talk to her, she listens as no-one else I've ever known has done. I feel like the only person in the world when she looks at me. And I know others feel the same."

Zoe had put her fork down.

She thrust her hands into her lap and clenched her fists under the table.

As the meal drew to a close, bright chatter still filled the air, together with the sound of cutlery clinking against china. Zoe got up and moved to the space in front of the kitchen door. At the other end of the room, Theo also rose and came across to join her.

Zoe picked up a spoon and tapped it against a glass.

"A few words, please." The conversation faded as eyes turned in their direction. "I hope you all enjoyed your lunch."

Cutlery banged on tables. Gareth punched the air.

Zoe smiled. "First, two bits of news: you'll be glad to know Theo's doing an extra workshop tonight, after dinner. It's in the upper room in the barn."

"It's called *All That Breathes*," said Theo, "and will be a celebration of creation and the poet, Caedmon."

A cheer went up.

Zoe looked at Alice's face, visible between the shoulders of Heidi and Cynthia, two tables away from her. She wore a grave expression.

"Now, one more favour we need to ask of you," said Theo.

Sounds lessened, though three guests still clattered cutlery against their plates.

"We're hoping someone may be able to help us. A few items are missing from the ceramics cupboard in the studio. The cobalt-blue communion set: the jug, the large plate, and both goblets. We wondered whether there's been some misunderstanding. Bernie has the only other spare set of keys."

Theo stopped. Zoe took over from him.

"Does anyone know what's happened to the set?"

All eyes fixed on her. Zoe's face blushed beet-red. She began to stammer.

Theo came to the rescue.

"We're not accusing anybody."

"Oh no," said Zoe. "We just want to know if anyone's seen the missing stuff."

Whispers began to arise. Zoe saw the expressions shift on faces around the room. Smiles faded. Glances flicked to left and right. She bit her lip.

"No? Nobody knows anything?" said Theo.

Zoe wanted to throw her arms round Theo and comfort him, but didn't move. It was as if they'd both strayed onto quicksand and begun to sink.

"It's OK," said Zoe. "No worries."

"Finish your lunch, everyone," said Theo. "First afternoon session doesn't start till two o'clock. We meet in the barn."

The guests finished their meal in silence. The good humour and relaxed atmosphere had vanished, along with something precious which Zoe knew to be much more important than the recovery of missing items. In their place was a forcefield that resisted her body with every move. She glanced around, half-expecting that Natasha had come in. But there was no sign of the healer. And then, she told herself, if Natasha had entered, she'd know straightaway by the guests' reaction.

Zoe located James once more. He was sipping coffee with his little finger crooked. She felt something wringing her out. There was no way he could be involved, and yet...She shuddered. James's eyes met hers. They gleamed. She scurried through the doorway into the kitchen.

"Everything OK, Zoe?" said Miles.

"No," said Zoe, and shared with him what had happened.

"I'm sure you misunderstood their reaction," said Miles. "They would all have known you had to ask."

The door opened and Alice came in.

"How are you; OK?"

"No. Oh God, we made a hash of it. Or at least, I did."

"Nonsense. You were fine."

Zoe shook her head. "Judging by today's performance... load of good I'd be as an actress, wouldn't I?"

"Rubbish. Don't make this personal," said Miles.

"They all acted like I'd accused them of theft."

"No they didn't. Stop worrying about it."

But Zoe stood, gripping her upper arms, and she cast her eyes down so neither Alice nor Miles could see her tears.

"I'm calling an emergency team meeting," said Theo. "In the office. Are you able to join us too, Alice?"

"Yeah, that should be all right," said Alice.

A couple of minutes later, Bernie put the *Closed for half an hour* notice up outside the reception door then locked it behind him, and they all seated themselves.

"Sorry, Theo, can I ask why James is with us?" said Griff.

"Ah," said Theo, "that's because James has shared some information about Natasha with me, which is relevant to this."

Zoe tried to catch Alice's eye. But she was looking at James.

A sense of dread welled up in Zoe.

"We all know a number of incidents have happened here in the last few days," said Theo.

His audience remained still and silent.

"And we've dealt with things as they've arisen, as best we can. Cynthia's fall downstairs was our first shock. That was Saturday night. Then on Sunday there was the damage to the barn window; and we still don't know who threw the stone. Or what's happened to the communion set. That's been missing since yesterday morning. Of course, nothing else may happen. And those three events may prove random pieces of bad luck."

James crossed one leg over the other and tapped his fingers against his knee.

"Sometimes," said Theo, "when negative things happen, there's no message; it's just life. But I've an instinct something deeper's going on here."

Zoe moistened her lips, but made no comment.

"In addition," said Theo, "both Alice and Zoe have recently met a small child who then vanished. And they found that disturbing. I make no assumptions: I just mention it. And I don't necessarily connect these events. I'm simply listing them."

"But then, Theo," broke in Griff, "we also have Natasha here, and that's good, isn't it?"

"Good?" repeated Zoe, her heart pounding.

Griff stared at her.

"Of course," he said. "Everyone loves her. And she has the most amazing healing gift."

"Yes," said Theo hastily, "and it may be true that God is using her. I've now heard several guests call her a *miracle worker*; and an *angel*. But even so…"

"I think that answers all your concerns, Theo," began James. "You've no need to…"

"Nevertheless," broke in Theo, "I believe we must agree on a new way forward. And I've made a decision."

Zoe flushed with relief. Now Theo had acknowledged *something deeper* was going on, she felt a great burden had been lifted from her. On the other hand, two fresh doubts gnawed at her. Firstly, she was unconvinced by the reason he'd given for including James in this discussion. As a guest, James had no place at a team meeting. Theo was acting as if he trusted him. And secondly, Theo still seemed to think it possible that God was using Natasha. Zoe felt sick thinking about it. And yet, she tried to persuade herself, Theo surely knew what he was doing.

Meanwhile, Alice, Bernie and Griff all kept their eyes fixed on Theo. Zoe couldn't wait to hear his decision. She shot a glance at James. He looked as if he was paying his respects at the house of a deceased relative.

"I propose to hold a house blessing," said Theo.

Zoe started.

"A house blessing?" asked Alice.

"A sacramental act for a place which attracts negative events," said Theo. "It may include prayer, the sprinkling of blessed water and the signing of a cross on doors."

"Natasha will do that for us," said Griff.

"No she won't. I'll do it," said Theo.

Zoe felt numb inside. Theo hadn't said it, but the word *exorcism* was written in letters of blood across her mental screen.

Bernie and Griff exchanged puzzled glances. A chill gripped Zoe's fingers, and spread up her arms, before trickling down through her throat, her chest and her belly. James gave her a piercing look.

"You all right, Zoe?" asked Theo.

"Y-yes. But… which parts of the house will you do?"

She inclined to think he should be focusing on James and Natasha, not the house. Then she chided herself. Next, she'd be imagining Theo holding a cross up to them both and hanging garlic from the beams wherever they went!

To the eye of the superficial observer, James cut an immaculate and impressive figure, and had been charming and courteous, despite occasional flashes of arrogance. Meanwhile, Natasha had enchanted everyone – except Alice and Zoe. And several guests thought she was on a hotline to a higher power, at the very least. Certainly Zoe had no hope of convincing anyone otherwise without giving them cause to doubt her own state of mind.

"Good question," said Theo. "It would be a bit of an overreaction to do every single room. So I suggest we concentrate on the studio where the ceramics went missing, the staircase where Cynthia fell, and the barn where the window was smashed."

"Thank you, Theo," James said in a slightly sardonic tone of voice. "Your plan sounds admirable. Glad to see you tackling the problem on a spiritual level."

Zoe frowned at him. She considered he had no right to pass comment. She sprang to her feet.

"James, you…" she began then started coughing. Theo came across behind her desk, and rubbed her on the back.

"All right?" he murmured.

Zoe nodded. She felt agitated. She didn't dare look at James. And she tried not to think of Natasha.

"When will you start, Theo?" asked James.

"And will you involve the other guests?" asked Zoe.

"No," said Theo, "only those who feel comfortable with what I'm doing. Several won't, and I respect that. I'd like to do it straightaway. But the workshop starts in twenty minutes so we'll do it after that finishes. I'm sorry you won't be here at that time, Alice. But Griff, Bernie, Zoe – meet me at the front door at four thirty."

Zoe swallowed hard. All the other people in the room grew dim, except James, whose silhouette – in Zoe's eyes – held an unnatural intensity and darkness. Zoe's fingers tingled as she tried to visualise the house blessings Theo proposed. So, he did believe these bad events had a spiritual cause. Psychic influence lay behind them.

On the face of it, the worst she could say of James for certain was that he showed a disturbing tendency to muscle in on the work of the centre staff, rather than behaving like a guest. But as for Natasha: with her around, Zoe doubted that the house blessings would have any positive effect at all. She didn't believe they'd lift Theo out of his low mood. Nor did she suppose, even for a second, that they'd put her own mind at rest regarding Natasha. Rather, she suspected the opposite.

All the time a dark undercurrent reminded her that her opinion of Natasha ran counter to everyone else's. She only had Alice's instincts to justify this. And if she was wrong, and everyone else was right… she feared she might be going mad.

Theo began the blessings at four thirty that afternoon as promised. Griff, Bernie, Miles, Natasha, James and two other guests joined Theo and Zoe at the front door. Theo led them into the entrance hall and blessed the staircase Cynthia had fallen down. From there, they all filed through to the office, where Theo meant to add another blessing. They couldn't all get in, but Theo stood in the doorway and they heard his words.

"Bless the work done here," began Theo, "so it reflects the peace and order of creation. Bless the relationships between the people who work here. Bring a spirit of respect and gentleness and courtesy."

At this, one of the guests wiped tears away from her face. Zoe glanced at James. His lips curved but his expression remained serious.

They then walked across the courtyard to the barn, where Theo blessed the window that had been broken and the place from which they guessed the stone had been thrown.

Natasha stood apart from everyone else. Zoe noticed the expression in her eyes kept changing. In one moment, they flared with light. In the next, they clouded over, a lake beneath a stormy sky. Then they found Zoe, and focused on her, with an intensity that was almost like a knife-thrust.

Fidgeting, shifting her weight from one foot to the other, Zoe broke out into a cold sweat.

CHAPTER TEN

Theo finished the blessings at the front door. He stood with the door open, while guests and staff gathered round him in a semicircle.

"I bless this house, built upon the rock of rocks, the rock of Christ; no onslaught will undermine it, and no ill winds unsettle it. The guardian angel will welcome all who enter this place and repel all that would harm it."

He raised a small jug and sprinkled water from it on the door, then made the sign of the cross upon it with his finger.

Zoe watched Natasha. The healer's eyes were now fixed on Theo. Zoe shivered. Then Natasha's concentration on Theo cut out and switched back to Zoe. At once Zoe felt like a vole targeted by a kestrel wheeling overhead. She recoiled and nearly lost her balance.

"Are you all right, Zoe?" asked Miles. "What happened there?"

"No idea," she said. "But I'm fine, thanks." She pasted a smile onto her face, and hoped he didn't notice the tremor in her voice. She turned back to Theo, who looked ready to collapse. She grasped his arm to steady him.

James too had noticed.

"You know, Theo," he remarked, "I think the blessings have exhausted you. Sometimes, I imagine, intense prayer can do this. When people become open and vulnerable through prayer, they can lay themselves bare to all sorts of influences.

In this case, I think it's nervous strain. A lot's been going on around here, hasn't it, in the last couple of days?"

Zoe's jaw dropped. James's patronizing tone had caught her unawares. She itched to slap James's face, but knew it would do no good. She dropped her hand to her side and Theo put his arm round her.

"Come along, Zoe," he said. "It's getting colder now. Let's go inside. Come into the library with me and we'll sit down for a few minutes and relax."

The last thing Zoe saw, before Natasha allowed James to guide her along the path through the conifers to the goose house, was Natasha's face. It seemed to sway in and out of focus. Zoe felt as if she was viewing it through a gauze screen. Then James and Natasha disappeared from view. The others, too, had now started to disperse.

"Come on, Zoe; the library," said Theo.

"Good idea."

Once inside the library, with the door closed behind them, they went to sit on the sofa. Zoe took one end and Theo, turning towards her, searched her face.

"I can see you're not happy. What more do you expect of me, Zoe? I've done my very best."

"No you haven't," she said. "The best thing you could do is throw Natasha out."

He frowned. Then he took her hand in his and held it tight. At this, a wave of love and remorse swept through her. She drew a deep breath. Surely, this was her chance to pour out her fears about Theo and Natasha. But she couldn't bring herself to accuse him.

Instead, she said, "James is bad news. And Natasha's much, much worse."

"Now, come on, Zoe…" he protested. "How can you possibly say that?"

"Nothing bad happened before they came."

"It may seem so," he said, "but remember, we've had our setbacks in the past. And now we've done the house blessings, we must trust that we'll have the protection we've asked for."

"I don't believe we will."

A line appeared on Theo's forehead.

"It's Natasha and her healings, isn't it?" he said. "You're still worried about how she does it."

"That's right. I am. And I can't seem to get through to you. Why don't you see how dangerous she is?"

"Dangerous?" He looked perplexed.

"Yes," insisted Zoe, her heart pounding. "Natasha isn't 'normal'. And it's not just the healings. It's everything about her; but if you want to start with the healings... I don't believe they come from God. Not by a long way."

Theo's eyes widened.

"You believe she's using occult power?" he said.

She nodded, released her hand from his and folded her arms tight.

"Look," said Theo, "if she was, I'd know about it. I've come up against it a few times in my ministry – we're talking physical manifestations."

"What d'you mean by that?"

"Face changing, and an irrational, disproportionate reaction. You need two or three different sorts of evidence before you can be sure you're looking at that kind of power. So set your mind at rest. Nothing of the sort has happened with Natasha. I must admit, at first, I was so taken aback, I did wonder. But now I feel confident she has a special gift from God. So trust me; stop worrying." Theo drew her into his arms and held her tight, kissing her hair, cheeks, and ears. "What more can I do to reassure you? I love you so much. You have nothing to fear."

But Zoe's heart was still pumping fast. And she believed Theo was wrong.

Then she realised the door stood ajar. She thought Theo had closed it. But now, she could see through to the entrance hall beyond. James walked past the chink. She stiffened. She'd not long before seen him head off to the goose house with Natasha. What was he doing back here in the house so soon? As she thought this, James moved out of sight.

After dinner, Theo took several of the guests to the barn for his *All That Breathes* workshop in the upper room. Being off duty for an hour or so, Zoe went straight to their private study for some peace. As she sank into one of the easy chairs there was a knock at the door.

"Come in," she called, not moving. The door opened and James stood there. She jumped to her feet, angry to feel herself flushing.

"James! Why aren't you at Theo's workshop?" she asked.

"Not my scene, the ancient Celts," he said. "Contemporary poets are more my style. Relax. Why don't you come back downstairs instead, to the sitting room, where we can have a drink together and a little talk?"

"No thanks, James. Say what you want to now."

He came in and sat down with her. She bit her lip.

"Zoe," he began, "you seem to have picked up some very odd ideas about me and Natasha. I'm here to put things right between us."

She felt an uneasy stirring in her stomach.

"Go ahead. What would you like to say?"

"Just this: I have no sinister agenda. I feel connected to this house. I have an affinity with it."

"An affinity?" She folded her arms, frowning.

"I believe I'm meant to be here," went on James. "I've had an acting career, but now I'm ready to move on."

"Oh? Why's that?" She felt interested, despite herself.

"This will be something you'll already know from chats with Alice. An actor's life is very unstable. Rivalry's vicious. You can't trust anyone. You've got to be tough to survive, and very determined."

"I'm sure that's true," said Zoe. "And Alice *is* tough, and determined."

"Good, good. Glad to hear it. It's pretty nasty in the acting world; very bitchy, very cruel. And I've had enough of it."

"You're saying you've quit acting?" Zoe uncrossed her arms and folded her hands in her lap instead.

"Yes. I want a more level kind of life."

"Hmmm." She followed this, up to a point, though if anyone was able to cope with a cruel and bitchy world, she felt sure that person would be James.

She looked at him. His confident manner might be just a display, masking a sensitivity she'd given him no credit for. He may have simply decided he wanted to spend more time with Natasha: a difficult thing for a busy actor. And perhaps her own personal insecurity had made her misinterpret his behaviour as arrogance when it seemed that he tried to take over in the office, and after the incident with the stone...

"It would be good," said James, "if you and I could get on, Zoe, here in the house I feel so drawn to, the house my ancestor built."

Resting her elbow on one crossed knee, she sat with chin in hand.

"That may be so, James," she replied, "and I never treat our guests with anything other than respect and courtesy. But Natasha terrifies me."

He looked at her narrowly.

"Theo has every confidence in her. Why don't you?"

"I think Theo has been deceived." Then she felt a guilty

black tug at the bottom of her stomach for having said so much to James.

A sly expression came into his eyes.

"Do I detect a lack of trust there?" he enquired. "I imagine life can be quite as bruising for a priest as it can be for an actor. I understand from Natasha that Theo has not always been as strong as he appears to be now."

"And why would Natasha know that?" Zoe flashed, her heart starting to hammer.

"Oh, she's had a few helpful chats with him in private. Not that I'd like you to think she's betrayed Theo's confidences to me. But none of us are proof against times of weakness and stress, are we, least of all those of us who're vulnerable to depression?" He clasped his hands together before him and wore a look of solicitous concern.

Zoe started. "That's the past. All happened before I met him."

"But you must know quite a bit about it."

Her face burned. "He lived alone in a cottage on the north Norfolk coast for eighteen months."

"Cut himself off, you mean. Nervous breakdown?"

"No. He suffered mild depression and anxiety; and recovered."

James's gaze sharpened.

"That's encouraging. Let's leave the subject for now. I can see it upsets you. Goodbye."

He walked out. Zoe sat with her hand clasped over her mouth. She couldn't believe James had drawn this much information out of her. But worse than that was the realization that Theo had been chatting privately to Natasha, without her knowledge, and had shared with her some very personal details about his past life. She angrily rubbed her eyes.

CHAPTER ELEVEN

"Zoe, don't let this prey on your mind," said Alice the next morning in the office. "Go and find Theo and talk to him."

"I can't," said Zoe. "He was up early this morning and I haven't caught him alone since. Have you?"

Alice shook her head. Her eyes were warm as she leaned forward, elbows on her desk, looking at Zoe. "This is really weighing on your spirits, Zoe. In the last few days you've changed so much."

"Alice, I need your help," pleaded Zoe.

"And I *will* give it to you. I'll do all I can, you know that," promised Alice, "but the first move has to come from you. *You*'ve got to fight Natasha."

Thinking of Alice's words earlier, alone in the office that afternoon Zoe's hands felt cold and clammy. Her head, shoulders and neck ached. In the past she'd counted her blessings. But now her mind ranged over the circumstances of her marriage to Theo. When she'd agreed to marry him, she'd known she'd be up against two things; first, his vocation as a priest; and second, the possible recurrence of his depression.

She'd accepted that, in his role as priest, there would be times when he counselled people one-to-one, and she'd play no part in that. But he'd also explained the 'rules of engagement': he spoke to people on neutral territory, or in a public location. But now Zoe suspected Theo of going to see Natasha in her bedroom in the goose house. The words *unfaithful* and *betrayal* kept needling her.

Turning to her email screen, she was about to begin scanning the new messages. The door burst open and she glanced up. Griff hurried into the office.

"What is it, Griff?"

"Natasha just offered to heal Theo. And he refused. I can't understand it, neither can anyone else."

Zoe raised her eyebrows. "Heal him of what?"

Griff stared at Zoe wide-eyed.

"This virus or whatever it is he has. We can all see he's not well."

"He doesn't need Natasha to 'heal' him," said Zoe sharply.

Griff looked shocked. "Of course he does. What's up with you? We have someone with miraculous healing power, close by, and he…"

"Stop, Griff," ordered Zoe, her anger rising, "I don't want to listen to this."

Griff studied her burning face. "Look, Zoe, I can see something's not right between you and Theo. Come and sit here. Tell me about it."

"I've got lots to do, Griff, but… " They both sat on the easy chairs.

Zoe longed to share her true feelings about Theo and Natasha. But to name these seemed an act of betrayal. So, instead, she spoke of her fear that Theo's past depression might return.

"Since I've known him," she said, "he's never been depressed at all."

Griff nodded, his brown eyes full of empathy.

"I first met him three years ago, on Midsummer's Eve," said Zoe. "We fell for each other straightaway. All I cared about was the Theo I knew. And we wanted to hear each other's stories. We spent hours, sharing those."

"Of course you did," murmured Griff. "But you never wondered how you'd cope if his depression returned?"

"No."

"Do the trustees know about this?" he asked.

"His depression? I'm not sure. I've never asked Theo." She hesitated, then added, "I married him eight months after we met."

Griff's lips curved, but he said nothing.

"You think we married too soon, don't you?" said Zoe.

"Not at all. Look, can I take over here? I'll help for the next hour. I can deal with the emails for you, and take phone calls, and look after any guests who drop in. Go and find Theo now. He'll put all your fears to rest."

Zoe went first to the sitting room, where she found a guest and learned from her Theo had gone to the first-floor study.

Zoe hurried upstairs and ran along the passageway. Pulling the study door open she went in. James occupied one of the chairs by the coffee table, Jessica sat opposite and Theo behind his desk. They all looked at her, unsmiling, as she entered. The atmosphere was tense.

"Theo, Jessica. I didn't realise you planned a meeting." Her mouth went dry.

"Yes," said Jessica. "Sorry, Zoe, we should have let you know, but it was so last-minute. I'm glad you're here. Come and join us."

Zoe desperately wanted to speak to Theo alone. But now it wasn't possible. She took the third easy chair and sat with crossed arms and clenched fists.

"Why's James here?" she asked.

"Because he has special information that's relevant to this centre," said Jessica.

Zoe pursed her lips. She'd heard this before; and the next time someone said it to her, she felt sure she'd hit them.

"I'm afraid, Zoe, that Theo's just given me some disturbing news," said Jessica.

"About Natasha?" said Zoe. New hope flared up in her. Perhaps Theo had seen through Natasha at last and reported his concern to Jessica.

"No," said Jessica, "it's not about Natasha at all; it's about Theo's mental health."

Zoe's arms and fingers tingled as blood rushed to her face.

"I don't understand," she said, aware that her voice was trembling.

"Don't you?" responded Jessica. "Well, I'm very sorry to hear that because I've just discovered that back when the Trust appointed you and Theo to your posts in this centre, Theo failed to disclose to us that he'd had, in the recent past, a severe mental breakdown."

Zoe gasped. She jumped up, unable to bear any more of this.

"You've got it wrong about Theo. He's only suffered a bit of depression now and again. He's never had a mental breakdown."

Silence fell. She gazed at Theo, who failed to meet her eye.

Zoe's heart hammered.

"I'm sorry about this, Zoe," said Jessica, "especially as it seems you may not even know the full story yourself. 'Bit of depression now and again' doesn't fit the case. We're talking about eighteen months of severe depression and psychosis. That's what Theo has now admitted to me, following James's encouragement."

Zoe gasped and spun to face Theo again.

"I'm sorry, Zoe," he said. "I told you as much as I thought you could bear. Why should I talk about the… the full horror and wretchedness of it?" His voice dropped. "I was afraid you'd think twice about marrying me."

Jessica drew her breath in between her teeth.

Zoe looked desperately at James. What part had he played in stirring this up with Jessica? She felt like tearing him limb from limb. Meanwhile, James's facial expression was like that of a brown bear crouching with its paw out over white-water rapids, ready to catch a salmon. She felt a rush of fury at his betrayal.

"Have you been listening to lies from James?" she asked.

Jessica wore a look of deep disapproval.

"Zoe," said Theo, "please, don't say any more."

She ignored Theo; instead, clenching her fists, she glared at James. If she hit him now, in front of Jessica and Theo, at this critical moment, she knew she'd destroy whatever remaining chances they may have of holding onto their positions at this centre; and she'd never forgive herself.

"Zoe," pleaded Theo, "please understand, I'm in the wrong. I should have told the trustees the full story, before they appointed me. And I'm sorry, Jessica, that I held back from telling you the truth at the beginning."

Before Jessica could answer, James interjected.

"Of course, Theo, we sympathise with you, for what you've suffered. And I cannot be insensitive to these things, in the world in which I move. I've met numerous creative people, in both theatre and the film industry, whose mental health is fragile. But I also feel for Jessica, in her position. She must do what's best for us guests."

To Zoe's fury, tears escaped from her eyes and began to trickle down her cheeks. Theo came out from behind the desk and went straight to Zoe, putting his arms around her and holding her tight. But her tears continued to roll, staining his shirt and soaking it. Then she pulled back from him; and he covered his face with his hands.

James's voice flowed on. "Far be it from me, as a guest, to intrude at this moment of crisis, Jessica, but I may be able to offer help."

"No," said Theo, who now began pacing the room in agitation. "There's no way you need get involved, James. We'll manage this. I don't believe my work here has suffered."

"May I make a suggestion?" said Jessica, rising to her feet. "James and I would be much better discussing this in private later. I don't want to distress you and Zoe any more, Theo."

"Oh, I do agree," said James, also getting up to stand beside Jessica. The two of them faced Theo and Zoe.

Zoe clasped her hands to her head. "Oh, for God's sake!" she cried, dropping her hands to her side again. "What can you and James possibly have to say to one another about this in private, Jessica?" With a desperate effort Zoe restrained herself from lunging forward, seizing Jessica's arm and shaking some sense into her. "Why can't you see the truth about James? Why can't you see through his lies?"

Theo, Jessica and James all stared at her, aghast.

CHAPTER TWELVE

As soon as Jessica and James had left the room together, having agreed to ignore Zoe's last words to them all, and with an avowed intention on Jessica's part to call a further meeting of the trustees, Zoe turned to Theo and seized both his hands.

"Theo, tell me. Depression I understand. But what's psychosis?"

She could feel the tension in his muscles.

"It's as if someone else has climbed into your mind and taken control of it. You say and do things you cannot remember later. You only have what other people tell you to go by. And eventually you have to accept what they claim you did."

"And... what things *did* you do?"

"Well, the police later told me I was found in a field with a shotgun. I said I was going to catch a rabbit for the pot."

She stared at him. She wanted to laugh, and cry at the same time.

"But," she whispered, "you did get better again."

"Yes, Zoe, I did."

"Did you take medication?"

"To my shame, no. It was prescribed for me. Though quite honestly there's a lot I can't remember."

Zoe's eyes widened.

"Had it ever happened before that?" she asked.

"Well," he said, "my first attempt at theological training failed. Something similar happened then. I took a course of medication to help me through. But, you know, my first marriage... I married very young. That was a big mistake. It all broke down during my ordination training, though I later convinced the selection board to put me forward again."

Zoe squeezed his hands. "This stuff is all history. Now, it's you and me. And what just happened in this room isn't what you deserve." He kissed her on the forehead. Her words tumbled over each other as she released his hands. "Theo, you must speak to Jessica alone. We can't let her involve James like this."

Theo shook his head. "I'm keeping out of it. Jessica can take this to the trustees and let them make of it what they will." He adjusted his watchstrap, arm across his body.

"But James will be pouring poison into Jessica's ears right now," insisted Zoe desperately. "You can't run the risk of being sacked over this. Go to Jessica straight away."

"No."

Zoe's face burned.

"If you won't do it, I *will!*"

She stormed out of the room and slammed the door behind her. Then she stood with her back against the door, trembling. Any moment a guest would emerge from a bedroom to see what was wrong. Since it was six o'clock she expected to find a few around. As if on cue, a bedroom door opened and Cynthia appeared, wide-eyed.

"Anything wrong, Zoe? I heard a door bang. It made me jump. Must admit, when I hear that, it reminds me of the last row I had with my ex before I walked out on him."

Zoe cleared her throat.

"Sorry Cynthia. I was a bit rough with the door. Everything OK with you?"

"Oh yes," said Cynthia, "couldn't be better. I'm so glad I came here, Zoe. I could never have dreamed I'd meet someone like Natasha. It's almost too good to be true."

Zoe was speechless. Cynthia threw her a brilliant smile and then trod lightly along the corridor and down the stairs.

Zoe drew a deep, calming breath. She'd managed to control her trembling lips while speaking to Cynthia. The effort of hiding her true feelings had stirred nausea in her stomach. Theo's refusal to confront Jessica hit her again with full force. And Jessica's high opinion of James baffled and angered Zoe.

For half a minute she stood torn by indecision, debating whether to rush back into the study and make it up with Theo, or fly downstairs and find out where Jessica and James were meeting. The second option would be best, she decided. A few seconds later she walked into the sitting room, looking for them, and instead found herself face-to-face with Natasha.

The healer had draped herself across the sofa. She'd twisted some sprigs of autumn leaves into her hair. She seemed to have detached herself from the misty landscape and floated in.

But as Zoe looked at her she remembered Alice's image of the tarantula crawling over the jewelled mask, together with all that it meant for her: the glitter and light and glamour of a masked ball; and the silence and poise of the spider, its stealth, its watchfulness, its gracefulness… and its murderous intent towards its prey. Zoe's breathing became quicker and shallower.

Once again, Natasha's eyes reminded Zoe of a woodland pool which reflected a rapidly changing sky; one moment dark clouds massed overhead then they vanished to be replaced by translucent sapphire.

Natasha gazed at Zoe. Zoe struggled to break the eye contact, yet she was held against her will. Indeed, even while her mind rebelled, she could hardly bear to stop looking at her, because Natasha was so enchantingly beautiful.

"How's poor Theo?" asked Natasha softly.

Zoe started. "Poor Theo? What do you mean?"

"He's not well at all," Natasha said. "I know it. And so do the other guests."

"He's been a bit low. But he'll be fine tomorrow."

Natasha raised her eyebrows.

The words Zoe had planned to say swirled into a marshy wasteland. Instead, she opened her mouth and said something unexpected.

"Natasha, what do you do with Theo when you meet him alone?"

Natasha smiled. "What a curious question," she said. "We chat. What else do you think we do? He's such a sweet man. You're very lucky to have him, Zoe."

But not for much longer if you have your way, thought Zoe. A white-hot flame seared up through her, as if she'd spoken those words aloud. Then she felt a heavy pressure on her chest.

"I feel your fear and your uncertainty, Zoe," said Natasha. "Why don't you let me set you free? I can heal Theo of his depression too. All you need to do is ask me first." Her eyes began to draw Zoe in.

Zoe started perspiring. She flexed her fingers and they slithered against her moist palms. Her breathing became shallower. She felt Natasha's psyche reaching out to her.

She made a desperate effort to pull herself away.

"Let go of me, Natasha," she gasped. "I'll never put myself in *your* power." At this, she spun round and ran out of the room. In the hall she stopped to try and calm her ragged breathing. She'd lost all track of time. Glancing at her watch she saw it was half past seven; the guests would all be in the dining room right now. That scene with Natasha had destroyed any appetite she herself might have. She covered her mouth with her hand as she asked herself yet again why nobody but she and Alice saw the evil in Natasha. She dropped her hands and scrubbed them two or three times against the sides of her trousers, then, taking some calming breaths, set off upstairs, intending to return to the study.

As she turned along the first-floor passageway, she drew her breath in sharply. Theo lay on his back on the floor outside the study door, eyes closed.

"Theo!" she cried, rushing over to him and falling onto her knees beside him. "What's happened?"

He didn't respond. She slid one arm under him, held him close and listened to his breathing. She sat back on her heels, hand clamped to her mouth. She was shaking. There would be no-one around to help. She pulled out her mobile.

Griff was just going into the dining room.

"Of course, Zoe, I'll come at once," he said.

Zoe crouched beside Theo, repeating his name, but getting no reply. She could see no sign of injury and his breathing was regular. With a tremendous effort, supporting his head and shoulders, she lifted him into a sitting position and held him in her arms.

"What's happened, Theo? Speak to me."

He began to open his eyes then clutched at her with both hands.

"Zoe, I tried to stop you and make you come back. Then my head started whirling. The room spun round and round."

She heard footsteps running upstairs and soon Griff appeared.

"Griff, thank you!" she cried. "I need your help."

He hurried to join her. Theo's weight against Zoe grew heavier, though he was a slim man. She struggled to support him.

"Come on, let's lift him back onto his feet," said Griff. "You take that side, Zoe, and I'll take this. He needs to be in bed. Then we can call Natasha."

"Natasha?" It took all Zoe's self-command not to swear at Griff. "No, he needs a doctor!"

Griff looked at her sceptically.

"But…" he began then stopped.

With them both to help him, Theo managed to get himself to a standing position, but then clasped both hands to his head.

"God, I can't see. My head's spinning. And my neck… it feels so stiff."

"Come on, Theo," said Griff. "Let's get you into the bedroom."

They guided him through the doorway and manoeuvred him across to the bed. He fell onto it and lay still. Zoe reached over to switch on the bedside lamp.

"No!" he gasped. "Can't bear it; turn it off."

Trembling, Zoe did as he asked. He pressed both hands over his eyes. Zoe sat down on the bed beside him, stroking his hair.

"I really do believe Natasha would…" Griff began.

"No!" rapped Zoe.

Griff looked startled.

Theo moved his hands from his eyes then groaned. "The ceiling won't stop whirling. I can't bear to look at it. It's making me seasick." He covered his eyes again.

Sweat trickled down Zoe's forehead. Her heart raced.

"Theo, this doesn't make sense. You were fine in the study an hour ago." Then Natasha's recent words came to her: *How's poor Theo?* The truth was he hadn't been fine at all. And Natasha knew. Theo's health had been steadily worsening over the last few days. And Zoe had been in denial about it.

"I feel terrible; can't seem to control my thoughts. Zoe, tell Jessica. I've let everyone down. I'm the wrong person for this job."

"That's crazy, Theo. You're perfect for the job."

"I'm not. Zoe, someone's watching me."

"Yes. Me. And I love you!"

"No, not you," he said. "I mean someone else. All the time."

"I'll go and get Natasha," said Griff.

"Shut up, Griff!" flashed Zoe. *Ignore him, ignore him*, she repeated to herself.

"The guests know I'm a fraud," muttered Theo. "They believe in Natasha, not me. I'm hopeless. I wish I could die."

Zoe's heart was hammering.

"I'm no good and I've never been any good," said Theo. "I've always been depressed and I've messed up my life. I want to hide away. I'm so ashamed, so guilty…"

Zoe snatched at fragments of information about clinical depression, bits and pieces she'd picked up from the internet: *A descent into a smooth-sided black pit; no way to get out.* This could be a relapse. But worse, much worse than that, it could instead be something Natasha had done to him.

Conviction flooded through her. Natasha could very well have done it. From all Zoe had seen of Natasha's activities – and from her interpretation of these – Zoe had no trouble at all believing Natasha could launch such an attack. Natasha had cursed Theo!

Zoe threw her body around Theo and pulled him in, as if trying to shield him. Then Theo screamed and rolled over, hurling Zoe off again.

"My head! My head!" He slammed his head into the pillow and started biting the pillowslip. His body jerked as if he was going into convulsions.

"Griff, call an ambulance," sobbed Zoe.

"I will, I will." Griff, white with shock, pulled out his mobile and obeyed.

CHAPTER THIRTEEN

The following events passed in a dream for Zoe and she remembered very little of what happened before she found herself sitting in the ambulance, holding Theo's hand, as they sped away from the centre and headed for Gloucestershire Royal Hospital.

It was eleven o'clock by the time Zoe's taxi drew up at the centre that evening. She felt numb. In the past few hours she'd swerved and lurched between terror, panic and bewilderment. Although it seemed Theo was now being 'stabilised' at the hospital Zoe believed he still remained under Natasha's curse; and she felt convinced that the whole situation was being manipulated by Natasha's dark psychic power. On the way home in the taxi she had several times asked herself if she was going mad.

Her one source of reassurance was the knowledge that in a few minutes, so long as she could be sure no-one else was listening, she'd call Alice and share all this with her; she felt Alice was the only person right now who could convince her she was still sane.

As she walked into the entrance hall Griff hurried to meet her.

"How is he?" Griff asked.

She gathered herself together. There was no way she'd share her fears about Natasha's curse with Griff.

"Bad," she said. "Terribly depressed, Griff. But thank

God it's not an aneurysm as you suspected. They found no evidence of that."

"What a relief," he said, drawing her through into the sitting room which was empty of guests. "Come and sit down. You must be exhausted. How long will he be in?"

"I've no idea," she said, sinking into an armchair, as Griff took the one adjacent to hers. "The doctors said a period of inpatient care will be the best thing for him right now, to stabilise him with medication. Do any of the guests know about this?"

"No. I kept quiet about it, as you asked me to. I've told Bernie and Miles, of course. Obviously we'll have to tell the guests something tomorrow."

"Yes. But I don't want to frighten them."

"Of course not," he said, eyeing her narrowly.

"Griff," she said, "what's going to happen? Who'll manage the centre while Theo's gone?"

"Jessica," said Griff.

Zoe felt deflated. "But she has a business to run in Birmingham. I could do it, until Theo gets back."

"You?" A line appeared on Griff's forehead. "It's not my business to say. The trustees will decide."

"I know. But what do *you* think, Griff?"

"What do I think? Come on, Zoe. Your time's fully taken up with the administrator job. They'll have to find somebody to act in Theo's role."

Zoe bit her lip. Griff was going to be no help at all. He didn't believe in her, Zoe told herself. And neither did anyone else. That was bad enough. But what she really feared was that she might be judged insane before she had a chance to unmask Natasha to everyone.

Once she was back in her bedroom, and alone, she'd ring Alice.

The next day, Thursday, at ten thirty in the morning, Zoe was trying to concentrate on the spreadsheet on her computer screen in the office. But the figures danced before her eyes. She had just returned from visiting Theo in hospital. He seemed worse than last night. The drugs had deadened his reactions. She'd been in tears all the way through her drive back to the farmhouse. And now, having walked from the car park, let herself into the house and gone straight through to the office to rejoin Alice, she'd answered the phone to further bad news.

Jessica, she learned, had contacted the other six trustees. She'd managed to get four of them to make themselves available for a meeting that morning in the Corinium Hotel in Cirencester. The meeting had taken place at nine o'clock, while Zoe was visiting Theo. And James had been invited to it.

Zoe boiled with fury. James had no right to be involved at all. She deeply mistrusted him and could not guess what his motivation might be. But at the meeting he had, she discovered, outlined his career, background and experience to the satisfaction of them all, explained his present situation and availability, and convinced them that he could take on the role of acting centre manager in Theo's absence.

Zoe ended the call and put the phone down. Then she covered her face with her hands.

Alice jumped from her seat and went over to her at once.

"From your side of the conversation, I can guess what that was about. Zoe, remember I'm on your side. When you're ready to act against Natasha and James, I'll be with you every step of the way."

Ten minutes later the door opened and Jessica stood there. James was behind her.

"With the greatest possible respect for Theo," James said

as he walked in behind Jessica, "I do feel it was careless of him not to consider the possible consequences of a relapse, and to leave Zoe unprotected and at risk, together with the safe operation of the centre."

He followed Jessica into the office and closed the door behind him.

"How dare you criticise Theo, James," burst out Zoe.

Jessica hurried round Zoe's desk and took both her hands. A wave of her Dior perfume swept over Zoe. Her warmth and sympathy seemed so genuine, Zoe momentarily softened. "This has been a terrible shock for you. We're determined to support you in every way possible." She smiled at Zoe. Chic and poised, she appeared in control. She wore a straight navy skirt, a crisp pearl-buttoned blouse and tailored jacket.

She went to take one of the easy chairs. James seated himself in the one diagonally opposite. Alice remained behind her own desk, watchful and alert.

Jessica addressed herself to all three of them. "I've always held Theo in the highest regard…"

"As indeed have I," interjected James smoothly, "ever since I first met him."

Zoe drew some deep, calming breaths, and willed herself not to jump up and punch James in the nose.

Jessica went on. "Theo had the backing of every trustee. But we didn't know the full picture. And now – we hope he gets well as soon as possible, of course, but meanwhile, I'm so grateful to have James here. Your connections are impeccable, James; you're experienced in handling people at every level and we're convinced of your managerial skills."

"Thank you, Jessica," said James.

Zoe tried to speak, but her voice cracked and she swallowed two or three times.

"I assure you", said James smoothly, "that I'll do all in my power to guide the centre through this crisis."

A crisis which Natasha created with a curse, thought Zoe bitterly.

Now was not the moment to tell James exactly what she thought of him. It would have to wait till later. She turned her head away from Jessica and James to hide the tears in her eyes.

CHAPTER FOURTEEN

At a quarter past eight the next morning, Zoe crossed the courtyard beneath a dismal, overcast sky. But as she headed for the office, her eye was distracted by a flash of movement to the south. In the distance, beyond the barn, she saw Alice vault over the woodland fence. She smiled. Alice didn't often bother to unlatch the gate and walk through. She'd done gymnastics as a teenager and always took the more energetic route from the car park.

"Hi, Alice," she said, as the familiar figure in a burgundy jacket and black trousers ran towards her.

"Zoe," said Alice, "it happened again. Last night."

"What did?"

"I saw the child again."

Zoe drew in her breath sharply. "You're joking."

"No."

"Look," said Zoe, "come into the office. Tell me there."

They both went through the office doorway. Zoe shut the door behind them and they sat behind their desks.

"Tell me what happened," said Zoe.

"Last night: in Cirencester. I was walking up Gosditch Street just as James and Natasha came out of Graze Bar and Brasserie. It was eleven o'clock."

Zoe stiffened. Alice touched her hand then continued. "I saw the child with James."

"What?"

"I blurted out, 'James! Where did you find Poppy?' I don't even know why I said that, and why I identified the child as being called Poppy. James and Natasha both gawped at me. James said, 'What are you talking about?' I said, 'The little girl'. And he said 'There's no little girl'."

"Did the child speak?" asked Zoe.

"No."

"And James denied she was there?"

"Yes."

"How long did you see the child for?"

"Less than a minute; then she disappeared. I was rambling, I was so shocked. They both looked at me as if I was mad. James then suggested I get checked out by a doctor. I said I was as sane as the next person. I'd now seen the child three times. Then I left them."

"I guess you haven't come across James or Natasha yet this morning?"

"No, I haven't."

"Right; when you do see one of them, say nothing about this."

Silence fell between them. Then something seemed to snap inside Zoe.

"Oh my God, Theo's not here and I need him!" she cried.

Alice seized hold of Zoe by both shoulders and fixed her eyes on her. "Zoe, Theo's not coming back any time soon. Don't you see? There's just one person to get a grip on this: You."

Zoe stared at her, pulse racing, fists and teeth clenched. "Me? Why? They don't believe I'm good enough to run this place!"

She realised this reaction was out of all proportion to what Alice had said; because deep down Zoe knew Alice was right. Her palms felt clammy.

"What's this ghost child trying to tell us?" she asked.

"I don't know," said Alice. "But one thing I do believe: until we sort out what she's trying to say to us, she'll keep coming."

The door opened and Bernie put his head in.

"Zoe, one of the guests has just seen the vagrant lurking among the trees near the entrance. I'm off up there."

Zoe jumped up. "I'll come with you, Bernie. You OK to look after things here for half an hour, Alice?"

"Sure."

"Come on," said Bernie, "let's go. Take a waterproof. We're in for a downpour."

Zoe hurried through the internal doorway into the passage beyond and grabbed a waterproof from a hook on the wall of the utility area. She wondered where Vito was. She whistled to see if he was anywhere in the house and waited for him to come bounding down the passageway. But there was no sign of him. She hurried out of the back door to meet Bernie in the courtyard.

"Come on," said Bernie, "let's nail this guy."

"Yes," she said as they walked across the courtyard.

The gloom overhead had thickened since Zoe crossed the courtyard earlier. She didn't care. She needed to get to grips with at least one of the mysteries in this place, and if it was the vagrant, so much the better. She and Bernie walked round the house and across the forecourt and set off up the driveway to the main entrance.

When they were still twenty metres from the car park entrance, she glimpsed movement to her right. She spun, staring into the trees, her heart beating fast.

"There he is, Bernie," she said.

At once the thought flashed into her mind: Bernie would protect her if necessary. Not that the tramp had tried to assault her yet, but she no longer wanted to meet up with him while she was on her own. She now felt people like him needed to be visited in pairs.

"Hello," called Bernie. "Come on out. We know you're there. Talk to us."

Branches swayed. Twigs cracked. She jumped back as the vagrant appeared. Her fingers tightened into a ball. There he was: same filthy old coat; same thick beard and matted hair. His eyes snapped at her and Bernie; bloodshot, challenging.

She took a grip on herself, swallowed a couple of times. "Sorry, haven't got anything for you to eat."

"Come down to the house with us," said Bernie. "We can help you there."

He snorted then spat on the ground. Zoe couldn't stop a grimace of disgust from springing to her face. Then, without warning, he leapt forward and seized her by the hand. Immediately Bernie grabbed hold of his arm.

"Let her go," he ordered, forcing the tramp to release his grip.

The vagrant growled something indistinct, wiped his sleeve across his face, glared at them one more time, then swept round and disappeared back in among the trees.

"Right, I'll follow him," said Bernie. "You go back to the house, Zoe. I'll take care of this." He plunged after the tramp.

Zoe was about to follow Bernie, despite his words, but then thought better of it. Instead, she turned and hurried down the drive again towards the house. She chided herself for her unprofessional behaviour. She was the centre administrator. She should have gone with Bernie into the trees to flush their unwanted visitor out.

Her heart was pumping so fast she thought it might jump out of her chest. She longed to wash and scrub her hand, the one he'd grabbed. Bending down, she wiped it hard on the damp grass.

She had in the past, especially as a student, had huge amounts of sympathy for those on the edge of society, the dispossessed and the marginalised. But there was something different about this individual that disturbed her. Something that hinted all was not as it appeared to be.

A brisk walk along the path through the conifers did little to calm her. Then she felt the first drops of rain. The expected downpour was about to materialise. She continued to brood upon her own sense of self-doubt. In Theo's absence, she should be able to take charge of this situation. But instead she felt powerless, superfluous, and utterly miserable; and increasingly uneasy at herself for relying so heavily on Alice's support. How was she ever to fight Natasha in this frame of mind? As the rain intensified, she returned to the office. There, she found James waiting for her.

"Ah, Zoe," he said, "fresh, full of energy and ready for us to start working together. Excellent."

She gave him a hard stare.

"Where's Alice?" she asked.

A shadow flitted through James's eyes.

"Alice?" he said. "I've sacked her."

CHAPTER FIFTEEN

"You've sacked Alice?" Zoe gasped, rain still dripping from her waterproof, as she confronted James. "That's impossible."

James anchored himself on the corner of Alice's desk.

"Not at all," he said. "I simply told her we no longer need her services here."

Zoe stood with her hands on her hips, trying to combat a mounting sense of panic and paranoia. "But that's rubbish. We do need her – more than ever."

"I disagree." James slipped down from his perch.

She stood her ground, her heart pounding.

He held his hands out, palms uppermost. "What's the big deal? This was only a temporary thing for her. She's an actress waiting for her agent to ring. She'll get that part of hers soon."

"I'm amazed at you, James," said Zoe. "You, an actor, saying this? You know how much this means to her, and why she's here instead of living and working in London. Until she gets the part she deserves, this job is a lifesaver for her."

He sighed. "It's insecure, the life of an actor. But I'm not one any more, am I? I'm standing in the gap here at this centre, saving it for the future."

She gasped. Impervious to her reaction, he threw himself into an easy chair and sprawled in an indolent pose.

Zoe started towards him. "Call Alice right now," she said, her body tense, hands clenched by her side. "Tell her she has this job as long as she needs it."

James's eyes narrowed. He rested his right ankle on his left knee and drummed his fingers on the other knee.

"Listen," he said, "Alice was here because *you* wanted her. Yes, I know the background. Jessica's told me. And I agree, at the time, it suited Alice too. Well, now, *I'm* in charge. And I make the decisions, in the best interest of all of us. I've decided to let her go. You'll need to respect that."

"Never," she said.

"Too late," he replied. "Alice cleared her desk and left ten minutes ago."

Zoe spun round, flew from the office and out into the damp courtyard. Ahead of her, a group of guests were making their way towards the barn, chatting: Gareth, Cynthia and Heidi. She nearly crashed into Gareth.

He turned with a startled expression and the other two stopped and looked round at them both.

"Oh, sorry, Gareth," she said.

"No problem," he replied.

"We'll be so sad to leave tomorrow," said Heidi. "This week has been unbelievable!"

"But we'll all be seeing Natasha again, though," added Cynthia.

"What?" said Zoe.

"Oh yes, how could anyone possibly let her go, once having found her?"

"See you later," said Zoe, "must dash." Then she hurried away from them and onto the path leading to the car park.

"Alice!"

Alice stopped and turned as Zoe entered the car park through the woodland gate. Zoe ran up to her, panting. "Alice, don't go."

"I must. James has fired me."

"James can go to hell as far as I'm concerned. And so can Natasha"

Alice put a warning hand on Zoe's arm. Both girls turned. Natasha had materialised as if from nowhere. She would have had to walk up to the car park along the path, same as anyone else. But Zoe hadn't seen her. Normally, she'd have noticed out of the corner of her eye, or felt Natasha behind her.

"Hello, Natasha," said Alice.

Natasha said nothing. Her eyes settled upon Zoe's, and began once again to draw her in. Zoe felt as if she was sinking down a deep well into a subterranean cavern far away from all questions, doubts and memories. All she could see was Natasha's face in its perfection, her almond-shaped eyes, her soft, glowing complexion, her exquisitely-defined cheekbones. She seemed the very prototype of idealised feminine beauty; past, present and future. Zoe felt in that moment exactly what it was to equate this with moral superiority. *Truth is beauty, beauty's truth, that's all you know on earth and all you need to know...* Surely she could trust this lovely woman?

Then she began to fight desperately. As she did so, Natasha swayed, the lines which defined her seemed to blur, she became more obscure, then faded back, receding into the distance.

Alice's voice tugged at Zoe, sharp and insistent.

"Zoe! Let's go!"

Alice shoved Zoe into the front passenger seat of her car. Then she slammed the door closed behind her, and raced round to the driver's side. The next thing Zoe knew, the engine had started and the car leapt forward. In the rear-view mirror, Zoe saw Natasha's ethereal form behind them, seeming to float above the tarmac surface of the car park.

Zoe put her hand to her mouth. She was breathing fast. "Quick getaway," she said.

"Yeah, she started to hypnotise you."

"It was worse than that, Alice. She was trying to possess me. And she nearly succeeded."

Alice shot a glance at Zoe, as she powered up the driveway, out through the main entrance, and swung left. A sense of solidity and reality returned. Zoe tried to calm her breathing.

"What you just said," began Alice, "did you mean it?"

"Yes, I did."

"I'm glad," said Alice, "because now you are beginning to see properly for the first time."

Zoe stared at her. "Is Natasha demonic?" she asked, and shuddered. "Sorry, I can't stop shaking."

"Take your time," said Alice, slowing down as they drew closer to a farm tractor in front of them. "Oh, come on," she said to the back of the tractor.

"Tell me what you think, Alice," pleaded Zoe.

Alice started indicating right and edging out behind the tractor.

"What I think", she said, "is based upon my experience of playing Lady Macbeth. You see, sometimes, being an actor can be psychologically very dangerous because you're stripping yourself away, your character, and taking on board someone else and their spiritual and mental state. If you're playing someone evil, it's almost as if, for that period of time, you take on…"

She hesitated.

"… Their heart of darkness?" supplied Zoe.

Alice nodded.

Zoe studied her. "Do you recognise the power Natasha is using, Alice?"

"I believe so, yes."

"So what shall I do about Natasha?"

"Do? What you do about this, Zoe, is take it into your own hands."

"But I don't understand… Natasha is so strong. Whatever this power is that she uses, I cannot overcome it."

"You fight it every time you encounter her, Zoe. You're strong, much stronger than you think." Alice stepped on the accelerator and sped round the tractor and on up the lane, leaving it far behind. "Listen. I know you and Theo are Christians, and I respect that. I don't believe quite the way you do, and not in exactly the same things. But this is where you and I do agree, Zoe. Natasha is using negative spiritual power and we can't beat that on a physical level. You can fight it only on the same level, but with power that comes from a different source."

"I do believe that," said Zoe. "But where do I go from here?"

"Put it this way," said Alice. "You believe in ghosts, you and Theo, but what about spirits? Spirits in the house?"

Zoe gave a nervous laugh. "You don't mean the spirit of James's ancestor, do you?"

"No. Many people have been associated with the story of that house. Their spirits would have been absorbed into the walls. I've never met anyone in the acting profession who didn't accept this idea. You know the relic wall at the Royal Shakespeare Theatre in Stratford-upon-Avon? Why do you think they had to retain that wall? Because so many actors insisted that it be preserved, knowing the spirits of the great actors in the past had been absorbed into the fabric of the wall."

Alice reached the end of the lane, looked to the right, checked the road was clear, and accelerated onto the A road.

Zoe drew in her breath between her teeth. "I know the house 'has a personality of its own'. Lots of people have commented on it."

"They have. And when people say such things, there's far more to it."

The speedometer started racing up to seventy.

"Oh, Alice, it sounds weird. I know if Theo properly understood the danger, he'd pray about it."

Alice made a small grimace, which Zoe didn't miss.

"Pray to his God? Well, yes, of course. That's what my mum would say. But, Zoe, will you try my way as well?"

Zoe bit her lip.

"Spirits?" she said.

"Yes. The house has many. They've been absorbed into it over the course of nearly five centuries."

The road streamed behind them.

"But what makes you think they'd be on my side, and Theo's, against James?"

Despite her scepticism, Zoe focused on Alice, intent on every word she spoke.

"I believe they would. And you can make them move against James and Natasha, if you ask."

"I'm not sure, Alice, I can still hear Theo saying 'it would be best to pray about it'."

Alice raised her hands and smacked them back down onto the steering wheel. "Well," she said, "perhaps Theo has the patience to wait for those prayers to be answered. But have we?"

CHAPTER SIXTEEN

Alice and Zoe made their way upstairs to the first floor. The evening meal was due to begin in ten minutes in the dining area across the courtyard. Zoe had asked Alice to return to the house at this time, as the best way to avoid awkward encounters with James and with inquisitive guests.

The footfall of centuries had passed over these timber treads, wearing them smooth. As always, when Zoe placed her feet on the silken surface of the oak she felt in danger of slipping. At the top she placed her hand on the structural post to her right which was helping to support the floor above. She'd long wondered about the fissures in the timber. It was possible that a few Roundheads had tested the point of their swords as they searched the house for hidden priests or monks.

Zoe found the atmosphere of the house dreamy and serene, despite being caught up in the power struggle going on within its walls. Several guests had mentioned this gentle, inviting presence which could be felt throughout the building – but they, of course, knew nothing of any conflict among the centre staff.

At least, so Zoe hoped.

Floorboards creaked as Zoe followed Alice along the passageway. Zoe had asked Alice to show her what she meant. Alice clearly hoped Zoe would recognise the spirits as real and engage with them. Zoe didn't feel at all sure about what Alice intended to do. But curiosity and a sense of intrigue led her on.

Raised voices intervened. James and Bernie were in the study. And the conversation sounded heated.

Alice and Zoe stopped. They exchanged a quick glance and flattened themselves against the wall adjacent to the study door. Heavy footsteps paced to and fro across the floorboards of the study.

Bernie's voice broke in.

"James, so far we've been grateful for your help. But I cannot agree with this. Alice has shown herself to be a hard-working member of staff in the short time she's been here. I know it's a temporary job." Bernie seemed to have reached the window, swung round, and began pacing back again across the study, towards the door. "But she should stay with us until she gets her next professional acting role. As house manager, I rely on her. Where will Jessica get a replacement at such short notice? Please ring Alice right now and tell her to come back."

James's laugh sounded thin.

A book smacked down hard on the desk.

"I make the decisions now, Bernie," said James. "Jessica authorised it. You must trust that I act for the best of reasons."

The floorboards creaked again. "Well, it's hard to see any sense in *this* decision. I know Theo's ill, and Jessica's put you in charge for the time being. But I still believe you might have consulted me over this business with Alice."

Alice and Zoe gave each other a subtle thumbs-up.

A chair scraped back across the floor. "Sorry, Bernie, but I don't have to consult you. Jessica gave me power to hire and fire."

More protest from the floorboards.

"No she didn't. I was there when she spoke to you. She gave you no such power."

"She did," insisted James. "I've asked Alice to leave. And

she's gone. As for Zoe – I must say, pretty as she is, and hard to resist, she's also very naive." The chair creaked again. "Nobody suggested *she* was fit to take over during Theo's absence. After all, Jessica could easily have done that, and recruited a couple of temporary secretaries, if she had so chosen. I propose we contact an employment agency, though I don't see that Zoe needs to continue in her current role during this period, either, since I have things so well in hand. I'm going to suggest she gives herself a break from this centre for a while."

Zoe would listen no more. She leapt forward, flung the door open, and stormed in.

"How dare you, James?"

Bernie, whose back had been turned, whirled round to face her, his eyes wide with dismay.

Beyond him, James sat in the chair, placed to the side of the desk. His jaw hung as he took in Zoe's entry.

Removing his hand from the desk, James rose to his feet, scrutinising Zoe.

"I'm surprised you've broken in on us like this," he said, "but it gives me a good chance to say what I want to say to you. Listen, you're young, and charming, and I'm sure you've worked hard at the centre administration. But now Theo's ill… why not take a break? A couple of months, at least, I suggest."

Zoe strode across the room past Bernie, to face James.

"Spirits, attack!" hissed Alice behind her.

Zoe fought to combat Alice's words but failed. Instead, she raised her hand and slapped James's face. The sharp crack forced a reaction from Alice.

"Zoe!" she cried.

James let out a noise between a bark and a yowl. He staggered back, hitting the chair and knocking it over, then slammed into the bookcase. As he crumpled to the floor, the timbers vibrated beneath Zoe's feet. She absorbed the impact in her own body.

"Zoe! What have you done?" cried Bernie.

"Oh my God," gasped Zoe. "He's not moving. I've killed him."

CHAPTER SEVENTEEN

Alice had sprung forward into the middle of the room. Bernie pushed past Zoe and dropped to his knees beside James's prone form. James was unconscious. Blood poured across the oak timbers from a gash above his right temple. The chair lay on its side and three spindles had snapped off and rolled in different directions. Alice opened her mouth to speak, but Zoe got there first.

"Alice. Bernie. What shall we do now?" she breathed.

Bernie was already taking charge. He squatted down close to James, picked up one wrist, and felt his pulse.

"Don't panic," he said. "He's breathing."

Zoe's heart was pounding so fast, she clutched both hands to her chest. Alice put her arms round Zoe and held her tight. Zoe knew Alice was trying to reassure her. But she was shaking.

The door banged back and Griff stood on the threshold. Alice released Zoe.

"What on earth…" he began then caught sight of James's body.

He rushed into the room and squatted down beside James's head.

A lightning swift glance ran between Alice and Bernie. Zoe saw it. She read a plea in Alice's eyes; as if Alice was saying, *Just this once, Bernie, for Zoe's sake.*

"James fell off his chair and hit his head," said Bernie.

Zoe swallowed several times. Her mouth was dry and her face burned.

"Bernie checked he's still breathing," added Alice.

Zoe allowed her eyes to flicker up and meet Griff's. Her stomach flipped. Mutual understanding flashed between them. He pulled out his mobile phone and began to tap.

The ambulance sped back up the drive half an hour later, unseen by the guests who were all in the dining room, impervious to that evening's new turn of events. It carried James away from the house and off to Gloucestershire Royal Hospital. The witnesses had co-operated well in answering the paramedics' questions. Zoe and Alice corroborated each other in every part of the story, and Bernie agreed with them; James had been the victim of an unfortunate accident. The chairs were old. The leg on that chair must have been weak.

The only guest aware of the new crisis was Natasha. She'd appeared without warning just as James was being loaded into the ambulance. She listened to Bernie's explanation in silence. Zoe studied her face. She sensed that Natasha knew exactly what had happened but was saying nothing.

"I'm so sorry, Natasha," said Bernie. "I'm sure you'll want to ring the hospital a bit later after they've run a few tests to make sure he hasn't sustained any serious brain damage. We must hope for the best."

"Of course," she said, her eyes calm.

Zoe shuddered. Natasha was supposed to love this man. But she betrayed no emotion.

Then Natasha turned to look at Zoe. Zoe avoided eye contact. She knew Natasha was set on breaking down her resistance to her.

Griff said as little as possible.

Alice and Zoe felt no temptation to speak. The speed with which Zoe had acted robbed both girls of further words.

The following day was Saturday, the day their current guests were due to leave; and it passed in what felt like a drug-induced haze for Zoe. Natasha had visited James, who, it seemed, had not been seriously hurt, and was expected to make a good recovery. She'd then returned to the centre. She'd phoned Jessica, who'd asked her to take charge until she, Jessica, could be there, first thing on Monday morning. All the departing guests had arranged to see Natasha again, in whose spiritual authority they totally believed. Zoe was left in no doubt at all that Natasha would target the hearts and minds of the new intake of guests the following afternoon.

She herself felt powerless. A strange torpor hung over her. She had neither the energy nor the will to go and visit Theo, who she realised with a sense of dread, was now probably in the same ward as James. Neither did she have the strength to make any decisions. And so the weekend passed, the new guests arrived, and Zoe sunk into a deep sleep that night.

The next day, Monday, she'd regained some of her vitality. When she crossed the courtyard from the dining area beneath a cold but bright, clear sky she saw two people in the office. She hurried through the doorway. Jessica stood in the far corner and Alice sat behind her desk.

"Alice! You're back!"

Zoe ran behind the desk and hugged her.

"Yes," said Alice, as Zoe released her from the embrace. "After Friday night's drama, Jessica called me and asked me to come in again this morning. She said there'd *been a misunderstanding.*"

She grinned, her white teeth contrasting with her milk-chocolate-coloured skin. Her eyes danced.

Jessica, who'd been going through some folders in the filing cabinet, turned to face Zoe and Alice. She wore a tailored French-blue trouser suit. Zoe was about to hug her, too, until she saw the expression on Jessica's face.

Zoe moved out from behind Alice's desk and crossed the office towards Jessica.

"Thank you, Jessica," she said. "Now James is in hospital, I'm willing to take over. I can do his job as well as my own – until Theo returns."

"Not so fast, Zoe," said Jessica. "I'm afraid you've misjudged the situation. And I'm a bit concerned at your cavalier attitude to James's awful accident."

Zoe cleared her throat. "Yes, of course."

"Though Natasha has given me the good news from the hospital that they expect James to make a full recovery," said Jessica.

Zoe twisted the wedding ring on her finger, and made no reply.

"That being said, what matters next is the centre. And our guests," said Jessica. She walked over towards where Alice sat. Zoe followed her. Jessica perched herself on the corner of Alice's desk.

Zoe stood facing her.

"Since we have no guests in the room right now," said Jessica, "I can speak frankly to you, Zoe."

"Good," said Zoe.

Alice threw her a quick warning glance.

"Before you say anything," said Zoe, "I want you to be clear that I fully realize the guests come first. And they've booked on this course believing Theo would be leading and supporting them. The centre needs Theo. Over the years we've been open, and through the courses we've run, the guests have all warmed to him straightaway. Why do you think so many come back again and again?"

Jessica sank her forehead into her hands.

When she looked up, Zoe saw lines around her eyes she hadn't noticed before.

"You all right, Jessica? Not getting one of your migraines?"

"No; though if we carry on this way, I might do. Listen, Zoe, I've always had the highest regard for Theo. But I don't feel secure about him any more; not now I know how fragile his mental health is."

Zoe's mouth went dry as sawdust.

Jessica continued. "Zoe, it's a big responsibility being manager, warden *and* creative director of a centre like this, along with the one-to-one counselling he does for those who request it." Jessica held both her hands aloft. "We need someone strong."

Alice got up from her chair and, coming round to Zoe, laid her hand on her shoulder.

"Theo has been strong in the past," said Zoe. "And he will be again, when he has recovered."

When Jessica spoke, her voice seemed to have dropped a few notes down the scale.

"OK. Let's stop talking about the warden and creative director role, and instead look at the manager post. That job *is* too big for Theo. But it's perfect for James, when he's fully recovered."

Zoe ran her hands through her hair, her breath coming faster.

"It's not enough for the guests to be fond of Theo," went on Jessica. "And I'm sure the other trustees would agree with me there. We'll meet tomorrow to discuss the situation."

Alice massaged Zoe's arm.

"Take it easy, Zoe," she murmured. "Let Jessica speak."

Zoe shook Alice off. "Jessica," she burst out, "why in God's name do you trust James so much? What is it with him, and you?"

Jessica's eyes widened at this. "I don't have to explain myself to you," she said. "I'm confident my instincts about James are correct. I have considerable knowledge of him to go on. His life experience puts him in a very special place to manage this centre. And other trustees share that view."

Zoe turned away from Jessica. She swallowed hard.

Alice took her hand and squeezed it. Then Zoe spun round again, startling Alice.

"God forbid that James recovers from his injury!" said Zoe. "He could return stronger than ever, take over again, and triumph!"

"Oh, come on, Zoe," said Jessica in a sharp voice.

But now neither Alice nor Zoe could restrain their laughter.

Zoe considered wild scenarios: the Celtic Knot, perhaps, renamed The James Willoughby Centre. James might use the property to rally embittered out-of-work actors to his cause – whatever that might be. Or maybe he'd provide a home-from-home for desperate academics who'd been refused research grants and were now prepared to follow illegal paths to achieve their goals. But in truth she considered James's ultimate objective to be far worse than those two possibilities: she felt sure his plans for the centre involved handing over full control to Natasha.

And meanwhile, thought Zoe, Natasha herself circulated among the guests, making them feel they were precious to her, inspiring them to confide in her, learning of their joys and sorrows, their troubles and medical problems, and offering them the 'sweet reward' of healing in return for access to their souls.

Healing them by the power everyone else said came from God but which only Zoe and Alice believed came from a much darker source.

Jessica walked across to the group of easy chairs and sat down in one of them. Zoe had fallen silent but could not master her trembling limbs.

"I plan to visit James in hospital this afternoon," said

Jessica. "We'll have a chat, and I'll find out the true story of what happened to him on Friday night."

A lump rose in Zoe's throat. She nodded, but could not trust herself to speak.

Zoe returned from visiting Theo in the neurology ward at lunchtime to find Alice waiting for her in the entrance hall.

"Alice! Still here?"

"Yes, I had to stay. How's Theo?"

Zoe shook her head.

"Hopeless, Alice, hopeless."

Alice led Zoe into the library and made her sit on one of the chairs at the round table.

Alice took Zoe's face between her two hands. "I want to see your sparkle back again." Dropping her hands to her side she pulled out the seat close to Zoe's, then turned it to face Zoe. Sinking into it, she said, "I've got exciting news, Zoe. My agent rang. I have an audition. I'm meeting a casting director in Covent Garden on Friday at ten o'clock."

Zoe clapped her hands together. "Brilliant, Alice. I'm so happy for you."

"Thank you. It means I won't be in that morning."

"Of course, of course. That's fine, Alice. I do hope you'll get the part."

"Bless you, Zoe. But now it's all the more urgent I help you and Theo out of this mess as soon as possible. I can't bear to leave with you two still in it up to your neck."

"Sorry, Alice, but you may have to." Zoe felt close to tears. "I'm so happy for you. I want you to have a great career."

"I know you do, Zoe. And I want you and Theo to be happy, too."

Alice got to her feet, pulling Zoe up. "Come on." Zoe followed her to the far corner, well away from the door.

They stood together, close by the bookcase, and spoke in low voices.

"The situation's dire," said Zoe. "Jessica's visiting James later. He'll tell her what happened. Then I'll get arrested, charged with assault, and put on trial. I could end up in prison."

"Rubbish," said Alice. "Not a chance of it." She grabbed one of the books from the bookshelf and waved it in the air to emphasise her words. "James *might* tell Jessica you hit him. But I don't believe he will. He's too crafty."

She opened the book apparently at random.

"Searching for inspiration?" said Zoe.

Alice laughed. "Could be."

She placed the book in Zoe's hands. Zoe looked at the page. At once her eyes fell on a group of words: *evidence that demands a verdict*. As she considered this, Alice spoke again, in a low but intense voice.

"Spirits, give me inspiration!"

Then Alice held her head in both hands. "Think, think, think," she murmured, walking to and fro across the rug.

Zoe watched her, beginning to feel dizzy. Then she looked back down at the book in her hands. Again, the same words jumped out at her.

"Evidence that demands a verdict," she said.

"What?"Alice had stopped. Now she whirled to face Zoe and seized her by both shoulders.

"It's in this book," said Zoe. "The words jumped out at me."

"Right, OK," said Alice. "Don't you see, Zoe, what they're telling you?"

"Yes. Yes, I do see," whispered Zoe, "evidence against James, strong enough to convince Jessica. And how do we get it?"

"James is out of the way," said Alice. "For how long, we don't know. Shall we search his room?"

Their eyes met and held.

"Your one chance," said Alice. "Or the centre falls into James and Natasha's hands."

Zoe threw her arms round Alice. "Thank you, Alice. Thank you," she said in an urgent voice. "Would *you* do it?"

Alice nodded.

"But be careful. Don't let anyone see you. Go through his papers, USB sticks, business cards… See if you can find his mobile."

"I expect Natasha's taken that to give him."

Alice hurried across to the door. Then she turned back.

"This could crack it for you, Zoe! I'm going on up to James's room. Obviously, if there's anyone around who might see me, I won't do it. I'd have to choose another time. But I'll text you later." Alice pulled the door open. Zoe followed her into the entrance hall, and Alice sped upstairs.

Zoe was just about to go back through the house into the office. But the front door opened and Bernie appeared.

"There you are, Zoe," he said. "Jessica rang James's ward. He's doing well and they expect to discharge him Wednesday morning."

Zoe folded her arms.

"I'm sorry, Zoe," said Bernie in a low voice. "You know I'm loyal to you. And I lied to protect you. But I can't condone what you did to James." He raised his voice again. "I'm off with Jessica to see James later on."

Jessica put her head in through the doorway.

"Zoe, will you come too?"

"Won't Griff need me to help prepare for the evening workshop?"

"No. Why should he? Griff's handling everything perfectly," said Jessica. "I'd like you to visit James with us."

"If you say so, Jessica," said Zoe. "Right now, there's work to be done. I'm going back to the office."

"You do," said Jessica. "We'll call for you at five-thirty."

Zoe walked through to the office with a heavy heart.

Just one thing now gave her any hope: the chance Alice might find something incriminating in James's room. She thrust her hands in her pockets and squeezed both her fists. Evidence, that's what they needed.

CHAPTER EIGHTEEN

When Jessica, Bernie and Zoe entered James's private room at the hospital that evening, James was sitting up in bed, a bandage round his head, reading the latest issue of *The Stage*, and wearing black silk pyjamas. Zoe gathered Natasha had brought these to him when she visited him that morning.

Jessica went straight up to James and began enquiring after his well-being, whilst Bernie stood behind her. Zoe did her best to keep a low profile, taking a chair at the far corner of the room. But it was soon clear James didn't mean to let her get away with this.

"Zoe," he said, "come closer. I want a word with you."

Gritting her teeth, Zoe approached his bed. He met her gaze with a knowing expression. She refused to be intimidated.

"No serious damage, I hear, James?" she remarked.

"No. I'll be out on Wednesday."

She waited.

"I hope," he said, "when I return, you and I, Zoe, will be able to get our relationship onto a more civilised footing."

"Oh?" She made no attempt to hide her astonishment.

"Yes, time for us both to move forward." And with this, he tapped her on the shoulder with his rolled-up magazine in a light, jocular manner. She flinched.

He laughed to see this.

"Come on, Zoe," he said in a breezy tone of voice. "D'you agree? Shall we put all these misunderstandings behind us?"

Zoe regarded him, tight-lipped.

"An excellent idea," declared Jessica, "a fresh start for all of us. For my part, I'm so relieved and grateful your injuries aren't serious, James."

"No, no, I'm stronger than many realise," said James, reaching for a large glass of sparkling mineral water at his bedside. He drank. "It would take a lot to beat me. Knock me down and I spring up again."

"So I see," said Zoe. She walked across to the door. She had to get out of this room; and what better reason for that than to go and visit Theo, who was in another sideroom on the same ward.

Bernie looked at her, a line in his forehead.

"Where are you going?" asked James.

"I'm off to visit Theo. Do excuse me."

She darted out of the room before anyone could stop her.

As she burst into Theo's room, he got up from his chair and came halfway across the room to meet her. She flung her arms round him and kissed him hard.

"What's happening at the centre?" he asked during a pause for breath. "Can't remember what you told me last time."

Zoe quickly marshalled the facts, trying to recall what she'd already shared with him. Yesterday, she'd felt too low in spirits to come and visit him. Natasha. Zoe thought she should begin with her.

"Natasha... everyone still believes she's a miracle-worker." She filled him in on the news, not letting go of him. Natasha's increasing spiritual influence, Alice's latest ghost sighting, James's accident...

Theo pulled himself away from her and held her at arm's length.

"What accident?" he demanded.

"I slapped him. He fell and hit his head."

"What?" He went over to his chair and stood behind it, steadying himself with his hands on the chair-back. His face was ashen.

"You hit him?"

"Yes, Theo." She hurried across to join him, her words tumbling over each other as she recounted the story. "If James presses charges, I'll be arrested. The others won't escape either. They're accessories after the fact. Theo, we could all go to prison."

At this, Theo gripped the chair-back, leaning his weight on it. The chair buckled beneath him, then slid aside. She hurtled forward and grabbed hold of him just in time, as the chair hit the floor.

"Oh God, Zoe, what have you done?" he cried. "This is horrendous." He passed the back of one hand across his forehead. "I must get out of here."

She swung him round in a wild dance of joy. Whether he thought ill of her for what she'd done, she didn't know, but all that mattered was that this news seemed to have sparked him up again and motivated him to return to the centre with her.

"Will they let you go?"

"Who cares? I'll discharge myself," said Theo.

"I love you!" she cried. All his strength, will to live and appetite for problem-solving seemed to have kicked back into full throttle once more. Theo was coming back. Theo had recovered. Zoe's spirit was humming. Whatever doubts she may have had about the suddenness of his recovery, she dismissed. "Theo, where's your suitcase? I'll throw in everything I can see. You can always send for other stuff later."

"Yes, Zoe, hurry."

A duty nurse walked into the room.

"What's going on here?" she asked.

"I'm discharging myself. I'm going home."

"You can't do that. I'll call the duty doctor."

Soon a junior doctor and another nurse had joined them. Both asserted that Theo was in no state to be discharged. Zoe listened to the argument. They all insisted Theo stay. Then Jessica and Bernie came into the room.

"Zoe? We're ready to leave," said Bernie.

"What's up?" asked Jessica. When the situation was explained to her, she said, "Of course Theo must stay! It's out of the question for him to return to the centre right now! James will be out on Wednesday; he'll be in top form to take over Theo's role again…"

Zoe clenched her fists. Before she could speak, Bernie stepped forward.

"Take it easy, Zoe," he murmured.

The doctor and nurses looked from Zoe to Jessica to Bernie and back again. Theo had sunk into his chair once more. Zoe marched over to the doctor and confronted him. "You must discharge Theo!"

"Zoe," said Jessica, taking hold of her arm.

"Let the doctor decide, Zoe," said Bernie.

The doctor spoke to Zoe in a low voice.

"I've never seen anyone with clinical depression recover so quickly," he murmured. "This kind of depression can last several months at least."

"OK. I'll wait till I see the consultant this evening," said Theo. "Then I can explain how I feel, and together we'll reach a decision."

This seemed acceptable to them. But Zoe could see they didn't hold out much hope. She rubbed her eyes. Then her phone beeped. It was a text from Alice.

Found something in J's room. V interesting. Will sho u 2moro. Alicex.

At once, Zoe's heart lifted.

CHAPTER NINETEEN

After breakfast the following morning, Zoe went straight to the office. She felt sick at heart, having been forced to spend the meal listening to the guests speak of Natasha's spiritual gifts, which had been their sole topic of conversation in the dining area. Zoe was now anxious to learn Alice's news about her search of James's room. But she was equally impatient to hear from the hospital about Theo's discharge.

Before she had the chance to call the hospital, Alice appeared wearing a warm fur-trimmed jacket and carrying a backpack.

"Hi Alice," said Zoe, as Alice took her jacket off and hung it up. "Well done for yesterday. What did you find?"

Alice cast a nervous glance at the door.

"Can't tell you now, Zoe; anyone could come in."

As she spoke there was a knock on the door.

"See what I mean?" said Alice, heading for her desk and stowing the backpack away underneath it. "Let's go to the hermitage after I finish at lunchtime. I'll bring this with me. You can look through what I found and then we'll talk."

"Fine," said Zoe. "Come in," she called.

The door opened, and two guests entered.

Zoe and Alice were kept busy all morning with queries, phone calls, bookings and emails. Zoe rang the hospital twice for news of Theo. But the consultant had not yet made a decision.

She hoped too for a phone call from Jessica to give her the outcome of the trustees' meeting which would be taking place right then in Birmingham. But no call came from Jessica. The meeting had been due to start at nine thirty, and may have lasted a couple of hours. She hadn't really expected to be informed so soon of their decision.

At twelve thirty Alice closed down her computer, and then, wearing their warm jackets, both of them left the office. Alice held her backpack in her arms.

As she locked the office door behind her, Zoe realised the stone-hard chill in the air had intensified even further since the early morning, beneath a dull, uniform cloud cover. There were no guests around; they seemed to be still in Griff's morning workshop. Alice and Zoe crossed the courtyard to the north-west, hurrying between the studio and dining area.

They climbed the stile in the woodland fence and set off up the track which led to the top of the ridge. Halfway to the ridge, another track branched off to the right, and they took this. After a short walk they reached a small clearing. There before them was the simple tongue-and-groove pine cabin, known to them all as 'the hermitage'. It was another place for silent retreat and solitary contemplation.

Zoe unlocked the door and they hurried in through the doorway. Alice sat in one of the wicker chairs and put her backpack down on the floor beside her.

"Shut the door then sit here, Zoe."

Zoe obeyed. Alice unzipped her backpack, reached in and brought out a well-stuffed A4 document wallet. "Letters, bank statements and copies of emails."

Zoe's heart-rate increased. "Anything of interest?"

"You bet. Letters to Natasha's sister, Sonya."

"Natasha's sister? Oh yes, I remember James mentioning

her. He said he'd known Natasha and her sister for a few years."

"Yes. Sonya and Natasha were both born and brought up in the New Forest area. I must admit I'd like to know how James first came to know them both. However, the main thing right now is that a large sum of money changed hands between Sonya and James. But I don't know why."

"Large sum? How large?"

"You just see." Zoe took the paperwork from Alice.

She studied the documents.

"My God," she murmured. "Massive. What would that be about?"

Alice shrugged.

"She's bankrolling him for something," she said.

"The mystery is – for what? There's no clue here."

"And if he has all *that* money, why does he need the manager job?" said Zoe.

Alice shook her head. "I don't know."

She took the documents back from Zoe.

"By the way," she said, "in case you wondered, I've photocopied what seemed to me the most important documents. I have them here too. I'll return the originals to James's room as soon as possible."

"Thanks."

Alice began to tidy them away again into the wallet she'd brought with her. Then twigs snapped outside the hermitage window. Zoe looked in that direction. Branches swayed, as if disturbed by some heavy body passing by.

Alice was looking too. They both held their breath. Then their eyes locked. The undergrowth outside crackled. They twisted round and stared through the window.

"What was that?" asked Alice.

"No idea. Didn't hear anyone come up the path behind

me. Rabbit perhaps? Stoat? Fox?" Leaves rustled. They looked at each other again.

"Birds foraging?"

Alice got up. "Let's go and investigate." She opened the door and walked out, followed by Zoe.

They could see nothing but maples and rowans and the leaf-strewn woodland track. They heard only gusts of wind, intensifying the chill-factor; no birds sang. There was no sign of any person or animal moving among the trees.

Zoe's mobile buzzed in her pocket. She took the call.

"Theo!" she cried.

"I'm back, Zoe. I'm in the office right now."

"Thank God!"

"Where are you?" he asked.

"I'm outside the hermitage. Wait right there. I'll be with you in two seconds!"

Zoe stuffed the phone back into her pocket and spun round to Alice.

"Theo's back. He's out! I can't wait to see him."

"You go on," said Alice, "I'll collect the stuff together and put it in my backpack."

"Ok. Speak to you later."

"Yeah, I'll give you a call."

Zoe sped back down the woodland track.

Climbing over the stile and jumping down into courtyard, Zoe hurried along the path between studio and dining area. Looking across to the office and through the window, she could see Theo and Bernie. She ran across the courtyard and in through the open doorway.

Theo had been talking to Bernie. But now he turned towards Zoe. His eyes looked bright and engaged; his stance strong and upright. He appeared, to Zoe, as he had done on their wedding day.

132

A flare of light surged through her body. Her cheeks burned. She sprang forward, just avoiding Bernie, into Theo's arms.

"Theo, you're back. You look so much better. This is wonderful."

Theo held her tight, kissing her, squeezing her.

"Thank God you're all right, Zoe," he said. "I was so worried about you."

"Me?" she said. "I'm all right. All I care about is you."

Bernie cleared his throat.

They both glanced round at the same time then released their hold of each other. Zoe was still enveloped in an aura of brilliance and warmth. All her fears of the past week had melted. Everything would come good now, she felt sure. Her suspicions about Natasha were temporarily forgotten. She gazed at Bernie. He was wreathed in smiles.

"I'm so happy for you both," said Bernie. "Can't tell you how relieved I am to see you back again, Theo. I hope to God everything will return to normal now."

"Bernie, no need to worry yourself," said Theo. "I'll put things right. When Zoe visited me yesterday, she told me everything. It shocked me out of my malaise. I'm back, I'm strong again, and determined to sort things out."

Zoe held Theo's hand tight. Her heart was so full, there was so much she wanted to say but no words emerged. She went and sat down behind the desk. Everything would be fine now, she felt convinced.

Half an hour later, Theo and Zoe parted. Theo headed for the barn to join Griff in leading a workshop and Zoe called Alice. She'd said nothing to Theo about what she and Alice had been up to; it seemed inappropriate. First she needed to check that Alice had got those documents back to James's room unseen, and gone safely home. Then they both needed to do some thinking and work out what they were going to do with their new information about Sonya and James.

However, Alice's mobile was turned off. Zoe bit her lip. She longed to know what had happened. She'd have thought Alice would at least keep her mobile on. Oh well, she decided, there was nothing for it but to get on with her work. She trusted Alice would call or text her very soon.

However, another hour passed with no news from Alice. Frowning, Zoe called Alice's mobile again. It was still turned off. Zoe left a voicemail message asking Alice to call her.

"This doesn't make sense," said Zoe aloud. Alice's last words to her had been *I'll give you a call*. It was unlike her to fall out of contact. But then, thought Zoe, perhaps something had come up which had far higher priority than their minor troubles here at the centre. Maybe Alice had heard from her agent, with an even more urgent call to another audition. Certainly, Zoe understood that would have made her drop everything. Alice's acting career came first. Zoe needed to be patient. Alice would call or text when she had time.

But an hour later, when Zoe called Alice's mobile a third time, it was still turned off. By now, she might have expected a text, even if Alice had caught the next train to London. Then Zoe rang Alice's home landline and spoke to her mother, Leila.

"I've seen nothing of Alice all day," said Leila. "She left the house before I was up, to go to work."

"Yes," said Zoe. "She was with me as usual this morning. I last saw her at one o' clock. She said she'd call me later, but I've heard nothing. Her mobile's been turned off all afternoon. I thought perhaps she'd had news of another audition and gone to London."

"Not to my knowledge," replied Leila. "She'd certainly have texted me. I'll ask her to call you as soon as I hear anything."

"Thank you," said Zoe.

Puzzled and uneasy, she went over the last time she'd seen Alice, their words to each other, and what she imagined Alice would have done after they parted. She'd have gone back to the house and up to James's room, replaced the original documents, then left the house with the photocopies safely in her backpack, walked up to the car park and driven home to Cirencester.

Zoe decided to check whether Alice's car was missing from the car park. She put her warm jacket on again, went out of the office, locking the door behind her, and hurried round the house and up the drive to the car park. Alice's car was nowhere to be seen.

Zoe frowned. OK, so Alice had driven away, but she still couldn't understand why there'd been no contact since. Her mind ranged over possible scenarios. If she'd gone to catch a train, her car would be in the station car park.

The more Zoe thought about it, the more troubled she became. She fought against her darkening mood, chiding herself that she was overreacting. But this failed to calm her. There was nothing else for it. She got into her own car and drove off to Kemble Station to search for Alice's car. There was no sign of it.

Zoe rang Leila again at seven and still there had been no news from Alice. Dinner at the centre was at seven-thirty but Zoe had lost her appetite. She went in search of Theo, and found him near the barn, walking along the path from the goose house.

"I've been talking to Natasha," he said.

A dark shadow sprang up from her solar plexus. She made a conscious effort to rein in her paranoid fears. Theo took her hand. As she looked at him, she sensed he was hiding something from her.

"What is it?" he asked.

Zoe's stomach felt queasy. It seemed so out of character for Alice to disappear and make no contact. Zoe was used to Alice's efficiency and had come to expect that Alice would always keep her informed if she changed her plans. Zoe told Theo all this, but didn't mention James's documents.

"Well," said Theo, "as her car's gone, we can be sure she's driven away. But who knows where she might have gone? What can we do, but wait to hear further, either from Alice herself, or from her mother? Come on, let's go to dinner."

He set off across the courtyard ahead of Zoe, expecting her to follow. Instead though, Zoe hesitated. She shivered. A sense of isolation and loneliness crept over her. In every season, daylight or darkness, Zoe had always felt in harmony with this place. But now, for the first time ever, she felt something hostile waited at the centre of the night.

She hurried after Theo.

At nine o'clock, Zoe called Leila again to ask if Alice had made contact. Leila's voice sounded high-pitched and jerky. She gabbled and Zoe failed to catch several phrases. But she gathered that Leila was now considering other possibilities, aside from Alice having gone to London. Alice did often meet friends locally, in the evenings. However, she would normally text her mother to let her know of her plans. Today Leila had heard nothing and had, like Zoe, been unable to get through to Alice on her mobile. She planned to wait up until Alice came in later.

Zoe's mouth went dry. She said goodbye to Leila and went through into the sitting room where Theo sat chatting to three guests.

"Theo, can I have a quick word?"

"Of course. Be back with you a little later," said Theo to the guests, and went through into the library with Zoe.

She repeated Leila's news. Then she added, "Theo, there's something I need to tell you." She shared all that had happened with Alice and the fact that Alice had borrowed documents from James's room, and photocopied them, and the circumstances of her disappearance.

Upon hearing this, Theo became thoughtful.

Then he said, "Since Alice had the documents and the photocopies with her when you last saw her, and you now have no access to them, I don't see how we can use them or the information in them as the basis for any further investigation, until Alice gets in touch again."

Zoe's heart chilled. She wanted to say, *Theo, now I've shared this about James and Natasha's sister I want you to open up. You've been to see Natasha earlier today. Tell me what you talked about. What's going on with her and James? You never hid anything from me before.*

But the words wouldn't come. Natasha's face floated before her, and silenced her.

And then Zoe remembered certain information that Alice had shared with her about the character of Lady Macbeth, and the power of the Weird Sisters. "They used this power to corrupt people's minds," Alice had told her, "together with prophecies that spread evil through falsehood." *Fair is foul and foul is fair*, Zoe thought, her heart pounding.

CHAPTER TWENTY

The next morning, Wednesday, dawned; and Zoe rang Leila at eight-thirty. But Leila had still not heard from Alice, and had already made a phone call to Alice's agent, who said she'd not been in touch with Alice at all the day before. Leila was about to start contacting Alice's friends both locally and in London.

At ten o'clock, Theo made sure all the guests in the barn had plenty to occupy them in the icon-painting workshop.

"All the staff will be in an emergency team meeting for the next half an hour," he said. Then he went to summon Zoe, Griff, Miles and Bernie into the library.

When everyone was seated around the circular table, Theo spoke. "We've drawn a blank on Alice's whereabouts. Her mother Leila has rung Alice's agent, and has started getting in touch with her actor friends in London. She's turned up no news so far and I've just taken a call from Leila to say she's going to the police."

The atmosphere chilled. The door opened. Zoe twisted round, expecting to see her friend, with the familiar milk-chocolate skin, chestnut eyes and black hair. But instead it was Jessica, accompanied by James.

Zoe scrutinised him.

"James," she said. "You're back."

James nodded, smiling. His face was flushed, as if in anticipation of some remarkable news or event. He was as sharply-dressed as ever. The brightness of his eyes spoke of restored health. A flesh-coloured elastoplast across his cheekbone was the only evidence of his injury.

Zoe lapsed into silence. There was nothing in James's manner to suggest he'd found the documents missing from his room. She could only conclude that Alice had succeeded in returning the originals, before she mysteriously disappeared.

"I'm so glad to find you all here together," said Jessica. "Now James is back with us again, I can give you the full verdict of the trustees at our meeting yesterday." She turned to her companion.

"Do sit down, James," she said, taking one of the remaining two seats at the table. James obeyed.

Theo cleared his throat.

"Before you do that, Jessica, I must share disturbing news. Alice has disappeared. Zoe last saw her yesterday afternoon at one o'clock. Then Alice left. Zoe needed to speak to her later and was expecting her to call, but Alice made no contact and her mobile was turned off all afternoon. Zoe rang her mother; Alice never returned home. There's been no news of Alice this morning either. I believe her mother is on the phone to the police right now to report her missing."

Jessica's face drained of colour.

"That's terrible. I'm so sorry."

Zoe noted that James's eyes widened. But he said nothing.

"We hope of course," continued Theo, "that she'll be found soon and will return to us. But at the moment we cannot tell what has happened."

"Of course, of course," murmured James. "Have you considered that she may have gone to London? I would imagine…"

"Yes James," interrupted Zoe. "Her mother has already thought of all that and acted upon it. I must add, too, that I drove to the station car park and there was no sign of her car, which would surely be there, if she'd caught a train to London."

"Not necessarily," said James. "She might have been planning to stay a few days with friends, and driven there."

"If she had," said Zoe, "she'd have let me know; and her mother."

"Most puzzling," said James. "But I'm sure the mystery will soon be cleared up." He scratched his nose.

Zoe gave him a piercing look. Something about him didn't ring true.

"It falls to me to pass on some very important news to you all," said Jessica, "and I'm very sorry that I bring it to you when you're all so anxious about Alice."

Zoe glanced at Theo. She wanted to take his hand and squeeze it. But something restrained her. Already Zoe's mistrust and her sense of Jessica's betrayal, and Theo's failure so far to protest against it, stood between her and Theo, a physical presence.

"As you know, the trustees met yesterday," said Jessica, leaning forward, elbows on the table, and interlacing her fingers. "We considered all the events in the centre during the last couple of weeks, together with their implications. And we reached a decision about who can best rescue us over the next few months. Our decision is in favour of James."

Zoe studied James's face. He wore the expression of a satisfied, well-fed cat.

"One thing more," said Jessica. "Difficult news, I'm afraid. The trustees also decided we must ask Theo – and Zoe too, of course – to start researching possible alternative ways forward for their future."

Zoe gasped – as did Griff, Bernie, Miles and Theo.

"What?" Zoe blurted.

"But…" began Griff, sitting up straight.

"Do you mean you're asking them to leave?" asked Bernie. "Why?" asked Miles.

Theo remained silent and ashen-faced. Jessica continued to speak, in a low, even voice.

"I know this news will sadden you. We appreciate all that Theo and Zoe have done for us. But we cannot continue in this present state of insecurity."

"We're not insecure," said Griff. "Theo's back. All will be well again."

"None of the trustees shares your optimistic view of Theo's health," said Jessica.

Bernie shook his head and frowned.

Jessica turned to Theo. "I'm sure, Theo, you'll acknowledge this yourself: we need someone whose strength and good health we can rely on."

Theo bowed his head. Zoe was about to spring up from her seat, but Theo held her hand and restrained her.

"Our next task," continued Jessica, "is to put our new centre manager in place. James has been asked if he'll take on the role in an acting capacity until such time as we make a permanent appointment."

Zoe cast a wild glance at Theo. He said nothing. She glared at James.

He wore an enigmatic smile. "You've done me a great honour, Jessica," he said in silky tones, "and I promise I'll do my utmost to take the centre in a direction which will ensure its continued and increasing success."

Zoe's face burned.

"James's first task, of course, will be to oversee the appointment of a new creative director," said Jessica.

James now shifted his position and sat back in his chair with folded arms. "That's true," he said, "and Jessica has already approved my choice: Natasha."

"Natasha?" croaked Zoe. She began to cough. Theo rubbed her on the back.

Zoe swung to face him, knocking his hand away from her. "Theo! You must fight this!"

"Zoe, my love…" Theo placed a warning hand on her arm. She snatched it away. The others all looked at them. Zoe jumped to her feet.

As if in response to this, James too stood up and moved to take his position in the centre of the rug, commanding everyone's attention. "It's natural, Zoe, for you to feel emotional…"

Zoe's hands itched to pick up a table-lamp, swing it at his head and restore his previous injury.

Instead, she said, "Where *is* Natasha?"

Jessica frowned."Where she is right now is no concern of yours, Zoe. I don't need her here in order to share the news of her appointment."

Zoe turned on Jessica, who also then rose to her feet. "Give me one good reason why the trustees think James is right for the job, Jessica."

"Very well," said Jessica, smoothing her hair back. "James has superb connections for fundraising purposes. We can think of no-one better to carry us forward and increase our revenue."

"Revenue?" Zoe choked. "But that's not all we're about. Since when has that been a problem?" She pounced on Theo. "Theo! You're not going to accept this, are you?"

"I'm not prepared to argue with anyone here, in this room, right now," said Theo. "Jessica and I will speak in private, later."

Zoe felt blood drain from her face.

"The thought of James running this place, with Natasha in tow, makes me feel sick."

"Come on, Zoe," said Jessica. "You're not feeling well, so why don't you go on through into the sitting room and lie down on the sofa."

Zoe tossed her a contemptuous glance. Jessica took hold of her arm and began trying to shepherd her towards the library doorway. Zoe resisted and pushed her away.

Jessica gave up on Zoe and turned to Theo. "Theo, rest assured, we've no intention of asking you and Zoe to leave for another couple of months yet. You may both stay at the Trust's expense, until you've made alternative arrangements."

Then James stepped forward.

"I shall, of course, need to seek a replacement for Alice," he said, "because, before the recent worrying turn of events, I'd already made my feelings clear about her position here, given her continuous psychic experiences."

"And what's wrong with them? Nothing she's said or done has been any more psychic – or dare I say 'occult' – than Natasha's healings," said Zoe.

Dead silence fell.

Bernie took a deep breath and shifted the subject. "As far as Alice is concerned," he said, "we've no idea how long she'll be missing, but when she's found safe, and she comes back..."

"She won't be back," said James.

"How do you know? You're talking as if she's dead," said Zoe.

All eyes turned to James.

CHAPTER TWENTY-ONE

Zoe was still shaking from her recent altercation with James about Alice. It turned out that James had not meant to imply Alice was dead at all, and he had apologised profusely for giving this impression. But Zoe's stomach still turned at the very thought. And meanwhile, as if determined to make Zoe feel even worse, Jessica had aired her views about Theo's 'supposed recovery'. She had described Theo's recovery as 'unnatural', and not to be trusted – which was of course, she emphasised, why the trustees had appointed James in his place.

Back in the office the phone rang. Zoe snatched the receiver.

"Zoe."

"Leila! Any news?"

"Yes," replied Leila, in a thin voice. "The police officer's only just left me. Constable Hardwick his name was. He asked me lots of questions about Alice and filled in a form. He told me they'd treat the case as medium risk, whatever that means."

Zoe's heart thudded.

"And then?" she prompted.

"That was it. He said he'd go back to base and put everything in place for the investigation."

"And what about her car? Can't they do anything to trace that?"

"Yes, he said they'd put a marker on her car on their computer."

Zoe chewed her lip. "And then what?"

"Another police officer will come and visit you. Should arrive any moment now."

Zoe put the phone down, her fingers shaking. It didn't make sense for Alice to vanish without trace on the edge of a new opportunity in her career. She was due to meet a casting director in London on Friday morning. Zoe could only pray that the friends and contacts Leila had not yet spoken to might have some information to share.

And, meanwhile, she had other bad news to deal with too. She swallowed repeatedly as she thought of the trustees' most recent decision. They were supposed to have the best interests of the centre at heart. And then Zoe turned over in her mind the question of Theo's past secret meetings with Natasha.

Running counter to the thoughts, feelings and perceptions of everyone else here at this centre, Zoe believed herself, specifically, to be the focus of Natasha's malice. She felt so alone. Without Alice to back her up, she feared she may fall back again into doubting her own sanity. And she still couldn't avoid the conviction that the only reason why Theo had recovered so quickly was because Natasha had chosen to lift her curse. Natasha had new plans, Zoe felt sure of it. Immediately upon Theo's return to the centre she'd targeted him again. And now she'd made him compliant.

Zoe desperately needed to keep an eye on Theo, and watch out for any evidence of him falling under Natasha's influence. But it would be difficult for her to keep that up all hours of the day or night. Meanwhile, Jessica had granted them a two-month period during which they could research options for their future, and wind down their work at the centre, preparing for the stage when they were ready to move on to something new.

Theo was back in the icon-painting workshop right then, and James had vanished once more. Where Natasha was,

Zoe had no idea. She never seemed to attend workshops. Meanwhile, Zoe still had to keep the office running, even without Alice's support.

The door opened, and a female police officer walked in.

"Good morning. Are you Zoe Lucas? I'm here to speak to you about Alice Nazari."

By four o'clock that afternoon, Theo had returned to the office. Griff was leading the guests in the afternoon workshop. Zoe looked at Theo. With the one exception of his recent period of depression, whenever she'd been with him in the past, she'd usually felt buoyant and happy; but not now.

She had found her conversation with the police officer agonising. While she wanted to be open and honest with Constable Morley, she nevertheless shrank from sharing the story of how Alice had taken private and confidential documents from James's bedroom, photocopied them and then met up with Zoe at the hermitage to discuss them. She felt she'd eventually be pressed to reveal their reasons for this course of action – and that would have led on to a messy attempt to avoid all the details of her fears about James and Natasha. So she kept quiet about those details, terrified all the while that her failure to reveal them might prejudice the search for Alice. Those details might even turn out to be the key to her discovery – though Zoe couldn't imagine why.

The atmosphere seemed to be leeching energy from her. The harder she struggled against it, the stronger this feeling became. In every room she entered she felt the walls were closing in on her. What had happened to the friendly spirits of the house that Alice had placed her trust in? Perhaps they, too, had been overwhelmed by Natasha's malevolent psychic influence.

"Where's Natasha?" she asked. "Is she at Griff's workshop?"

"No," said Theo.

"Where is she then? What's she doing?"

"Can't say."

Zoe felt a flash of anger. "Probably enticing another of the guests – and maybe throwing in a miracle healing, again without bothering to invite you along to oversee it."

Theo studied her. "What's happened to you, Zoe? This attitude is so out of character for you." He came round the desk towards her and took her face tenderly between his two hands. "Look, it's no good torturing yourself about what's happened. That's the way things are."

"No!" She grasped his hands and thrust them away from her. "You had your chance when you spoke to Jessica. You could have fought the trustees' decision. But instead, you accepted it."

He shook his head. "Do you suggest we defy the trustees?"

"Yes. They're wrong. And you know it." She pressed her hands to her head. "If Alice was here, she'd help us!"

Theo frowned.

"I know Alice is missing, and we're all worried. But you have tended to rely on her a little too much. Try not to fret over her, Zoe. There's probably a very good explanation for why she's gone."

"Not Alice!" cried Zoe tearfully. "Not without telling me."

Theo took a few steps away from her, seemed to hesitate then made a decision. He dropped into Alice's seat and pulled the phone closer to him.

"I need to speak to Neville and find out which parishes are looking for new incumbents."

"No, Theo!" she said.

He looked at her, startled. "Why not?"

She swallowed. "Yours is a creative ministry! You can't go into a parish!"

"I'm sorry. It's my only option right now."

147

"But Neville... he's vocations adviser. He'll foist you off on some obscure rural parish with a haunted vicarage."

Theo's eyes widened. Then he burst out laughing.

"A haunted vicarage? Why on earth do you say that?"

"Natasha must have got to me." She seized Theo's arm. "Don't you see? These healings of hers; they'll all be reversed. There's a reason why the writers of fairy tales have always insisted the good effect of spells only lasts till midnight."

He stared. "Spells? Fairy tales? Zoe, are you quite well?"

Her stomach clenched. He was totally off her wavelength. Then, unkind words and phrases began to scroll through her head: *Blind, unimaginative, literal-minded; weak, indecisive, short-sighted.* Things she'd never, ever, thought about Theo before. And now, she in her turn began to doubt that Theo's mental stability would last.

CHAPTER TWENTY-TWO

By the next day, Theo had spoken to Neville, who'd agreed to look out for suitable parish vacancies. Meanwhile, whenever Zoe saw Natasha, she was surrounded by admirers, gazing at her, hanging on to her every word. And when Zoe found herself in conversation with those admirers, she heard the same thing again and again.

"Natasha's the loveliest person I've ever known."

"I can't understand why you don't seem to like her, Zoe."

"She's so caring, and so beautiful. I feel she really understands me. I want to listen to her and look at her all day."

Zoe skilfully fielded these remarks, whilst managing to appear composed. But with every response she made, she felt she was sinking into a deep, sticky marshland. Natasha herself Zoe couldn't seem to pin down. Whenever Zoe tried to find her alone for a few words, she was nowhere to be seen.

Without Alice, Zoe remained unsupported and with no-one else to validate her opinion; it came as a shock to realise how much she needed Alice to reassure her that she was seeing things correctly, and wasn't going into psychosis herself. She rubbed her throat as she thought this. She must do something about Natasha soon: but what?

The phone rang and she snatched it up to hear Leila's voice again, sounding tearful.

"Zoe, it's Leila."

Zoe's heart began to pound again.

"Leila! What news of Alice?"

"None. I've just finished speaking to the Missing Persons Co-ordinator, Carol. Very nice lady."

Zoe could tell Leila was trying to keep an iron grip on her emotions. She, too, fought the urge to panic.

"Carol told me Alice's mobile number has been 'pinged' but her mobile found to be dead," said Leila.

Her voice faded away. Zoe sensed her wrestling with her fears, as she herself began to visualise the worst that might have happened to Alice.

"Alice's bank account has been checked," said Leila. "The police have obtained a live trace on her card and checked out her Facebook and Twitter profiles for any clues. And they've loaded her photo onto their database."

"So what happens next?"

"They'll contact local press, feature her on their website, and contact Radio Gloucester."

Zoe bit her lip and tears of frustration sprang to her eyes. The police were doing their very best, but it still all seemed so slow to her.

"I'm frightened, Zoe," whispered Leila.

Zoe remained silent.

Later, having not managed to eat much at lunch, Zoe excused herself to the guests who were still sitting chatting over their fruit course, and went to prepare the barn ready for that afternoon's workshop. She felt the best way right now to deal with her fears about Alice was to keep busy. She found that Griff had already done most of her work for her, and was finished in five minutes. That gave her quarter of an hour before she needed to be back in the office. She decided to take Vito for a quick walk. They walked up the driveway, across the car park and out through the gate on the west perimeter, to climb the steep side of the valley until she reached the public footpath at the top. There was an icy bite in the air today and she wore a warm jacket and scarf.

Halfway up the wooded slope, she felt an urge to turn and look back down towards the farmhouse and barn. Through the bare branches of the field maples, she could see down beyond the woodland fence and across the wide lawn to the goose house.

There she spotted Theo and Natasha, strolling along the path together. She stiffened. Vito looked up at Zoe and then nudged her side with his nose.

Zoe's eyes sharpened. Natasha had laid her hand on Theo's arm. Theo stopped and turned towards her. He was gazing into her face. Zoe held her breath, expecting him to kiss her. But it didn't happen. They continued walking along the path into the goose house.

Zoe's heart pounded against her ribcage.

She watched as they disappeared into the goose house.

Vito jumped up at Zoe with anxious eyes, pawing her arm. She plunged her face into her hands. Returning to all-fours, Vito nosed at her side and whined. She dropped her hands to her side and gazed down at him.

"Vito," she said urgently, "Natasha's evil. Alice was always right about her. I don't believe her healings will last. But no-one will listen to me. Alice would have done, but she's gone."

Tears trickled down her face. Wiping them away, she strode along the path back to the centre, Vito bounding at her side, both filled with new energy. She was determined to confront Theo. She'd face him with the truth.

Zoe caught up with Theo on the path which ran past the barn.

"Theo, this can't go on," she gasped.

He turned and looked at her. "Look, let's go back here behind the barn. Then no guests will see us."

She followed him onto the wide lawn, talking as she went. "We must deal with Natasha, fast."

"How do you mean?" He swung to face her.

"You should be the first person to suggest something. I've seen you alone with her several times now." Zoe slapped her hand against the trunk of a nearby pine tree, making her palm tingle and sending shooting pains down her arm. She quickly withdrew her hand and flexed her fingers. "Natasha's so sweet, so perfect, in the eyes of all our guests and staff. I hear nothing but *how caring she is, how spiritual*, even *how holy*. And these so-called 'healings': I believe they're false, and those she 'heals' put themselves into her power. And when it came to you, Theo, I'm sure she cursed you. And she only lifted the curse when it suited her."

"Come on, Zoe," he said, seizing her hands and gazing at her. "You can't expect me to take this seriously. It's way over the top."

"No, it isn't," she said, snatching her hands away and putting them on her hips. "I'm dead serious, Theo. And I do wonder if she's even normal flesh and blood."

"Oh, she's *that*, all right," he said with a misjudged smile.

Zoe froze. "Theo, what exactly are you suggesting?"

Theo's eyes, normally a gentle grey, now looked black. He grasped her by both shoulders.

"Zoe, you're running wild. Don't say things you'll regret later."

"Regret?" With a violent twist, she shook herself free of him.

"Zoe, listen to me!" He gripped her again. She tried to pull away, but this time he held on. She hoped no guests would walk round the south-east corner of the barn.

"Let go, Theo. Listen, it's clear Jessica doesn't trust you and she's asked you to leave. And now I'm beginning to understand why. We can't carry on like this in our marriage. When we leave here, I want us to separate."

He let go of her, a shocked expression on his face.

"Zoe, Zoe…" he cried.

She hurried away in the direction of the house, leaving him stunned.

CHAPTER TWENTY-THREE

Zoe looked up from her PC the following morning, Friday, as James walked through the office doorway. The clock said nine. Zoe was acutely aware that Alice should now be heading for her appointment with the casting director in Covent Garden. Her agent would have withdrawn her name and, most likely, some other actress would be on her way to the audition, rejoicing that the coveted part was likely to fall into her hands instead. Zoe clenched her fists and her stomach churned when she allowed her imagination free rein on what might have happened to Alice. She could even have lost her memory and perhaps forgotten who she was. She might be found wandering around somewhere, lost. And yet... surely at least her car would be identified sometime soon?

Yesterday, Zoe had considered packing her bags, leaving Theo and the centre straightaway, and driving off to her sister in London, and asking to stay with her. Leila would be a phone call away and Zoe could keep in touch with her daily, tracing progress on the search for Alice. Then she'd thought better of the plan.

With Theo she'd preserved a cool, detached manner. But, this morning, swallowing her pride, she'd walked into the office again.

James wheeled to face her. "What's up between you and Theo?"

"Nothing that need concern you," she replied in a haughty tone.

James clasped both hands together on his chest.

"It'll be a wrench for you both to leave the centre, I see that. But I'm sure Theo will find something to move onto that will suit him much better."

She said nothing.

"Meanwhile, of course," he said, "you'll both be mourning the absence of Alice; it's a sad business." He sighed, and let his hands drop to his side. "But people are so unaccountable. It's a fact of life that sometimes they disappear without saying goodbye, and cut off all contact."

Zoe's fingers itched to pick up a well-stuffed lever-arch file and throw it at James's head. But she managed to resist the impulse.

"Let me settle myself down," said James, "then I've a favour to ask of you."

He walked across to the cafetière and reached for the bag of coffee.

Zoe's thoughts tumbled over each other. Theo had betrayed her. He'd failed to take a stand against Jessica and the rest of the trustees, he'd made no attempt to defend and protect the life he and Zoe had begun to build here. And Alice, whom she might have confided in, had vanished, and even now her life could be in danger.

Having poured hot water into the cafetière and replaced the lid, James pivoted on his heels, then strolled across to Alice's desk. He sat in Alice's chair and held Zoe in his gaze.

"Every time I look at you, Zoe," he said, "and see the amazing colour of your hair and eyes, I can't help thinking that if *you* wanted a film career, it would be yours for the taking."

Her heart skipped a beat. She could not believe the change of subject, the lack of consideration for her feelings about Alice's loss... but she could also not help wondering how he knew of her childhood dreams. Then she realised he probably didn't. He was just being the same, crass, insensitive old James. The remark was merely another sign of his falseness and insincerity.

She gave him a hard stare.

"There must be many casting directors who'd be eager to sign you up, if only they knew about you," continued James.

"Highly unlikely," she said.

He persisted. "I mean it, Zoe. Listen; there'd be no more menial tasks here in this office. Let me put it to you straight. I could give you an entrée into the film world. You'll be feted, admired and adored."

He leaned forward, both elbows on the desk, fingers laced together under his chin.

She frowned.

"I really can't think of this while I'm worrying about Alice."

"Maybe," he said, "but you won't help Alice by ignoring what I'm saying to you. I do have connections I could exploit to make this happen for you."

"I thought you were disenchanted with the acting world, James," she said. "You said so yourself. Why would you be encouraging anyone else to get into it?"

He smiled.

"It would be different for you, Zoe. You have a potential I could never touch. You're young, female, and stunning to look at. Often producers will only do a film if they get exactly the person they want for the star role. The producer is the power, the control and the money. If the producer wants someone who looks like you, you're the one the casting director will zero in on."

She remained silent.

"Listen," he said, unlacing his fingers and drumming them

against the desk top. "I have a producer friend. You'd be ideal for a role she has in mind. With your fragile beauty, you're a winner. You'd beat every other actress on the international celebrity circuit."

"So why didn't you tell Alice about this when she was with us?" Zoe asked.

"Because Alice is a black girl; very attractive, of course, but not right for this particular role."

Zoe sat back in her chair.

"OK. White, female, beautiful; why not suggest Natasha?"

James didn't hesitate. "Natasha isn't suitable. My friend's already confirmed that. Come on, Zoe. I see my offer intrigues you."

She didn't know whether to laugh or cry.

He jumped up. "And while you're thinking about it, let me go and make the coffee."

She put her elbows on the desk, and sunk her head in her hands, while James poured coffee into the cups, and brought one over to her. As he set the cup and saucer on her desk, she looked up. He locked her in an intense gaze.

"So, Zoe?"

The air seemed to ripple. Words sprang into her head. *Say yes, Zoe, this is what you've always dreamed of. What have you got to lose?* James's voice broke through.

"Give me the benefit of the doubt; just a few photos." He brought his smartphone out. "Thank you, Zoe. Perfect."

"Stop, Zoe. We need to talk," said Theo.

Zoe had met him whilst walking in the garden at nine o'clock that evening, after dinner. James was leading the final session of the week's programme and had enlisted Griff's help in preparing for it. So Theo and Zoe were both off duty. Though the temperature had been dropping all day, and the darkness was relieved by few stars, both of them felt an urge to go for an evening walk, well wrapped up, their thoughts sharpened by the flinty chill, in order to reflect on all that had happened in the last few days.

Zoe thrust her gloved hands into her pocket, and said nothing.

"Come and sit in the gazebo," Theo said. "Though we'll be warmer if we keep walking, I still feel it would be best to sit while we talk."

She followed him along the path through the leafless shrubbery. Theo opened the door of the gazebo, switched the light on, then walked in, holding the door for her as she passed through, and closing it behind her. They settled opposite each other on the redwood seats of the octagonal structure. The space between them felt vast.

"I've had my discussion with Neville," said Theo.

"I knew you'd spoken to him. What did he say?"

"He did his best to be helpful." Theo spoke in a reflective tone of voice. "We discussed my career and he suggested I try to discern God's leading in the events of my life. We looked at it as if it was a voyage along a river. Then he talked about how vast everything is." He held his hands out, palms uppermost. "This was vast, that was vast, the other was vast. I asked myself *why did God make the universe so vast if we're the sole planet with life on it?* Then I thought: *Perhaps God doesn't exist after all.*"

Zoe's heart fluttered. Whenever Theo had talked this way in the past, the spectre of his depression arose before her.

But she had no patience right now to follow through on his religious doubts. She was anxious to steer the conversation back to the problem of Natasha.

"Theo, I can't help you with that," she said. "Please, focus on what's happening to us, here at this centre. You need to stand up to Natasha." She folded her arms tightly.

Theo leaned forward, elbows on knees, head in hands. Then he lifted his head to look up at her.

"Listen, Zoe. The power Natasha has is incredible. It's quite beyond my experience. It's all-encompassing."

"Then resist it!" she cried, clenching her fists. "You believe in prayer."

"I did," he said. "But this power she has…"

Acid seemed to boil up from deep within Zoe.

"…is a power you can overcome! Just do it!" she cried.

He leapt to his feet, his face flushed. She felt an electric charge in the pit of her stomach. She'd last seen that expression in his eyes as they made love. But this was burning anger, not desire.

"Why let her ruin everything we've worked for here?" she demanded. "Our life at this centre, our marriage…"

His gaze remained fixed on her face. For a moment she thought he'd seize her and begin kissing her. Instead he withdrew, and sank back down onto the seat again. She urgently needed to shock him out of this passive state of mind.

"Theo, there's something I must tell you," she said. "James has made me an offer – which I'm thinking of accepting."

"What offer?" He sat up straight again.

She shared it with him.

"God! James and his arrogance!" said Theo. "Say you'll have nothing to do with it."

She got up and went to the door.

"I shall do what I like," she said. "After all, *you*'re not prepared to listen to my warnings about Natasha."

She pulled the door open then turned to face him on the threshold.

"Natasha's an entirely separate issue," he said.

"No, she isn't. Why are you so blind? I warn you, Theo. She's dangerous."

He fell silent, shaking his head.

Zoe fired up. "Tell Natasha you know where her power comes from! Defy her!"

Theo threw her a look full of doubt and distrust.

"She's entranced you," went on Zoe, her face burning. "The trouble is you won't acknowledge where that power comes from. Instead, you've put yourself under it. And if you don't get out now, it could destroy you."

"Nonsense. This is crazy talk, Zoe."

She turned her back on him and ran along the path through the shrubbery, towards the house.

CHAPTER TWENTY-FOUR

Zoe was cool towards Theo at breakfast on Saturday morning. The day itself had dawned muted and mild. She was thankful that none of the guests seemed to have noticed the rift between her and Theo. But the reason for this depressed her: Natasha had so absorbed their hearts and minds this week, she was the only thing they could think and talk about.

As Zoe said goodbye to each departing guest, she was even more disturbed to learn that, in common with those who'd left the Saturday before, these guests, too, had arranged to see Natasha again very soon, though where these meetings were to take place, Zoe had no idea.

The next day, Sunday, would see the arrival of a new set of guests for the following week's programme. More souls for Natasha to catch in her net, thought Zoe desperately, lured by the promise of a sweet reward. Zoe had several times searched her own conscience and mind and imagination to try to guess what Natasha's ultimate goal might be in all this; and she remained baffled, frightened and close to despair.

Meanwhile, Theo had made it clear to her that what Natasha offered him had a stronger hold on his heart than any idea of trying to save their marriage. Zoe's jaw tightened at the thought of this. And she needed to consider her future, the life she might lead, if she were to give up on Theo and leave the centre. She'd have to rethink her whole world. But right now it took all her strength just to keep from bursting into tears.

And then there was James, and the offer he'd made her. She knew she should reject that offer. She sensed he was trying to make inroads into her, just as Natasha had already succeeded in doing with Theo. And yet she also told herself that what he was offering could save her future life… though she hated herself for relying upon such false hope.

At eight o'clock she left the dining area and went straight through into the office. A light on the answering machine indicated a message; she picked it up and learnt that Jessica, who had planned to come in that morning and chat to the departing guests, sent her apologies. She had a migraine and was staying in bed. She asked Zoe to pass on her good wishes to all those leaving today.

Zoe worked at twice her usual pace for three hours, helping guests with suitcases and seeing them off. Meanwhile, Griff took over temporarily in the office. Against her own best instincts, Zoe had explained to Griff at breakfast her intention to go to a lunch appointment with James at midday. Griff had accepted this without comment, and now Zoe pulled her purple jacket on over her cream blouse and smart black trousers, picked up her crystal-studded shoulder-bag, and hurried through to the entrance hall. Opening the front door she walked out of the house.

She and James were due to meet James's producer friend in a hotel in Chipping Sodbury. She'd told nobody but Theo of the purpose of the meeting. And still she fought against her better judgement which told her to have nothing to do with James's offer.

James was already waiting for her in the Cayenne. The front passenger door was wide open. She got in.

"Right then," said James. "We're off to Chipping Sodbury. Sonya should be at the hotel waiting for us, with the lunch already ordered."

Sonya, Zoe wondered. That was a coincidence. Sonya was the name of Natasha's sister.

James hummed a jaunty tune to himself as he turned the Cayenne round and then sped back up the drive towards the exit gate.

As soon as James and Zoe walked into the hotel bar, and James introduced Zoe to his friend Sonya, Zoe knew for sure she was Natasha's sister.

"Hello, Zoe," said Sonya, uncurling herself from her velvet-upholstered chair, and rising to her feet.

Though her physical similarity to Natasha was clear, in many respects Sonya was very different. She boasted fine ash-blonde hair like Natasha's. But she wore it backcombed, and piled up high in a textured hive.

She stood at least ten centimetres taller than Zoe, and held her in a steel-hard gaze.

"It's good to meet you." Her voice was crisp.

"You're Natasha Morrigan's sister, aren't you?"

"That's right. But in a very different line of business, I can assure you." Sonya gave a small chuckle.

Zoe's spine prickled as she looked at Sonya. It would certainly be uncanny if both sisters held miraculous healing powers. Nevertheless, Sonya in her own way had a presence as formidable as Natasha's. And the dazzling white, sharply-tailored suit contributed to that image in no small measure.

"Do sit down, both of you," said Sonya. James and Zoe took chairs on either side of her. Zoe's eyes were drawn to Sonya's shoes; four-inch silver heels and pointed toes extended her legs even further.

Zoe returned her gaze to Sonya's face.

"Do have a drink, Zoe. I've taken the liberty of ordering one ready for you."

163

And Sonya indicated a psychedelic-looking cocktail.

"What's that?" asked Zoe.

Sonya named the drink. It didn't mean anything to Zoe, but she gave Sonya the benefit of the doubt and sipped it. The cunning blend of flavours in the cocktail sent a cascade of fire down into her stomach. She took a deep breath, setting the glass down on the table again.

"So how would you describe your sister's line of business?" Zoe asked.

"Spiritual healing, of course," said Sonya.

Zoe moistened her lips. Her discovery that Natasha's sister, the very person who'd paid a large sum of money to James, was in fact a film producer, did seem, on one level, to settle a major question in Zoe's mind. But James had already suggested that acting work was thin on the ground for him these days and that he was disillusioned with the acting scene and wanted to live a more level life. So she still didn't understand why such a large sum would have been paid to him.

"I suppose you must often cast James in your films, Sonya."

"No. Nothing suitable."

Zoe clasped her hands together and tried another topic.

"Do you and Natasha see a lot of each other?" she asked.

Sonya began to stroke one of the long, slender fingers on her right hand. Zoe noticed she wore several dazzling dress-rings.

"Oh yes," said Sonya. "We've had our differences in the past; but not now."

Sonya flicked a stray blonde hair off one of her white lapels and exchanged a swift glance with James. A line had appeared on James's forehead. He was about to speak when Zoe broke in with another question for Sonya.

"Where do you believe your sister's healing power comes from?" she asked.

Sonya's eyes narrowed as she looked at Zoe. "Natasha's

power?" she said. "From the same source that all spiritual power comes from: Some call it the 'Great Spirit', others the 'Ultimate Reality', or the 'Universe'. Now, Zoe, I understand you're interested in a part?" She reached down beside her to a large white leather handbag, snapped open the gold clasp, and brought out a document. "Here's the screenplay," she said, placing it on the table. "Let me talk you through it."

"Tell me about your film company first, Sonya," said Zoe.

Sonya searched her face. Then she named the company; one Zoe didn't recognise.

"What films does the company produce?"

Sonya began to describe them. Zoe had neither seen nor heard of them. As Sonya continued to speak, Zoe felt more and more unstable, as if she was trying to maintain her balance on a shifting deck in a high sea.

"Drink up," said Sonya. "But do have a look at the highlighted sections in the script first."

Zoe took the script and studied the highlighted parts. She began to wonder why she was considering this when she noted the foul language the character was to use. And she remained unsatisfied with the information Sonya had given her. Meanwhile, she was aware of a continuous murmur of James and Sonya conferring together in very low voices.

Then Sonya took the script away, put it back in her briefcase, and set another drink before Zoe.

"Lunch will arrive in a minute."

Zoe felt bewildered. "Has James told you about the trouble we've been having at the centre?" she asked abruptly. "And the fact that my friend, Alice, has disappeared?"

"Alice?" enquired Sonya. "Yes, I believe James did mention it to me. Sad. I understand the girl's an actress. I do hope she'll be found soon. But meanwhile, back to this part I have in mind for you. I must say, you're ideal. I need someone with your looks, your colouring and your manner. Most of all I want someone untrained and raw; innocent even."

Zoe stared at her. Something didn't ring true here.

"And yet the character seems very aggressive to me," she said.

"Ah, here's lunch," said Sonya.

When Zoe walked into the office later on, she found Theo sitting at her desk. He got up as she entered and came over to her.

"What happened at the meeting?" he asked.

"Can't talk to you about it now, Theo," she said.

At once, James, who'd followed, broke in.

"You've done the right thing."

"Zoe!" said Theo. "You haven't committed yourself to anything have you?"

She threw a cool glance at him then turned to James. "I didn't like the foul language."

"No problem," cut in James. "She said she'd get it changed."

Theo looked from Zoe to James and back again.

"Sonya will be in touch," said James.

Zoe nodded, but made no reply. She went to sit at her desk. As she did so, her worries took over again.

The meeting with Sonya had been all wrong. Zoe suspected that something had been added to those drinks she was given. And she mistrusted what James and Sonya had been murmuring together, out of her earshot. She felt tired, confused and irritable. And through all this Alice's name kept returning. Zoe instinctively felt responsible for her disappearance; though this seemed to have no logical cause.

Theo came behind Zoe's desk and laid a gentle hand on Zoe's arm. She stiffened and drew her breath in between her teeth. He was trying to conciliate her. But it was no good. Their relationship was damaged beyond repair – unless he stood up to Natasha. But she kept her lips clamped shut. If she signed a contract for a film role she'd soon be well out of it.

Sighing, Theo turned back to James. "I look forward to glancing over your schedule of workshops and learning the title of the ones I am to lead next week."

"Yes, yes," said James in a bright, jocular tone, thrusting his hand into his pocket and jingling keys against coins.

Zoe felt a pressure increasing over her scalp and above her right eye. *Oh no, not a headache.* The pulse on her wrist beat strongly. An image had flashed into her mind of Natasha sitting in the goose house with a voodoo doll of her, sticking pins into its head.

Then Theo spoke again.

"Griff has agreed to look after things in the office this afternoon," he said, "and that suits me well. I've set up a special meeting with Natasha."

Zoe and James both went on alert.

"Afternoon tea," he replied, "in the King's Head in Cirencester. I felt it best to choose neutral territory."

"And the occasion?"

"A heart-to-heart chat about Natasha's healings. Would you join us, Zoe?"

James opened his mouth, when Theo said, "You have a meeting with Jessica then, don't you? I checked in the office diary."

The skin stretched tight over James's cheekbones. "That's been postponed. Jessica, I understand, has a migraine. I'll join your meeting instead."

"As you wish," said Theo.

Zoe studied James. Shadows swirled across his features.

A short while later, both James and Theo were called from the office on different tasks, leaving Zoe alone. On impulse, Zoe went online, and entered some new keyword combinations together with James's name. The next moment, she was surveying a set of results she'd never seen before. And following information trails she'd previously been unaware of.

The phone rang. She grabbed it, hoping it might be the Missing Persons Co-ordinator to say Alice had been found. Instead, she heard Jessica's voice.

"How are you feeling?" she asked.

"Much better now, thank you, Zoe. I did have a meeting arranged with James this afternoon. We postponed it but I believe I could now make it."

"Don't worry about that, Jessica. James, Theo and I are meeting Natasha in the King's Head at three-thirty."

Jessica thought about this.

"Then I'll come too," she said.

CHAPTER TWENTY-FIVE

The hotel where Natasha had agreed to meet them presented an elegant facade on Market Place, with its stone-coloured paintwork. Inside there were several individual areas, and from one of these Natasha stepped forward to greet Theo and Zoe. Her cobweb hair flowed, as ever, over her shoulders and down the back of her ankle-length white silk dress. She held Zoe's gaze for two or three seconds. Zoe's muscles tensed. She thrust her fists into the pockets of her jacket.

"Do come and sit down," said Natasha. "Make yourselves comfortable."

They followed Natasha, finding Jessica and James already seated on one of the low brown leather sofas which were placed opposite each other near the feature fireplace. Afternoon tea had already been set out on the oak table between the two sofas. Natasha sat next to James, and Theo and Zoe settled themselves down facing the other three.

Natasha poured the tea. As she handed James his cup, he ran his finger down her bare arm. She shivered. Zoe watched, conscious of the current of erotic desire that passed between the two of them. Smiling, Natasha indicated the cake-stands. "Do help yourselves, everyone," she said.

"An excellent choice for afternoon tea, Natasha," said James.

"The credit's all Theo's," she said.

"So," said Jessica, "I understand this little get-together is to give Theo and Zoe one last chance to quiz you yet again. You're very kind, Natasha."

James crossed his legs and folded his arms, the finger of his right hand tapping against his other arm.

Natasha relaxed back into the sofa and nodded. "That's true, and I'm happy to answer their questions. It will allow me once again to explain my healings."

Zoe was bursting with questions.

Theo looked at her. "You begin, Zoe."

She started. "Of course." She turned back from him to face Natasha again. "Where does your power come from?" she asked.

Natasha's reply was given straightaway.

"There can be only one source," she said. "You would understand it as God."

James and Jessica both shifted uneasily.

Natasha herself looked perfectly serene.

"As you know," she said, "I've healed several of the guests over the past two weeks. I've banished minor injuries and also life-threatening disease. Some say I do miracles."

"Yes," said Jessica, "and both James and I can testify to that, too."

Zoe threw a startled glance at her.

"Mmm," said James, "Natasha healed a sporting injury of mine five years ago, sustained in a fall from a horse. I owe my present good state of health to Natasha." He flicked a speck off his trousers.

Zoe switched her attention to Jessica, who'd just sat forward.

"As you know," said Jessica, "I suffer from migraines. I woke up with one this morning. Later on, Natasha and I spoke on the phone; with a few words from her, it vanished."

Zoe could think of nothing to say.

Then Natasha's voice broke in. "I keep a record of all my healings." Zoe refocused on her. "You may look at it if you wish." Natasha produced a green velvet-covered notebook and handed it across the table to Zoe.

Zoe spent five minutes leafing through the book and studying it. It recorded healings from three years back. The names, addresses and telephone numbers of the sufferers, details of their ailments, dates when they'd visited Natasha, a description of the healing and how it had been confirmed.

Zoe looked up. "Do you keep in touch with all the people you've healed, Natasha?"

"Oh yes," she said with a smile, "very much so."

"Last week's guests," said Zoe; "do you expect to see them again in the future?"

Natasha nodded, keeping her eyes on Zoe's. Zoe sensed that a hidden meaning lay beneath her expression. Natasha sipped her tea.

"May I look at the book?" asked Theo.

Zoe passed the book to him. Meanwhile, James munched a strawberry tart, and exuded smug self-satisfaction. Zoe looked at Natasha again and tried to decide whether she recognised anything of Sonya in those eyes. As Natasha met her gaze, Zoe shivered. She felt as if her power source had started to fail; as if she was being broken up by a faulty electrical connection. Natasha was playing with her.

"What do you do first of all," she asked, "when you're with a sick or injured person?"

"Nothing, until they ask me to heal them," said Natasha. "That's very important. I never heal people who don't ask."

"And when they do ask, you pass your hands over them. Do you pray?"

"No."

James fidgeted. She glanced at him and noted a furtive shadow cross his face. He selected a meringue from the cake-stand and sunk his teeth into it.

171

Zoe refocused on Natasha. Though seated on a leather sofa in the King's Head Hotel, the healer looked to Zoe as if she was reclining against a tree in a glade of an ancient Celtic forest.

Zoe sat forward. She tried to guess what Theo might say or do now if he was his true self, and not influenced by Natasha. Zoe had met his colleagues in the deliverance ministry, two years before. She recalled the words they used if they felt real occult power was present. She had to give it a go.

"Do you believe in the power of Jesus Christ over all this, Natasha?" she asked.

Silence cut in. Zoe could no longer hear the murmur of other guests in the background. The healer's luminous gaze seemed to stalk Zoe, biding its time, ready to spring when the time was right, when Zoe was trapped in a corner with nowhere to run. Zoe fought to avoid eye-contact with Natasha. But it was impossible. Some kind of presence swam in the air between Natasha and herself, reaching out to Zoe, trying to suck her in.

"Tell me, Natasha," said Zoe. "Do you believe that *Jesus Christ is Lord*?"

Natasha's expression changed. Zoe was looking at a different person. Sharp, dark lines scored the healer's features. Her eyes glittered cold, impenetrable, venomous. The temperature in the room dropped ten degrees.

Zoe flinched. Something hard had hit her. It was a teacup. Hot tea splashed onto her lap. She dropped her own cup at once. It smashed as it landed on the floorboards. She leapt to her feet, crying aloud. A storm seemed to have whipped up around her. Teacups and cakes flew, and Natasha screamed. To Zoe, her appearance was no longer that of a beautiful young woman, but of a winged creature.

James, Jessica and Theo all leapt to their feet, shouting, struggling, as if fighting something off. A waitress hurried towards them, fear and shock etched on her face. All Zoe could hear was screams, cries and the beating of wings. Then someone grabbed her arm and pulled her from the individual area where they'd been sitting, and she stumbled past the bar, followed by airborne missiles, grazing her cheek.

Zoe had no sense at all of the reaction of the other guests in the hotel, as the main door shut behind them and they ran along Market Place in the direction of Castle Street.

Jessica stopped opposite the Church of St. John the Baptist, and turned to Theo, her hand clutched to her chest.

"What happened?"

"No idea. How did that bird get into the room?"

"Someone must have left a window open," said Jessica. "It was huge, and black; a raven, perhaps."

Zoe turned to James, and saw Natasha folded in his arms. Bewildered, Zoe was about to speak, when James's voice struck her.

"Why did you say those words, you little…?"

"That's enough, James! Back off." Theo's voice was razor-edged. He strode along the road, as Zoe hurried to catch up with him. She shot several glances around, searching for James and Natasha. But they'd already gone. Meanwhile, Jessica marched on ahead, cutting off all further opportunities for conversation.

Matching her pace to Theo's, Zoe seized his hand, bringing him to an abrupt halt.

"Why did you leave it to me?"

He turned on her, his face livid. "You had no right to do that; or to use those words. You played with fire in there." He grabbed her arm and held it in a fierce grip. "You've no idea what you're doing. No idea at all."

Tears streaming down her face, Zoe broke away from him and fled.

CHAPTER TWENTY-SIX

When Jessica stepped into the office at Zoe's request at five thirty that afternoon, Zoe was prepared to make the biggest plea she'd ever made in her whole life. No sooner had the door closed behind Jessica than Zoe confronted her. She raised both hands, palms uppermost.

"Jessica, please tell me. What will you do about Natasha? And James?"

Jessica pursed her lips and folded her arms. "First, let's get one thing clear. You tell me what *you* suppose happened in the King's Head earlier."

"It must have been obvious to everyone," said Zoe. "We saw clear evidence of demonic power."

Jessica stared at her. Then she walked across to the group of easy chairs and seated herself.

"All right," she said. "Shall we try being rational about this? I'm a bit concerned that you think something supernatural took place. Well, it didn't. A bird blundered into the room when someone left the door open. Frightening, I admit, but sometimes that does happen."

"And this is your last word on the subject?" said Zoe.

Jessica's eyes narrowed. "Yes. However," she added, "I *have* called another emergency meeting of the trustees; for Monday evening at six."

"Monday evening? We can't wait till then!"

"Wait for what exactly?" Jessica scrutinised Zoe's face like a psychiatrist about to reach a diagnosis.

It was clear to Zoe that Jessica thought she was unhinged.

"All right," she said. "I've one more thing to say. I believe James is involved in Alice's disappearance."

Jessica's eyes widened. "Oh, come on, Zoe."

"I've looked James up. And I learned three new things about him."

"OK," said Jessica with a visible effort to be patient. "What's the first?" She opened her handbag and produced a notebook and pen.

Zoe cleared her throat. "Six years ago, James stood in court, accused of the abduction and rape of a first-year undergraduate girl at Edinburgh. The case was dismissed due to 'unsafe' evidence."

Jessica began scribbling on her pad. Zoe guessed she was taking notes.

"And number two?" she said, without looking up.

"A certain actress lodged a complaint about him stalking her. The police investigated, he was held for questioning, but released without charge. The reason given was 'insufficient admissible evidence'."

A deep line appeared on Jessica's brow. "Go on," she said. "Let's hear number three."

"Did you realize James is divorced?" Zoe asked.

Jessica stabbed her pen into the page three times. "So? I don't see what…"

"His wife initiated the proceedings; and her grounds? Domestic violence and mental and emotional cruelty."

Jessica closed the book, capped the pen, and returned both to her handbag.

She stood up. "I won't, of course, take your word for any of this. Otherwise it's defamation. Show me the evidence."

"I will. I'll find it and print it out for you."

"You do that. As it happens, I'm meeting James again today – Cirencester again, not the same hotel by the way – I should imagine we'll probably be black-listed from it now – at nine o'clock this evening."

"Good. I'll get it to you before then."

The door opened and Theo came in.

"Ah, there you are, Zoe," he said. "May I interrupt? I'm sorry, Jessica, but it's very important."

"By all means, Theo, you're welcome," said Jessica. "Our conversation's at an end anyway, isn't it, Zoe?"

Zoe drew herself to her full height and levelled her gaze upon Jessica.

"Would you come with me, please, Zoe?" said Theo. "I want to talk to you. The Monk's Room's free," and he disappeared back through the internal doorway again.

The Monk's Room was a very simple room with whitewashed walls, which had been set aside for solitary contemplation and for counselling. It was furnished with two chairs and a small table. The room had once been used to hide fugitives from royal agents, hunting down those of 'the wrong religion' in the sixteenth and the seventeenth centuries.

On one wall, an artist had painted a life-size image of the Angel Gabriel in egg tempera. It had been copied and enlarged from an icon, the original of which hung in the Church of St Demetrius in Pskov, Russia.

Theo faced Zoe as she entered the room. She shut the door behind her and stood with her back against it. Before she could move, he strode forward and took hold of both her hands.

"Zoe, we can't carry on like this."

"No we can't," she snapped. "When are you going to open your eyes; see Natasha for who and what she really is; and do something about it?"

"Never. I don't accept that there is anything for me to 'do' about Natasha. We'll have to agree to disagree about her."

He shifted his hands to her wrists.

"But what I want you to listen to, Zoe, right now, is how I feel about the way you behaved this afternoon."

She twisted from side to side, trying to loosen his hold, her face burning with anger.

Theo's eyes were dark with frustration and, though she hardly dared to admit it, fear.

She fought to loosen his grip. But Theo held on.

"I feel betrayed, Zoe," he declared. "You had no right to say those words to Natasha earlier. When I introduced you to my colleagues before we married, I never expected you to abuse my trust. "

"What are you talking about?" she cried. "Someone had to do it! Since you weren't going to, it was left to me. You should be ashamed. I don't know how you dare accuse me."

He stared at her, disbelieving. "You've changed, Zoe. I can't cope with this. You make me feel desperate."

Zoe tried to break free, and he at first resisted her; but then, without warning, let go. She fell to the floor, knocking both chairs over. Theo plunged to his knees, ready to seize hold of her and lift her up. But she recoiled from him.

"Don't touch me," she sobbed. "You know in your heart of hearts I was right to say the things I did to Natasha. You were too cowardly. And if you love me, you'll admit it!"

"I don't admit it. I never thought you'd sink to emotional blackmail."

She scrambled to her feet, and raised her hand to hit him. A loud knock came on the door. Zoe started violently. Theo had frozen.

"Theo? Zoe? Are you two all right?" Griff called.

CHAPTER TWENTY-SEVEN

Forty-five minutes later, the sound of a car engine outside the sitting-room window caught Zoe's attention, as she glanced up from her iPad. But she refocused on the first page of information about James and his ex-wife. She'd make sure Jessica had the evidence she needed to hand, to present to the trustees on Monday so they could make an informed decision about James.

She intended to miss dinner. After her fourth confrontation of the day, twice with Theo, and once each with Jessica and Natasha, she'd lost all appetite, and was feeling weak and tired. Her wrists still throbbed from the pressure of Theo's grip on them. Right now she didn't trust herself to speak to anybody and was thankful no-one else had come into the room. She feared she'd lose control and burst into floods of tears.

She loved Theo and had meant to stay with him forever.

With fierce concentration she studied the screen. She must get back to that information about James and print it out for Jessica. She'd send it to their private printer, not the one in the office. This evidence in black and white seemed the sole chance right now of beginning to change Jessica's opinion of James and, in turn, that of the other trustees. That would be the first step, Zoe hoped, to break into the toxic chain of events that held them in its grip, together with every aspect of their lives. James and Natasha would be kicked out. And she and Theo would be back on the path of healing again; or so she reasoned to herself.

The door from the entrance hall opened. She looked up. It was Griff.

Zoe bit her lip.

"Hello, Zoe," said Griff.

"Hi," she said, and refocused on her screen.

She was aware that Griff hesitated and guessed he wanted to say something to her. But she ignored him. He walked through the room to the doorway beyond, and left.

If Alice was here, Zoe felt sure she'd know what to do. But nobody had a clue to where Alice might be, or what had happened to her. A tear escaped from the corner of her eye and trickled down her face.

She was so preoccupied she'd failed to notice a new arrival in the room, until a shadow fell over her. She looked up. It was James.

She caught her breath.

"James! What do you want? I didn't hear you come in."

"Yes, amazing how quiet I can be if it suits me." His gaze locked on hers.

She frowned. "You have something to say to me?"

"I do. In fact, I have an invitation for you."

"Another one? Your previous one didn't turn out very promising, did it? The chance to star in this dodgy film which Sonya's making?"

"Oh, that. So you're going to turn it down?"

She paused. "Let's put it like this; perhaps Sonya might be able to come up with something more acceptable to me."

His eyes narrowed. "No guarantee of *that*, I'm afraid. But I do have another suggestion, which will again involve a bit of a journey for you. I know the others are preparing for dinner right now. So I don't expect you'll be missed, at least in the next half-hour; which gives me a window of opportunity."

Inexplicably, a frisson of terror ran down her spine. *Another journey?* But she kept a straight expression, and when she spoke, her voice was steady. Her fingers, though, had turned cold. "You want me to come with you to Chipping Sodbury again?"

He chuckled.

"No. We'll be going in quite another direction. Time's running out for you, Zoe."

Her stomach flipped.

"I have an appointment with Jessica at nine o'clock in Cirencester," he said, "and I may still be able to make it. So here's my invitation, Zoe. I want you to be my guest. At a little place I've picked up, some distance from here."

Zoe's heart missed a beat.

"I don't want to be your guest. Get lost, James."

At this, he whipped the iPad from her hands, pocketed it, and grabbed her upper arm. She cried out in pain.

He held on. "You didn't say the right things about me to Jessica this afternoon, Zoe. I was listening behind the door. And I can guess what you were looking up just now."

She pulled away from him, lost her footing and fell sideways, landing on the floor, with one leg twisted under her. The shock registered in her right knee. She gasped. Before she could make a further noise, a scarf was whipped round her mouth and pulled tight.

"Up you get." He grabbed her by the armpits and lifted her, kicking and struggling. "Come on. I've a special treat for you. You'll be my guest, whether you want to or not."

He tucked her under one arm, carried her back out through the deserted entrance hall, and through the front doorway like a rolled-up carpet. A few strides took him to the waiting Cayenne, with open boot. She prayed fervently that someone would see them. But nobody intervened, and

James flung her into the boot. She landed on a blanket spread out ready for her.

"I do hope you'll be comfortable in there," he said, and closed the lid, plunging her into darkness.

As she beat on the metal with both her fists, the engine sprang into life, and the Cayenne rocketed away.

CHAPTER TWENTY-EIGHT

Zoe lay in the boot of the Cayenne, the darkness pressing in on her. Her heart thundered against her ribs. Her conscious mind had gone into overdrive, like a piece of speeded-up footage. In each shot, she saw a different scenario of what James meant to do to her. She wrestled the foul images her imagination started to lob at her. She managed to control her wrenching gut before throwing up.

James hadn't tied her arms and she tore off the gag. She screamed again and again then gave up, knowing the sound of the engine would have drowned her out. She subsided, sobbing, in the darkness. The Cayenne accelerated. No doubt he was on the A417 now. Her mind continued to race.

Theo would never find out where she was. There was no hope anyone would guess what had happened to Zoe. Jessica and Theo had both brushed Zoe's opinions about James and Natasha aside. Now the worst had happened, and it was too late.

Zoe began to form a plan. As soon as the car slowed down, she'd prepare herself. Every muscle would be primed for her to spring at James the moment he opened the boot. She'd claw his face. She'd knee him in the groin – if her injured knee would allow. The pain throbbed, sending stabs up her right thigh.

She ran through his words once more. He intended to take her to *a little place* he'd *picked up, some distance from here*. That could mean a disused shack, or a lock-up, or even a fortified cellar.

And there was no way of guessing what he meant by 'some distance'. It could be out of Gloucestershire. It might mean ten miles, fifty miles, a hundred miles. He'd said he still planned to make a meeting with Jessica in Cirencester at nine o'clock. It must have been about seven o'clock when he threw Zoe into the boot. That meant he was giving himself two hours to deal with her and get to the meeting.

She was able, at least, to change position; there was nothing else in the boot besides her and the blanket. Her heart chilled. He'd have kept this clear so he could abduct her. Then her mind shot back to what she could do when he opened the boot. If she managed to knee him in the groin and throw him off, she might still only have at most three seconds to escape.

New, bizarre images intervened. Perhaps he meant to rape and strangle her. And then he'd dump her body in a ditch. Or he planned to lock her up behind a series of high-security doors. Zoe sobbed as her imagination flipped through ever more gothic scenarios. Theo might not miss her for hours. And then he'd waste time searching in all the wrong places. He'd have no idea where to begin.

Tears spilled from her eyes and coursed down her face, tracking around her neck, soaking the collar of her jacket and the blouse underneath, and the blanket on which she lay. She willed herself to crush those negative thoughts and concentrated on forming a detailed plan. As soon as the car stopped, the engine turned off, and she heard James walk round to the boot, that would be her cue. She'd brace every muscle, every nerve, ready to spring out as soon as the boot opened. She'd scream so loud, she'd pierce his eardrum. She'd knee him in the crotch. Then she'd run for it, screaming: "Help! Kidnap! Murder!"

The Cayenne made a wide turn and began to bump along what felt like an uneven track or dirt road, and to take sharp twists and follow round big bends. It levelled out, and slowed. This was her chance. The engine stopped.

Every nerve screamed; every sense was on high alert. She scrambled to a squatting position. The driver's door opened and closed, and footsteps approached the boot. Her heart pounded so fast she thought it would break from her chest.

The boot began to open. She sprang – into an enveloping blanket. Strong arms rolled her in it within a second. She opened her mouth to bite or scream. But it was stuffed full of blanket. She tried to kick, squirm, flail out with hands and nails, but her limbs were held fast.

An inferno raged inside her: frustration, panic, terror; all feeding the flames. Now he lifted her up, heaved her over his shoulder, and walked with long strides. A door closed. They were on the move again: Then stillness; silence.

God! Help me! screamed a voice in her head.

James carried her up some stairs. She calculated that he climbed three flights. Then he stopped. A door was unbolted and unlocked. A few further steps, then without warning, she fell and hit the floor. Still wrapped in the blanket, she squirmed and kicked. Meanwhile footsteps receded, a door opened and closed, a bolt slid, a key turned in a lock. James had dumped her, and gone. She clawed her way out of the blanket.

Gasping for breath, she opened her eyes wide. She was in a dark room, where the sole light-source seemed to be burning candles. Then a torch beam was directed into her face. She blinked and covered her eyes.

"Sorry," a voice whispered. She took her hand away and saw the torch was now placed lowdown, so it cast light around, but not straight at her. Struggling into a sitting position, she found herself staring into a female face. The whites of her eyes gleamed.

"Alice!" she gasped.

Alice flung her arms around Zoe and hugged her.

"Alice!" Zoe repeated. "Thank God you're alive."

The two girls clung together for several seconds. When they released each other, Zoe studied her fellow-prisoner once more. Alice's black hair, no longer tied up in the high ponytail, spread wild and bushy around her head. Her eyes still held fire. James might have roughed her up a bit, thought Zoe; but her spirit was unbroken.

"You've been *here* since Tuesday night?"

Alice nodded, still gazing at Zoe, as if unable to believe she'd come to share her prison and to break into her ordeal.

Zoe clasped both hands to her face. "And James...?" she whispered.

Alice took a deep breath. "He must have been watching and listening to us in the hermitage. Somehow he'd got himself out of that hospital by Tuesday. After you left me, I went back to his room to replace the documents. Then I went to the car park. After that, all I remember is reaching into my pocket for my car key. And then, my head hurt, and I was lying on the floor here."

Zoe swallowed, appalled at this stark evidence of James's true nature. "So he knocked you out?" she gasped. Then she glimpsed movement behind Alice. She froze.

"Who's that?" she asked.

A small girl came into view and placed her hand in Alice's.

Zoe's heart jumped. The child looked about five years old. Her fair hair hung in long, untidy strands over her forehead and shoulders. She wore a bright green dress. She looked at Zoe with huge, haunted blue eyes. There was something familiar in her features, but Zoe couldn't work out where it came from or why she recognised the look in her eyes.

"Hello," she whispered. "What's your name?"

"Poppy," said the child.

CHAPTER TWENTY-NINE

Nobody missed Zoe back at the centre until two and a half hours after James had abducted her.

Theo, Griff, Miles and Bernie had been sitting at the farmhouse dining table, discussing Theo and Zoe's plans for the future. Theo did not take her threat to leave him seriously. He believed it was just a temporary rift, and Zoe would in time come round to his point of view. They were all aware Zoe hadn't appeared at dinner, and both Theo and Griff supposed the day's traumatic events had robbed her of hunger. They imagined she'd chosen to go to the library or study, and had explained this to the other two.

After they parted, Miles to return to his home in the nearby village, Theo had walked through to the sitting room. It was unoccupied. He then started touring other ground-floor rooms, unease beginning to stir in his stomach. Next he'd gone up to the first floor and looked in the study, then opened their bedroom door. No sign of Zoe. Theo pulled out his mobile and called her. Her mobile was turned off. Puzzled, he left a voicemail message. Surely, he told himself, she wouldn't have packed her bags and gone to stay with her sister in London without telling him. All her things were still in place.

Baffled and anxious, Theo went back along the passageway and looked into the study again. He found no-one there. Frowning, he went down to the library, and after that he surveyed every room he'd visited before.

"Perhaps she's taken Vito for a walk." He went through to the utility room and found Vito in his basket. As Theo entered the room, Vito got up and licked his hand.

"Where's Zoe, boy?" asked Theo.

Vito gave a woof and waved his tail.

Theo called Zoe again. Her mobile was still turned off. He left a second voicemail message. Then Vito accompanied him to the office, his tail swinging to and fro. Theo looked around. The room was deserted. He took Vito out through the external doorway, crossed the courtyard, and looked in the dining room and kitchen. He opened the studio door and checked inside there; next he went to the barn, and searched all around it and climbed the spiral stairs to the upper room. He found no sign of Zoe, went down again, and out of the barn.

Bernie approached along the path. "Anything the matter, Theo?"

"Have you seen Zoe? I can't find her anywhere."

"Perhaps she went for a walk."

"No. Vito's here. She always takes him if she goes for a walk." Theo took out his mobile and called Zoe yet again. Once more he was put through to voicemail.

"Is her car still in the car park?" asked Bernie, looking at Theo.

Theo's heart lurched. Zoe couldn't possibly have left him without saying goodbye. And there was no evidence she'd packed any bags.

"I'll walk up there and have a look," he said.

Theo ran up the drive, followed by Vito. Reaching the car park, he saw Zoe's car still in place. He returned to the house and waited in the entrance hall, in case she'd been for a solitary walk, and would soon return. Ten minutes later there was no sign of her. Bernie came for news and Theo shook his head.

"I'll walk round the grounds and look for her myself," said Bernie, grabbing the torch from the occasional table and going out into the night.

Theo called Griff.

"Have you any idea where she could be?" he asked.

"No, last I saw of her was in the sitting room, at seven o'clock. I walked in and found her on the sofa with her iPad. She was surfing the Net. I wanted to chat to her but she seemed distant. I gathered my company was unwelcome. So I went out again. You're sure she's not gone to bed? Taken herself off for a drive?"

"I've eliminated both those possibilities, and others. I've called her and her mobile's switched off."

"I'll have a go," said Griff.

Theo waited. "Nope," said Griff. "Voicemail message."

Theo now felt a heavy weight pressing on his chest. He tried to reason with himself. She could have gone on a long walk and for some unknown reason chosen not to take Vito with her. But she always had her mobile with her, and kept it switched on. It seemed a hopeless gesture but he called Zoe yet again and left another voicemail message.

"Zoe. Where are you? Please call me as soon as you pick this up."

Although they'd now fought and argued several times, he loved Zoe, and intended to beg her for forgiveness and to try to make things work between them.

The front door opened and Bernie came in. Theo started towards him then his mood dropped again.

"Has Zoe turned up yet?"

"No."

They looked at each other.

Theo began pacing the entrance hall. Vito accompanied him, tail low, eyes on his master with a doleful expression, aware something was very wrong. He nosed Theo's hand and gave it a lick. Bitter self-recrimination was already seeping through Theo's heart. He convinced himself Zoe had left him.

He called her mobile yet again.

"Zoe. Please call me. Please forgive me for what I said to you. Forget those fights we had. They mean nothing. I love you. Call back as soon as you get this message."

Theo then called Zoe's sister. He gave her an edited version of events and asked if she knew of Zoe's whereabouts. The answer was no. There'd been no contact from Zoe and nothing to suggest she was on her way to London.

Theo folded his arms, cast his eyes downwards, studying the silk rug, and tried to concentrate on alternative scenarios. Zoe could be on her way and not thought to have warned her sister beforehand. He'd wait a couple of hours and repeat the call, to see if Zoe had turned up.

While he was still waiting in the sitting room with Bernie and Griff, they all heard footsteps on the gravel forecourt, and the front door opened and someone came in. Theo leapt up and hurried through into the entrance hall, his heart alight with hope – to see James.

"Just been meeting Jessica at the Fleece," James said. "Went on later than expected. Jessica's on her way back to Birmingham now. You look down. What's the problem?"

Theo shared the situation with him.

James raised his eyebrows.

"How strange," he said. "I wonder what could have happened to her. Let me think. What about her sister? Have you considered…?"

"Yes, I've rung her sister," said Theo. "I've ruled that one out."

James had no further ideas to offer Theo, but did volunteer

to sit with him, Bernie and Griff until the mystery was cleared. Midnight came, and one o'clock in the morning, and still no-one had heard anything from Zoe.

An image of Alice swam into focus before Theo's mind's eye. Alice had been missing for five nights now, including this night, and the police had turned up no leads at all. Both she and Zoe may have been abducted. He felt sick. He shared his fears with the other three and then called the police to report Zoe missing.

Three police officers arrived within an hour. They all gathered in the library – Theo, Bernie, Griff and James – and Constable Davis initially took details from Theo and filled in the form as he did so, while the others listened.

David began by asking who else was on the property. When told all the guests had departed, he wanted to know when the last one left.

"And who was the last to see Zoe?" he enquired.

"Me," said Griff. "I passed through the sitting room at seven o'clock and she was on the sofa with her iPad."

Davis looked over at Theo. "When did you last see her?"

"In an upstairs room at six o'clock," said Theo.

He and Griff shot a quick glance at each other.

"We parted at a quarter past," Theo said. "I was expecting to see her at dinner. But there was no sign of her. I guessed she hadn't felt hungry. But round about ten I started wondering where she was."

"Any reason you can give as to why she might have gone away?"

Again Griff flicked a look at Theo.

"No, none," said Theo, his heart burning.

Griff studied the carpet.

"What do you think?" Theo asked the police officer anxiously.

The three police officers exchanged glances.

"We have to tell you that we consider Zoe's case to be High Risk because of Alice Nazari's recent disappearance from the same location. Alice's case will immediately be upgraded to High Risk as well."

Theo's heart missed a beat.

"Yes – yes, of course," he said, his voice trembling.

Constable Davis sent his two colleagues to start a search of the property and grounds while he continued to question Theo.

"You say you've rung her sister, and given her time to have made a journey to London and arrived there, and she hasn't turned up. Is there anywhere else she might have gone? Has Zoe any other relatives?"

"No other relatives," said Theo. "Both her parents are dead. There are, of course, plenty of friends. I have their details."

"Let's go over everything again," said Davis. "I'm sorry about this, but I want to make sure we miss nothing. I understand you were the last person to talk to Zoe before she disappeared."

"That's right. We parted before dinner at six o'clock, and I knew she was anxious about a number of things."

"Which are…?"

"Changes in staffing, and the disappearance of Alice last Tuesday afternoon."

James remained impassive.

"Understandable," said Davis. "Anything else?" he enquired.

"Well," said Theo, "she and I were soon to leave for new jobs. She was upset about what was to happen to us; and about our future."

"Ah," said Davis.

Theo drew his breath in between his teeth, and went on the defensive. "She understood the difficulties facing us. She accepted those. We were working them out."

He caught Griff's eye again. A deep line had scored itself across the poet's forehead.

"So," said Davis, "we have a young woman; emotional complications; facing big changes; feeling unstable…"

"No, that misrepresents – I don't see what this has to do with…" blurted Theo.

Griff put his hand on Theo's shoulder. "We can't afford to ignore it. It was very much on her mind when I last saw the two of you together."

"So, Griff," said Davis, facing the poet, "you were the last person to see her. You passed through the sitting room at seven and she was on the sofa with her iPad. Did you notice what she was looking at on the screen?"

"No."

Davis looked at James.

"And when was the last time you saw Zoe?"

"Half past four in the afternoon," said James, "at the King's Head in Cirencester."

Theo nodded. "And then we parted company."

"And did you have any idea what Zoe planned to do next?"

"I thought she'd come back to the office here and do some work," said James.

Griff put a reassuring hand on Theo's shoulder.

"Would you say Zoe's state of mind was at all disturbed?" Davis asked Theo.

"No."

"However," said James, "some of her reactions to recent events…"

Theo pressed his lips together.

"Sorry," said James.

Davis studied him. "What were you going to say about her reactions?"

"Zoe got more than a little upset over a few issues, that's all."

Davis kept his eyes on James for a few seconds without saying anything. Then he turned back to Theo.

"You may rest assured we'll do all in our power to find Zoe. Because both her case and Alice's are High Risk, an Incident Room will be set up and we'll call in extra support. Carol, our Missing Persons Co-ordinator, will keep in close touch with you. She'll keep you informed at every stage and will let you know as soon as we hear anything new."

"Thank you," said Theo.

When the three police officers had finally left, James turned to Theo and said, "We'll all support you in every way possible, Theo. Would it help for you to take Monday morning's workshop?"

Bernie and Griff looked doubtful.

But Theo said, "Right now I feel it may help me. So I'll say yes."

"That's settled then," said James. "And now we all need to get some sleep."

# CHAPTER THIRTY

"So… you're Poppy?" Zoe said.

"Yes. Daddy brought me here," said the little girl.

"Daddy?"

She nodded.

Zoe looked at Alice. "Who…?" she began.

"James," said Alice.

"What?" A sensation like an oil slick swept through Zoe. "James?"

"Yes, Zoe," said Alice. "I've pieced things together from what Poppy's told me. She thinks James is her daddy. And Natasha's her mummy. But I'm not sure."

Zoe swallowed several times.

"How can this be?" she said. "I thought Poppy was the little girl you babysat."

"Ah. Sorry. No," replied Alice. "I know you must be confused, Zoe. And I confess I still don't understand all the links here myself. But this little girl, though she shares the same name, is not the child I babysat."

Zoe struggled to assimilate this information. "But", she began again, "if the little girl we have with us now claims her parents are James and Natasha… why would they treat her like this?"

Alice held her palms out. "I don't know. Perhaps she might tell us more. We have to be very gentle."

Zoe started to shake. Alice let go of the child's hand and put her arms round her.

"A few deep breaths, Zoe. We'll talk more about Poppy in a minute; when you're ready."

"Yeah, OK. Thanks, Alice." Zoe managed to take a grip on herself, and stood back from Alice. "So – where are we?"

"My guess", said Alice, "is that this is an apartment in a converted building – a mill, perhaps. There's no electricity. But there is running water in the toilet and in the kitchen. The windows have been boarded up. I guess the place isn't supposed to be ready for occupation yet. It may be the developers ran out of money and mothballed the project."

"But in that case, wouldn't there be a security guard?"

"Not necessarily. They might not be able to pay one. Or maybe James bribed the guard."

Zoe groaned. "But even so, it must mean we won't be here long."

"In theory, yes; but how do we know? At any rate, we do have food. James brought a box of stuff with him, with Poppy."

"When did he do that?"

"A couple of hours after I first woke up here," said Alice, stroking Poppy's hair.

"What did he say to you?"

"Not a lot. Just: 'look after her'. He had some picture books with him. I started asking questions, but he told me to shut up."

"Has he been back at all since then?"

"Yeah. Two days later. He had Natasha with him. She was all over Poppy; but not James."

Zoe glanced at Poppy, and lowered her voice.

"How did Poppy react to Natasha?"

"Stiff, cold; didn't want to know. Natasha said to Poppy, 'hold on darling, one day soon, we'll be together forever'. And then she said, 'Alice won't remember anything of this'. God knows how she could be so sure of that. But one thing I do know. I questioned James. I couldn't believe how easily Jessica had been taken in by him. And he did tell me a bit more about their relationship when they were both younger. I learned that as a teenager Jessica had been desperately trying to escape from an alcoholic, violent father. She used to visit The Fringe in Edinburgh, meet up with actors, go to parties. James was her 'getaway' friend."

"OK, so that does explain a lot," said Zoe.

"'Course, James would never have told me that about Jessica if he thought I could ever do anything with the information," said Alice.

"And were there just the two visits from him?"

"No. There have been three altogether. The last time was yesterday. That was when I managed to have a few more words with Natasha. She said, 'Your friend Zoe's in deep trouble. We'll deal with her too'. I thought they meant to kill you."

Zoe said nothing.

Alice took her hands. "Zoe, this'll sound strange. I'm not pleased you've been abducted. But I'm so glad you're here with me."

"I understand." Zoe squeezed her hands then Alice released them. "Oh Alice, you were meant to meet that casting director yesterday morning! I'm so angry you missed out."

Alice chuckled.

"It's not funny, but right now, that's the least of my problems," she said.

"Suppose so. The important thing is to stay alive and get out of here. But Alice, can we find a way to escape?"

Alice shone her torch beam upwards. "See up there?"

Zoe came to join her. "Yes," she exclaimed, "a window that hasn't been boarded up; but very high and very small."

She went across to the wall, stretched herself against it, holding her arms high above her head and standing on tiptoe.

"How on earth would we reach it?" She fell back again, with a groan. "We couldn't squeeze out of it, either. It's tiny. But there is a skylight."

"Yes," said Alice. "In theory, that could be our escape route. But how? No furniture to climb on."

They looked at each other in the torchlight. Zoe clenched her fists to stop herself crying.

"What have you and Poppy been doing with yourselves all this while?"

"Playing games, reading stories."

"But what does James want with you both? And me?"

"God knows." Alice spread her hands.

Zoe's stomach muscles went into spasm. She shuddered and swallowed several times.

Then she glanced at Poppy again. The child was so calm. It seemed unnatural to Zoe. Zoe shook her head. "You two have kept each other sane," she remarked.

Alice looked at Poppy with a rueful smile. "Yes. I reckon we have," she said.

Zoe could well understand how a distant observer might take Poppy for a ghost child. She seemed aloof. Perhaps that was understandable, with what she had been through.

"The police are searching for you, Alice. Your mother's distraught. As to little Poppy – if she *is* James and Natasha's own child, who'd search for her?"

Alice spread her hands, palms uppermost. "Your guess is as good as mine. But at least Theo should have the police searching for you before the night's out, Zoe."

"Not necessarily," said Zoe. They both gazed at each other, Alice's expression more than a little puzzled.

"Shine your torch onto my watch, Alice."

Alice did so.

"Eight thirty. James kidnapped me an hour and a half ago. We can't be very far from the centre here."

Then she looked at Poppy again. The child remained still and seemed to be almost in a trancelike state.

Alice stirred.

"Not a shack," she said. "Not a soundproof cellar behind several sets of security doors. Not a torture chamber in a military detention centre. None of those things. The one thing it has in common with them is no possible means of communication with the outside world – except when James and Natasha return. We've both seen enough of that pair to know they're highly cunning. And there's no way we can find out what they're up to or why they've done this to us, until they come back."

CHAPTER THIRTY-ONE

"I'd hate to think you and I had misunderstood each other, Theo," said James the following morning at breakfast. "Just because the trustees have asked you to step down from the manager's role, there's no reason why you shouldn't continue to lead workshops this next week, when we'll need all the help we can get. I assure you I don't accept the idea that because you're ill, the Celtic Knot cannot use you."

"I'm not ill," said Theo.

James gave a low chuckle. "Oh no, not now; perhaps a better word would be *vulnerable.*"

"Does that surprise you?" retorted Theo. "My wife's missing. All I care about right now is getting her back again."

"Of course," murmured James in a soothing tone of voice. "We're all concerned about her, Theo. But at the same time we also need to think about the new guests who're due to arrive here this afternoon."

"And that's another problem," said Theo. "If Zoe doesn't return then I believe we should cancel this week's course."

James shook his head. "Out of the question," he said. "We must carry on as normal. It's no good putting the centre at risk, for the sake of…"

He stopped.

"Yes, James, for the sake of what?" enquired Theo.

"Nothing. Hate to sound callous. Naturally, you feel anxious."

Theo felt like hitting him. However, he kept a grip on himself.

"*Anxious* is an understatement," said Theo.

James nodded.

"I know this is a stressful time for you, Theo, but be sure the police will do all they can. They're sophisticated these days."

"Maybe, but not so sophisticated they've been able to turn up anything on Alice, after five days and nights of no news."

"True. Nevertheless, I feel sure they'll find out what's happened to Zoe. But we must get on. There's so much to do to prepare for the guests. I'll go over to the barn and set up for this evening's welcome. I have Natasha's action list. You'd be amazed how thorough she is. She thinks of everything. And so she should, since she'll be leading tonight."

Alice sat with her head in her hands.

Then she looked up. "I'd love to know what James is doing right now." She lowered her voice to a whisper. "Some men keep their sex slaves like this."

"Don't, Alice." Zoe recoiled. "I'd kill him. I promise you. I would."

"How?" asked Alice. "There's nothing here to hurt him, or at least threaten him with. What would you use? Blunt knives and forks? Plates or a can opener? There are plenty of candles and matches, though, and this torch."

"Well," said Zoe, "the torch could be a start, or a lighted candle." She paced up and down the room for a minute, then spun, and said, "No sharp knives?"

Alice shook her head.

"Or rope?"

"You kidding?"

Zoe relapsed into silence. She continued walking to and fro then went over to Poppy to see how she was doing.

The child was nestled into a pile of blankets in the corner, looking through a picture book by the light of the torch. Zoe crouched down beside her and glanced through some of the books. She looked at Poppy but got no response. The child kept her eyes fixed on the book.

Zoe stood up again and crossed the room to where Alice stood, arms folded, leaning against the wall.

"Another thing," said Alice in a low voice. "I think James has got this place bugged."

"What?"

"Yeah, I reckon it's like the Big Brother House. He's got CCTV cameras in here. He's listening in on us and watching us right now, back at the Celtic Knot."

"Oh, come on Alice."

"No, I'm serious."

Zoe felt a jolt in her stomach at these words.

"How would you know? Haven't seen any cameras, have you?"

Zoe grabbed the torch and shone it all around the walls, up to the ceiling, and along the coving, then down again to the floor.

"No," Alice admitted. "But I wouldn't put anything past James."

Zoe shuddered and hugged her arms round herself.

"I can imagine him, back at the centre, right now," went on Alice. "He's talking to Theo; making out he hasn't the slightest idea what's happened to us."

"But how much longer can we live like this?" cried Zoe tearfully. "No exercise, no fresh air. And if not for that tiny window, the skylight, and the candles, we'd be in total darkness. And it's cold. This room, I suppose, is meant to be a sitting room – or would be, if it was furnished. We have three rooms: this one, plus the kitchen; then the toilet and shower. And

201

nothing in the room for us to sit or lie on but a few blankets. That door must lead to other rooms, but it's locked."

"And no mobiles," said Alice. "We're really cut off. And James could be watching our every move; and listening to us. I'm tired now. Maybe it is only five o'clock. But I'm going to lie down." She stretched out on a blanket in a corner, and they both fell silent.

Icy fingers clawed at Zoe's solar plexus. She'd been here one night now, with Alice and Poppy, and today was Sunday. Poppy had put her book aside and had nestled into her pile of blankets, her eyes closed. This was unreal and weird. Despite Alice and Poppy's companionship, Zoe felt so alone. But Alice seemed to have come to terms with the bizarre situation, to a certain extent, during the time she'd been here.

Zoe hoped fervently that the police would track them down. And that James and Natasha would be unmasked and caught. Then she remembered her conversation with Alice about ropes and knives. Yes, it would be good to have a weapon by her, in case James returned. She imagined herself bashing James over the head with the torch. Though not big, it still might be used on him to good effect.

So she made her way into the kitchen, directing the torch beam ahead of her and around the shelves and into the cupboards, looking for something suitable to defend them all with. All she could come up with was, as Alice had suggested, a can opener. She took it back with her to the corner she'd chosen, and placed it under the pile of blankets.

She wondered whether James had the capacity to speak to them through an intercom. She feared that his voice might boom out without warning, giving instructions, or threatening them with physical or sexual abuse when he arrived.

She curled up on her own pile of blankets and tried to rest; but was instead tortured by regretful thoughts. She doubted that Theo would ever forgive her, even if she survived this. And she longed to know what he was doing now. Tears poured from her eyes; she hardly dared believe she would ever see him again.

Sunday afternoon passed for Theo and the centre staff with no further news of Alice or Zoe. The new guests arrived, and every effort was made to welcome them. At James's insistence, no mention was made of the crisis the centre was going through. Natasha led the welcome session in the barn, and many of the guests had already fallen under her spell by the time it finished. The evening passed, and the night.

Monday morning brought no further news about Alice or Zoe, though Carol, the Missing Persons Co-ordinator, rang Theo and visited him in the office later to introduce herself and offer every possible support. But the assurance that the police were taking the disappearance of the two girls seriously only served to stir up Theo's worst fears.

"This is such a nightmare," he said as he slumped at Zoe's desk in the office, ten minutes after Carol had gone. James squeezed his shoulder. Vito lay at Theo's feet, whimpering, pawing his leg, looking up at him with doleful eyes. "It feels wrong, and unnatural, not to tell the guests what's going on."

"I disagree," said James. "There's no point disturbing them. Zoe may even turn up again later today, for all we know."

At this Theo buried his head in his hands. "If Zoe has gone off, of her own free will, how could she torture me like this?" he asked. "I only need one word – just to know where Zoe is, and that she's all right."

"Yes, yes," said James. "Everything will work out for the best, I'm sure it will."

"I don't know," said Theo. "I'm afraid of what she could be suffering right now; whether I'll ever see her again. Whether she's been murdered and raped; whether her body will ever be found; whether I'll ever get the body back so I can hold a funeral. I've tried to pray but I can't. This is beyond prayer."

"Come, come," said James. "Stop this negative talk, Theo."

Bernie and Griff were both supporting Theo as well as they could, and he felt confident of their genuine sympathy and concern. James's attitude, though, struck a false note.

"I felt terrible when I rang Zoe's sister yesterday", said Theo, "and told her there's nothing she can do..."

"Don't you worry about her," said James. "She'll cope."

"How do you know?"

James cleared his throat. "Good point. I don't. Forget I said it."

Theo threw him a sharp glance.

"We all want Zoe to be safe," said James. "Have faith. Now, do you feel strong enough to take the workshop this morning?"

"Yes, I do," said Theo, and left the office.

Theo's workshop took place in the barn half an hour later. Griff sat alongside him, in case he needed moral support. Theo had no idea where Natasha was. He caught Griff's attention and locked eyes with him. Griff smiled at him then Theo swept his glance over the other guests, and said, "My workshop is about different ways to see the journeys of our lives. We're going to use a wide variety of art materials. There are plenty of items you may choose from to make a collage if you wish. It's up to you. To give you some ideas, you'll find at each of the four corners of this meeting space, an arrangement of objects. In a moment, I'll invite you to visit each one."

When the time came, they dispersed to visit the four stations. The guests went to the south corner where rough reddish-brown sand had been scattered over the floor, glass beads arranged among it, to resemble footsteps in the desert.

"You can raise the curtain on your life journey and get straight on with it," Theo said.

Then he led them to the west where they found a white lantern placed on a silver dish, glass beads scattered in a trail leading out from the candle.

"Where's the light in our journey?" asked Theo. "Who have we met along the path; who's helped us see? Have we had moments of clarity and vision? When? And what was going on for us at the time?"

They all went to the east and found rich Indian fabrics, silk in jewel-like colours which had been spread out on the floor. Strong spice candles burned. A tree was planted in a terracotta pot to represent a family tree. A water melon had been hacked in two, seeming to symbolise cruelty and violence.

"Sometimes," said Theo, "we may want to find a way to express the worst moments of our lives."

Then the guests went to the north. An earthy, organic smell issued from this corner; it came from a pile of straw impregnated with animal odours. There was also an Income Tax Return form.

"This corner represents that which is crude, filthy, painful," said Theo. "This corner speaks of heartbreak."

Then he broke down. He bent over, as sobs possessed him. Some of the guests hung back in consternation and dismay; others drew close, laying hands on him, and offering words of comfort. Meanwhile, Griff found himself with no alternative but to explain to them what had happened to Zoe, and why Theo was so upset.

"Oh, Theo, that's terrible."

"You poor thing; if only we'd known before…"

"I'm sure Zoe will soon be found safe, Theo."

Theo crouched on the floor, his shoulders heaving.

His own self-doubt elbowed the abduction scenario aside.

He was convinced Zoe had intentionally left him. They'd fought a number of times. Theo fully expected that she'd lost all trust in him. He blamed himself for being too harsh and judgmental with her. He felt wretched for having moralised at her, and lectured her when she was trying to help, doing the best she could. And now he'd lost her.

Then he became aware of Natasha kneeling beside him. She must have entered the barn in the last few minutes, without his knowledge. She placed one hand on Theo's head, and the other on his heart. He shuddered.

"No, Natasha," he said. "Leave me alone. I didn't ask for your help."

Natasha dropped her hands at once and stood up. Theo, too, quickly rose to his feet. He noticed that the guests had all now fanned out, and were gazing at Natasha with awed expressions.

"Don't touch me, please, Natasha," he said.

"Why not, Theo?" she asked. "I can heal your pain."

"I'd prefer that you didn't," he replied.

Her eyes burned.

"Very well, Theo," she said; and an icy sensation swept through Theo's entire body.

CHAPTER THIRTY-TWO

The next morning, Tuesday, brought with it a fine miasma of rain, which gathered strength throughout the middle of the day, fading out later in the afternoon, then hanging, uncertain, in the air. It was followed by an uncanny stillness.

Alice had now been missing for seven nights and Zoe for three. James had employed two new temporary staff from an agency in Cheltenham, one to act as administrator and the other as a secretary and domestic assistant. Three guests had already left because they felt uncomfortable about staying at the centre whilst Theo was in the midst of a personal tragedy. They'd resisted James's attempts to make them change their minds.

James had rationalised this to Jessica.

"With all this uncertainty, it's inevitable some will want to move on."

He promised that his planned publicity drive would bring in new guests, who'd be coming into a reorganised centre. Meanwhile, the police had still failed to turn up any leads at all in the search for Alice and Zoe.

While all this was going on, Natasha strengthened her hold on the remaining guests. She was now officially known as the 'creative director', and continued to gather guests around her, listening to them, counselling them, and laying healing hands upon them. But when questioned, she had no insights to offer as to where Zoe and Alice might be.

That afternoon, James told Theo he and Natasha were meeting Jessica in Cirencester. Theo called the remaining guests into the sitting room in the farmhouse. He played a DVD of Celtic music for flute and harp, and candles were lit for Zoe and for Alice, and everyone meditated. Theo explained that those who wished to could pray.

"Prayers? Whoever's taken the girls should be castrated," said one guest.

"Locked up for life," added another.

"Bring back hanging," added a third.

Theo couldn't speak.

Bernie cleared his throat and stood up. "I know we all have different angles on this. I intend to pray for whoever might be behind Alice and Zoe's disappearance, whether that's one, or more than one person. We could pray for a change of heart over what they've done; that they might let Zoe and Alice go. And turn themselves in to the police."

Amidst a mixed response, some murmurs of sympathy and not a few expressions of scepticism, they all fell into silent meditation.

Theo knew that Alice herself would have suggested communing with the spirits in the walls. This convinced him to pray more to the God he knew. But he still found it difficult to shake off his doubts. God might not answer in the way Theo wanted. Zoe could still turn up dead. Or –worse – Zoe may never be found again.

And so he wrestled with himself and with angels or demons, he could no longer tell one from the other. The afternoon passed with no news from Carol.

Back in the apartment where James had imprisoned the three girls, Zoe felt ready to ask Alice about the phantom child.

"Was she a ghost? Or was she Poppy?"

"I've been thinking about that a lot," said Alice. "Two of my sightings – and your one experience – I believe were genuine ghosts."

The two girls stood in the kitchen together. Poppy, to their knowledge, was curled up on a blanket in the apartment's sitting room, asleep. Even when awake, she said nothing. She'd maintained her silence since Zoe first saw her.

"You mean the ones you saw on the train and in the road?" persisted Zoe.

"Yes," said Alice. She leaned against the sink with her arms folded.

"But it was Poppy you saw outside Graze in Cirencester. The little girl we have here with us?"

Alice nodded.

Zoe squeezed Alice's shoulder. "James certainly hated you seeing her. And he tried to pretend she, too, was a ghost."

"Course he did," said Alice. "But I believe they were keeping her hidden in the goose house with Natasha. They must have been doing it for several days. It seems unbelievable and I cannot understand what they were up to, or why they've done this."

"Does Poppy herself know why?"

"I've asked her," murmured Alice, "but the poor little thing can't explain."

Zoe walked across the kitchen to the open door. "Come on. Let's see how she's getting on."

They both went through into the other room where they squatted down beside the sleeping child.

"I can't imagine how all this is affecting her," said Zoe. "She says so little."

"Yes," Alice murmured. She stroked the child's head as she slept. "I hope we – you and me – will make a big difference for her. I mean, loving her and caring for her."

Zoe felt tears spilling from her eyes again. She raised her hand and wiped them away. "I can't get my head round this," she said. "What of the little girl you looked after on those two evenings, also called Poppy?"

Alice sat back on her heels. "When I thought about the ghost child a few days after I encountered her", she said, "two facts jumped out at me – the child was four or five years old, just the same as little Poppy, who, it seemed, attracted the spooky visitor with the heavy footsteps. And this child, too, I realised, was no ordinary physical child. And that terrified me. All three of them were connected by a strange, paranormal element. Everything stems from that."

Zoe's heart fluttered. Despite its bizarre nature, on another level, in another dimension, it was beginning to make sense to her.

She heaved a deep sigh and smoothed back hair from Poppy's face.

"So," she said, looking up again, "James was scared witless by your ghost sightings. We've worked that one out."

"And he knew we'd got wind of his scam with Sonya – whatever that is."

"Oh my God," said Zoe, getting up. "Sonya. I met her on Saturday. James introduced us. We had lunch together in Chipping Sodbury."

"What?" said Alice.

She stood up. "Let's go over to the other side of the room, away from Poppy; in case she wakes and listens to us."

Zoe followed Alice, as she suggested. Then they continued talking in low voices.

"James took me to meet Sonya over lunch," said Zoe. "He told me she was a film producer, and could give me an acting role."

Alice blew air out through her parted lips.

"So what happened when you met her?"

"Not much," said Zoe with a frown. "She showed me the script, which was foul. I didn't like it at all. She told me the name of the production company, which I'd never heard of. And she gave me some odd-tasting drinks. And she and James did a lot of whispering in the background which I couldn't understand."

Alice drew a deep breath. "I think you've been taken in, Zoe. What did Sonya look like?"

Zoe described Sonya in detail: her hairstyle and appearance, and the way she was dressed and her similarity to Natasha together with the ways in which Zoe felt her to be very different.

"Yeah, I've got a good picture of her. And did she seem genuine?"

Zoe considered this. "At the time," she began, "she seemed plausible. And then…" She stopped. "When I arrived, Sonya had a drink ready for me; a toxic-looking cocktail."

"And you drank it?"

"Yes."

"Hmm. Don't know what it was all about, Zoe, but I think James was trying to draw you into some trap with Sonya."

Zoe sunk her head into her hands.

Then she sensed she was being watched. She raised her head, looked at Alice, and then turned in Poppy's direction, expecting to find her asleep. Instead, Poppy was sitting up, awake. She gazed at them, her eyes calm. How long she had been listening to their conversation, Zoe couldn't tell. She stared at the child, trying to work out whether anything in her eyes reminded her of James, her supposed father. Horror of horrors. What a burden to bear. Poor little child. A father like James…

"Poppy," she whispered. "Tell us about your daddy and mummy."

Poppy nodded. "Daddy's sick," she said.

"Sick?" Zoe repeated.

Poppy nodded, but would say no more.

Zoe turned to Alice, who was standing with her back against the wall with the window, facing Zoe and Poppy.

Zoe gazed at her, and at the wall. Then her eyes travelled up the wall, as it had done several times since she'd been here, to the window and beyond it to the skylight, then back down to Alice again.

Zoe stiffened. Every muscle tensed.

Alice scrutinised her. "What?"

"Listen, Alice. I can't believe I've been here three nights and not thought of this before. You're good at gymnastics, aren't you?"

"Gymnastics? I came top in my club when I was fourteen. And later, of course, I did a lot of physical work at drama school."

"Great! I think we *can* escape."

"How?"

"Look, I reckon if you stand on my shoulders, you could get to that window."

"Right. Yes," said Alice in a sceptical tone, as she looked up at the window.

"Then, once you've got a grip on the window ledge, couldn't you open the window? Then get onto the sill, balance yourself, and swing up to the skylight? And open it, and get out?"

Alice drew her breath in between her teeth.

"Yes."

They looked at each other.

"Then, walk across the roof and see if there's a tree near enough to jump onto," said Zoe.

"And then what?" said Alice. "What about you and Poppy?"

"Well, if you reckon we could jump onto a tree, you need to get us up too. I suggest you take a blanket with you, over your shoulder. You'd find something to tie it onto. Then lower the rest down for me to grab. If necessary I'll knot another one onto it. I could make a harness for Poppy then you lift her up. Untie her then let it down again for me."

Alice stared at Zoe, rubbing her chin.

"OK," she said.

Zoe turned to Poppy. "Are you up for this, Poppy?"

"Yes," said the child.

"Right," said Alice, "let's do it. Before James returns. But wait; it'll be cold outside."

"True. You've got a warm jacket. I have what I'm wearing. What does Poppy have with her? Anything extra she can put on? If the worst comes to the worst, we could be out there for hours."

"I'll sort that. Then let's go. James could be back any minute."

CHAPTER THIRTY-THREE

Sonya climbed out of a taxi at the entrance to the Church Street car park in Tetbury on Tuesday at three o'clock, and paid off the taxi driver. She was wearing a caramel-coloured Burberry raincoat and carrying a matching suitcase. A damp mist hung about the trees.

As soon as the taxi was out of sight, Sonya walked towards the waiting Cayenne.

The driver's door opened and James got out.

He buttoned his sheepskin jacket up and twisted his scarf round his neck twice.

"What miserable weather," he said. "But there's no alternative. We can't waste any more time."

"Not after all the trouble I've been to," said Sonya. "I've got the keys. And the details we need for the satnav when the time comes."

"Good," said James.

"And it's ideal weather for us, in fact," said Sonya. "Fewer people will be out."

"True," replied James, opening the boot and depositing the suitcase there, as Sonya slid into the back seat.

"Hello, Natasha," she said.

Natasha twisted round in the front passenger seat to acknowledge her sister, as James slipped behind the steering wheel once more.

Sonya showed her a bunch of keys.

"Well done," said Natasha, "and the directions?"

"All taken care of," replied Sonya.

"Fine. We can't afford to delay any longer," Natasha said. "Theo's resisting me more and more. We've got to be quick."

"Maybe. But he doesn't suspect us at all," said James. "We've been very clever. And you've been perfect, Natasha."

He reached across and stroked Natasha's face. Dressed, as usual, in white, she looked more insubstantial than ever. She wore a fur coat over her gown.

"God, you look so beautiful," he said. He leaned in, took her face between his hands, and kissed her on the lips.

Sonya heaved a deep sigh.

"Let's go," she said, "we've got a job to do."

"Sonya's right, of course," said Natasha. "We do." James ignored this and began to nibble Natasha's ear. She wriggled and laughed.

"This will all work out, I promise you," he murmured to her. "No-one will take Poppy from us."

"Of course not," whispered Natasha. "We'll keep her safe – many others will follow."

"They will. I'll make sure," said James. "You shall have all the children you need."

"Please, let's go now," said Sonya from the back. "We've no time to waste."

"Of course, Sonya," said James, turning the key in the ignition.

He fired up the engine and the Cayenne glided away.

An hour later, James brought the Cayenne to a halt on the driveway leading to the mill. Although visibility was lower now, they could discern the branches of the trees and the detail of the building ahead of them. Suddenly, Sonya electrified them with a scream.

"What is it?" yelped James.

"My God, I saw movement up on the roof."

"It's the girls," cried Natasha. "How did they get up *there*? Hurry, we must catch them."

They all leapt from the car.

Alice, clutching one end of the blanket, her teeth set together, her face screwed up with the effort she was putting into it, hauled Zoe out onto the pitch of the roof.

Poppy clung to Alice, her arms wrapped around Alice's neck.

Alice's breath was coming in raw gasps now, as Zoe leaned into the roof pitch, holding on to the parapet, straining to get her balance and feeling the cold air whipping around her face. She'd stuffed the torch into her jacket pocket.

"Well done, Zoe," panted Alice, letting go of the blanket and hugging her friend.

"What now?" gasped Zoe, shivering. She pulled the torch from her pocket and was about to switch it on, then thought better of it. Torchlight would attract attention to them, should James arrive unexpectedly. She returned the torch to her pocket.

"See that tree over there?" said Alice. "It's quite close. I can jump onto it."

She turned, and Zoe took Poppy from her. Alice pulled herself up onto the roof ridge, then leaned down, caught hold of Poppy once more, and pulled her up too. Zoe followed.

"Will you two be able to jump onto the tree as well?" asked Alice.

Zoe looked down at the frightened child she held in her arms. The whole plan started to appear in a different light. Then she threw a desperate glance at Alice. The whites of Alice's eyes shone brighter than ever against her dark skin.

Zoe pushed hair back from her face. "I don't know, Alice."

Then they heard the sound of a car engine. Zoe's stomach twisted. Poppy was trembling.

"Someone's coming," Zoe gasped. "Could be James."

She stood up drawing Poppy with her, holding the child's hand in hers, trying to get her balance on the ridge. The sharp chill cut into them and Poppy's face already looked pinched, despite the extra clothes they'd put on her.

"It *is* him," Zoe cried. "The Cayenne; it's pulling up."

"We've got to jump," Alice shouted. "It's our only hope."

Zoe's heart thudded against her chest. Now James had returned, there was a high chance they'd be caught. The edge of the branch was about half a metre from the eaves. Alice would be risking her life, or at least serious injury, by jumping.

"Are you really sure, Alice?"

"Never been surer. Wish me luck, Zoe."

"Go on, Alice," gasped Zoe. "You do it, and get help as soon as you can. I'll stay with Poppy."

Alice squatted, preparing to slide down the roof pitch to the eaves. As she did so, they both heard shouts and yells from ground level. Zoe stared desperately down to the scene below.

"He's got Natasha and Sonya with him. Natasha's going into...I think it's a garage block," she cried. "James and Sonya are heading round to this side of the building. Goodbye Alice. Good luck!"

Alice scrambled down the roof pitch, and jumped. She landed on the branch with a great snapping and cracking of twigs, and was snatched from view. Zoe had no idea whether Alice had gained a purchase on the branch, or fallen. But of one thing she was sure. It was out of the question for her to risk Poppy's life in a fall from the roof, or the tree. Then she clapped her hand to her head. She hadn't thought to give the torch to Alice. Light was fading fast, and Alice would need to find help within the next hour, or she'd be stumbling through fields and woods in the dark.

Zoe sat down on the ridge. For about ten minutes, she remained where she was, holding Poppy close. The low temperature was the least of her problems. Fear and indecision paralysed her.

Then a figure began to emerge through the open skylight: Long blonde hair, white fur jacket, white dress.

"God help me. Natasha," breathed Zoe.

Poppy pressed in at Zoe's side as Zoe rose to her feet; and they stood together on the ridge, staring at the healer. Natasha had hitched up her gown to enable her to climb the parapet and Zoe noted her feet were bare. It seemed incongruous in such a tense situation but she wondered how Natasha had managed to climb a ladder and haul herself onto a roof in that outfit. She and Alice had both benefited from the fact that they wore trousers and sturdy, flat-heeled shoes. The climb had already crumpled Natasha's gown, and stained silk and fur with brick dust.

Zoe and Poppy shivered as Natasha, having reached the top of the parapet, climbed onto the ridge to join them.

"Hello," said Natasha in her sweetest voice. "I came up via the old-fashioned method – on a ladder. This *was* silly of you, Zoe, risking Poppy's life. I suggest you both come down with me at once."

Poppy clung to Zoe. Zoe was so cold and frightened she couldn't move.

Natasha's eyes seemed to penetrate hers. Zoe shuddered.

"Cold up here, isn't it?" said Natasha. "Now, Zoe, give the child to me." She edged her way towards them, reaching out for the little girl who shrank away from her. "Come along, sweetheart. You can't stay up here all night and freeze. Come back down inside with me, into the warm again."

She trained her limpid eyes upon Zoe. Zoe felt her head swimming. Natasha took advantage of Zoe's distraction to reach out and grab hold of Poppy. She clutched the child in her arms.

"Alice, I expect, is dead at the bottom of the tree now. Dead or alive, she won't escape."

Holding onto the child, she clambered back down the parapet towards the eaves, then across to the skylight where she slipped back inside and onto the top rung of the ladder.

CHAPTER THIRTY-FOUR

Zoe scrambled back down the ladder after Natasha and Poppy. She fervently hoped that Alice had reached ground level with no bones broken, avoided recapture, and found her way to a road or lane to flag down a passing motorist. Meanwhile, her own priority was to protect the child at all costs.

Back in the apartment, Natasha started moving around, lighting new candles and setting them on the floor in each corner. Poppy went and sat on the pile of blankets again, where she withdrew into herself, knees drawn up to her chest, head bowed. Zoe longed to go and cuddle her. Instead, she stood in the space between Natasha and the little girl. She didn't expect to see James and Sonya for a while yet. They'd be too busy chasing Alice.

"Here we all are," said Natasha. "I'm glad you've seen sense, Zoe. I cannot achieve true spiritual union unless my helpers are wholeheartedly compliant."

"True spiritual union? Your helpers?"

"I'll explain before long," promised Natasha.

"Why are you doing this to Poppy?" asked Zoe.

"She's mine. I can do what I like," said Natasha. "I've got great plans for her – and for the others."

"The others?" repeated Zoe, puzzled.

"Yes," said Natasha. "I've yet to collect them. But they'll be companions for Poppy. She won't be alone."

Zoe stared at her. Her heart pounded.

"*Collect them*? How do you intend to *collect* children?"

Natasha trod lightly past Zoe and over to Poppy's corner. Zoe whirled. Natasha crouched down beside the little girl, but Poppy refused to look at her.

"You, my darling," Natasha said, stroking the child's cheek, "will soon be part of something more beautiful than you could ever have imagined." She stood up and turned to face Zoe again. "I need one hundred per cent devotion," she said. "And I have it, from my disciples. Not from you yet, Zoe, but it will come."

"Who *are* these disciples? Is James one of them?"

"Ah, so many questions. Let's answer the second first. Of course James is one of them. You'll meet a few more soon. My faithful disciples got Poppy for me. And since this has worked well so far, I hope soon to get others, too. They'll all be mine and will be kept hidden from the world."

Zoe swallowed. She knew that regardless of what she felt, she must stay calm, or it would be impossible to question Natasha and satisfy her curiosity.

"Where will you keep the children?" she asked.

"Where do you think?" said Natasha. She began to stroll back and forth across the room. "In the farmhouse."

"The Celtic Knot?"

"Yes. The house James's ancestor built," she said. "We'll buy it from the Trust."

Zoe drew a ragged breath. She remembered the funds Sonya had transferred to James's bank account.

"The Trust will never sell," she said, breaking into forced laughter, which soon faded away.

Natasha smiled. "Everyone has their price. Very soon, Zoe, I promise this will all make sense. You'll want to follow me then, as James and Sonya already do."

"Natasha, how can I? I don't know what your teachings are."

"I'll help you understand. First, you have to be in touch with the True Reality, not the veil of illusion which most people hide behind."

"And you're in touch with the True Reality?" asked Zoe. "How *do* you heal people?"

Natasha stopped walking and swung to face Zoe. She took several steps closer to her. Zoe tensed.

"The key to my healing", said Natasha, "is the elimination of memories."

Zoe moistened her lips. "*The elimination of memories?*" she repeated in a faint voice.

"Yes. Let me explain. Imagine you've asked me to heal you. I'll eliminate your memory of the pain, of the injury or the illness, whatever it is. And so it will vanish."

"Natasha, sorry, but I find that unbelievable." Zoe folded her arms across her chest and fixed her eyes on Natasha's face. The pulse of her right wrist throbbed against her left arm, beating faster and faster. Dropping her hands once again to her side, she went over to Poppy and encouraged her to stand up and keep close to her. Then she turned back to face Natasha, who'd remained where she was.

"Another question. What really happened in the King's Head on Saturday?"

Natasha shook with laughter. "As Jessica told you, a bird got in."

Zoe froze. James, of course, would have passed onto Natasha the details of Zoe's conversation with Jessica, which she knew he'd eavesdropped on.

"Yes, it can be frightening," said Natasha. "A wild bird trapped inside a room. But rest assured it soon flew to freedom."

Zoe took Poppy's hand and squeezed it.

"I know what you're thinking, Zoe," went on Natasha.

"I can see you don't trust me. But you will. I'm confident of that."

Then it seemed to Zoe that Natasha had thrown out an invisible rope which was now whirling around her. All the negative or self-doubting thoughts she'd had in the three years of her marriage to Theo rushed into her mind at once, tumbling over each other. *You're not good enough. You're too young. You don't have the right experience. You have doubts. You haven't got Theo's faith. How can he possibly respect you?*

Natasha's voice broke through. "So many high expectations, Zoe. Will Theo forgive you if you fall short?"

Zoe started to shake.

"Your instincts were right, Zoe, when you showed yourself ready to turn your back on your life with Theo. You wanted to be a film star, didn't you? Well, that might not work out. But I have another future for you, one you could never have imagined, but one far, far better."

As Natasha said this, she raised both hands in the air, and Zoe felt as if she'd been kicked in the stomach. She recoiled, letting go of Poppy's hand, and stumbled backwards. Her heart raced and her breath came in jagged gasps. Natasha could mean only one thing: she planned to kill her.

Then small fingers grasped hers. She looked down. Poppy was holding onto her hand again, tight. All Zoe's will to survive surged back, together with her huge responsibility for this child's life.

"No, Natasha!" she shouted.

Natasha withdrew a few paces. But Zoe knew she was preparing another spiritual assault.

"You don't seem to realise, do you?" said Zoe, swallowing hard, and trying to control her shaking hands and arms. "The police will find you here. And then you'll be arrested."

Natasha smiled. "Not so. You see, Zoe – how can I make you understand this? – I'm a shapeshifter."

Zoe's stomach clenched. Natasha was deranged. "What do you mean by that?" she asked.

"You don't know about shapeshifting?" said Natasha. "Let me explain. Shapeshifting is one of the skills of a shaman. It's part of the Celtic shamanic experience. Shamans are found in all parts of the world. One may be a sage, or a master, or a healer. Another may be a seer of the future, or a prophet, or a spiritual teacher. Yet another may be a shapeshifter. Shapeshifting is the ability to alter one's physical appearance; it's the transfer of inner personalities to the outside."

Zoe's mouth had gone dry. Her heart thudded painfully against her ribcage. And then, suddenly and even incongruously, she remembered Alice's words about the Weird Sisters, who used their power of mind corruption on Macbeth and his Lady. So Natasha was a shapeshifter, was she? Did that mean another of her forms was that of a *raven*?

Natasha went on. "When you first noticed my appearance shift, Zoe, you saw one of my inner personalities as if transferred to the outside."

"Your appearance?" Zoe shuddered, remembering the scene in the King's Head.

"Yes," said Natasha. "The Welsh bard, Taliesin, said to be the father of Celtic shamanism, often alluded to shapeshifting when he claimed: *I have been in many shapes… there is nothing in which I have not been.*"

As long as Poppy's hand remained in hers, Zoe felt she had the strength to fight Natasha's claims.

"Was Jesus a shaman, do you think?" she enquired.

"Of course," said Natasha. "The greatest of all: a divine Master."

Zoe moistened her lips. "I don't think Theo would agree with that."

"Who cares what Theo might think? He wouldn't dare oppose me," said Natasha.

"Yes he would!" burst out Zoe. "He has a far greater power than you on his side."

Natasha stared at her, a look of faint amusement growing in her eyes.

"If it makes you happy to believe that, do. But remember, you have a choice: two outcomes; negative and positive. You choose."

Zoe's heart thundered. She hoped Alice was with the police right now. And she prayed that they'd get here fast, before Natasha started putting her demented plans into action. At Zoe's side, Poppy had remained silent and still. Zoe still clutched her hand, though it felt moist and slippery. She searched Natasha's face, hoping for some sign of sanity and normality that she could appeal to.

"I hear your thoughts, Zoe," Natasha said in a low voice. "I know you think I'm insane. Often a shamanic healer has entered her own death, illness or madness, and found the path through it with the help of Spirit." She smiled. "I cannot be caged; not this time." Before Zoe could query her last phrase, Natasha went on. "I'll take flight. The police are powerless to stop me."

Someone fitted a key into the door-lock from the other side. Zoe tightened her hold on Poppy's hand. New hope flared that it might be Theo with the police. No, they'd be breaking the door down.

"Ah, James and Sonya," said Natasha, "with Alice."

Zoe started. She fixed her eyes on the door. Natasha glided across and opened it.

"Come in, James," she said. "And you, Sonya."

James entered, looking very different to how Zoe remembered him from their last conversation. His manner now was that of a disturbed ferret.

Sonya, behind him, was in a state of disarray. Her beehive hair had come undone and several strands of it hung around her face. There was no sign of Alice. Zoe's heart beat fast.

"Where's Alice?" asked Natasha sharply.

"She got away," said James.

Zoe's heart sang. She felt like punching the air. *God bless you and protect you, Alice,* she breathed.

Natasha screamed. "Why did I ever trust you?"

"Natasha," James pleaded, seizing hold of her hands.

Natasha snatched them from him. "You find that girl! Didn't she even hurt herself?"

"No idea," said Sonya. "She was gone long before we could find out."

But Sonya now seemed to have lost interest in the question of where Alice was. Instead, she'd fixed her gaze on Poppy, who clung to Zoe's hand. Slowly Sonya began to move towards the child, hands out, palms uppermost, ignoring Natasha and James.

"Go, James!" cried Natasha. "You must get her back. If she brings the police you two will be lost."

Zoe was perplexed by Natasha's last phrase. Surely, if the police came, all three of them would be arrested. Did Natasha consider herself somehow inviolable and beyond the force of the law?

"Take the Cayenne!" commanded Natasha. "Alice may keep to fields and woods at first, but will be desperate to get to a road. You'll be bound to pick her up sooner or later."

Zoe had never seen James so obedient. He scuttled off. Sonya, however, impervious to all else, had reached Poppy and was now squatting down in front of her, holding her free hand.

"What a perfect child," she whispered.

"Yes, yes," said Natasha. "I see you like her. Now, Sonya, come here. I need to talk to you."

Sonya tried to take Poppy into her arms. But the child clung to Zoe.

"Give her time, Sonya," said Natasha. "There's much to do yet. And remember, there'll be more, many more."

"Yes," cried Sonya, her face transfigured, as she rose to her feet and rejoined her sister. "Thank you, Natasha!"

Zoe bit her lip; she watched this little scene in mystification. Then she squeezed Poppy's hand, as the two sisters spoke together in an undertone.

"We'll need to act, fast," said Natasha. "Now Alice has got away, we must bring our plans forward."

"Yes," said Sonya.

Pulling Poppy with her, Zoe backed away from the two sisters. How they planned to kill them both, she had no idea. She could see no weapons on them. But even so they may have knives hidden from sight. All she knew was that she must protect Poppy.

The Cayenne sprang into life down below and James drove away. Zoe's eye flicked past Natasha. In his hurry to do Natasha's bidding, James had left the door ajar; and Natasha had failed to notice, distracted by Sonya's behaviour towards the child. Zoe silently thanked God for this lapse, and squeezed Poppy's hand, hoping to communicate a warning to her. Meanwhile, she focused on the two sisters.

Sonya's eyes were devouring Poppy once more.

"Sonya! Please tell me what this is all about," said Zoe. "You're not casting for a film, are you? What do you want with Poppy? What's this plan you and Natasha have been talking about?"

Sonya wore a pitying expression.

"All you need know, Zoe," said Sonya, "is that the little girl has come to us, and I'll be her protector."

"She's come to *me*. And right now, I'm her sole protector," said Natasha with a warning note in her voice.

227

Sonya flashed a shocked glance at Natasha. "What do you mean? I've turned over all my savings to you to make this possible."

Zoe moistened her lips as she listened to this.

"And I offered to look after Poppy for you," said Sonya.

"Yes," said Natasha. "And I've accepted your gift. Be patient. You'll have your reward. But in my timing."

This seemed to defuse Sonya's anxiety for a second or two. But then she said, "You did promise. You know I'm the only one who can do it. It will need a very special person."

"Even so," responded Natasha, "The final decision is mine. And it may be that I need to put you through the initiation again."

Natasha seemed to grow taller, as the two sisters faced each other.

Zoe, hand-in-hand with Poppy, began to edge towards the door. She kept a vigilant eye on the two sisters. Her heart raced.

"I thought we'd agreed about Poppy," said Sonya. "I was to have her. And I claim her. Whatever else you do, I must have Poppy."

Zoe had reached the door by now.

"Wait, and be patient," insisted Natasha.

"Are you testing me?" asked Sonya in an ominous tone of voice.

Zoe pulled Poppy's hand, and flew through the doorway.

And as she did so, she remembered her dream. The one which had woken her in terror, before she shared it with Theo and later recounted it to Alice. .And now she knew it was about to come true.

CHAPTER THIRTY-FIVE

As she stumbled over uneven, stony ground, clutching Poppy's hand, sweat drenched Zoe's blouse, sticking it to her skin, despite the dank chill in the air. Her heart pounded and Poppy's fingers kept slipping out of hers. She scrubbed her hand against her trousers and then felt her jacket pocket. With a sickening shock, she realised it was empty. She must have dropped the torch somewhere, soon after leaving the mill. She seized the child's hand again. The light was very low, and soon they'd be in darkness.

Once outside the mill, they'd fled round the side of the building through to the partially-landscaped garden at the back. She could glimpse water beyond the tall, tasselled reeds. She wondered whether to head down there and follow the course of the river. But it might be too obvious – and dangerous if they lost the path. The road was out of the question at this point. James would easily pick them up in his Cayenne.

Reaching the perimeter of the grounds, they scrambled over a wire fence, to find themselves on a narrow, bramble-choked path which skirted the edge of a wood. They ran along it, Zoe wincing and Poppy sobbing as spiky stems tore at their clothes and flesh, drawing blood.

After ten minutes, they came out into a field. Her chest burning, and tears stinging her eyes, Zoe paused to wipe sweat and hair away, both from her face and from Poppy's.

Dusk was already well-advanced. They'd need to accustom

their eyes to the dark to have any chance at all. They set off again, pounding along the edge of the field, avoiding open space. Zoe knew Natasha and Sonya must be close behind, and they'd have brought torches and possibly flashlights with them, and would be at an advantage. She held Poppy's hand tight as the cold intensified. Zoe clenched her teeth together to stop them from chattering. She wondered whether they could last the night out in the open, before hypothermia set in. Poppy only had a cardigan to keep her warm. She'd been brought to the apartment without any coat or jacket.

Zoe halted. In front of them was a ditch, filled with mud, half-hidden by low-hanging field maples. She twisted round and saw, in the distance, a glimmer of white. Natasha had burst out from among the trees on the opposite side of the field. Zoe seized Poppy in her arms and plunged into and across the ditch, fighting her way through the twigs and branches of the trees beyond it. As she set Poppy down again, soaked in mud, scratched and bruised, she glimpsed movement across the field – the dark shapes of a herd of cows.

Keeping to the wooded margins of the field, they stumbled along the dirt track. A sharp wind whipped them as they struggled along the path. Their breathing came fast and jagged, and they had miles ahead of them in gathering dark, with no chance of a rest.

Two crows arose from the thicket ahead of them. A buzzard which had been wheeling overhead dive-bombed the crows and the air became filled with angry shrieks.

Poppy shrank in to Zoe's side as the battle rose to a climax. Disordered thoughts jostled in Zoe's mind, along with pictures of Natasha shapeshifting and attacking them in feathered form. She forced the images away.

They hurried up to higher ground as a light aircraft replaced the birds. A vast open space lay before them, but the darkness prevented Zoe from discerning any details. By daylight, she may have identified different features of the landscape, perhaps recognizing a church spire, or another landmark, silhouetted against the sky. But right now it was impossible to orientate herself. All they could do was put as much distance as possible between themselves and their pursuers, and hope to reach a road or lane and stop a motorist.

She grabbed Poppy's hand and they bounded to the end of the field, and then descended into a plantation, losing all the height they'd walked up earlier. Every so often, Zoe turned to see if she could catch sight of Sonya or Natasha – or, indeed, James, for she'd no idea what he might choose to do, in the event of finding or giving up on Alice.

Their path skirted around a high bank before rising up a hill. Reaching the brow, they found themselves stumbling down to another wood, through a succession of fields. Still they'd found no lanes or farm tracks. On the point of entering the wood, she turned, and saw the flash of torchlight roughly twenty metres away. Her heart lurched.

Then she heard James's voice. "Give up," he shouted. "You don't stand a chance."

His presence must mean there was a road not far away, where he would have left the Cayenne. Zoe saw Sonya and Natasha beside him.

"Poppy! Hurry!" she gasped, as they stumbled forward into a dense clump of trees. Zoe had no idea whether or not they were following the main path. Pausing to look behind her, she saw another flash back at the entrance to the wood.

"You've no hope!" yelled James. "We've got you!"

They fled deeper into the wood, stumbling over tree roots and uneven ground. Poppy lost her footing and pitched forward into a pile of stones. Zoe bent to lift her up, knowing the darting beam of James's torch was hunting them down. The damp odour of decomposing leaf litter filled her nostrils.

"Come on, Poppy!" she coaxed the weeping child. "Come on! We can do this!"

Flailing fingers grazed her sleeve. She jerked herself from James's grasp.

"Run, Poppy, run!" she cried.

Poppy scurried away into the undergrowth. James instantly seized Zoe's arm in a fierce grip.

"She won't get far on her own," he snarled.

Zoe screamed, as another torch beam cut through the trees behind James. She lifted her right knee high then kicked back. He bellowed in pain and let her go. She made off at once, but an overhanging branch caught the collar of her jacket. As she struggled to free herself, strong hands lashed out and James was onto her.

"Natasha!" he yelled. "I've got her!"

"Hold on. I'll get Poppy." Natasha sprinted past.

Zoe gave a violent twist and pushed James away. She was about to launch herself off again, but he grabbed hold of her by one arm and swung her to face him. She raised her free hand and slapped his face hard.

He gasped then punched her in the ribs. The force of it sent her sprawling to the ground. But, despite the throbbing pain in her side, she scrambled to her feet and flung herself forward. She slid down a sharp incline of loose stones, and at the bottom, picked herself up and fled. After trampling a wide area of dying ferns and scrambling over at least half a dozen fallen branches, she halted, gasping, beside a tree-stump.

She turned to find James right there, directing his torch beam into her face. Dazzled, she shrank back. He kept the beam trained on her as he closed in.

"At last," he panted.

She struck him across the arm that held the torch, knocking it from his hand. As he cursed and stumbled, she dived onto the torch. She straightened and shone it into his face. He fell back a few paces, swearing. He looked as if he was on an SAS training exercise through challenging terrain. His face was smeared with dirt, and his eyes bloodshot.

They both waited, their chests heaving. But as she stared at him, wide-eyed with terror, a mental image clicked into place. Those bloodshot eyes were familiar. Holding the torch steady in her left hand, she bent and snatched up a rock from the ground with her right. Any moment he'd make another move towards her.

He sprang and she hurled the rock at him. It struck him in the stomach and he lurched backwards, landing with a crash in a bed of brambles. She kept the torch beam on him. As she watched, he began to sink. There was a dismal gurgle. The brambles had formed a masking screen across a bog. She gazed intently at James wallowing in fetid water.

Then she refocused. That memory again filled her mental screen.

A man lurched out of the trees, and swayed before her. He wore a long, filthy coat. Bloodshot eyes held her in scrutiny; thick beard and matted hair; half-full bottle of wine in his hand.

Her mind ricocheted further back, to her session of online research. Along with other pieces of information about James, she'd learned that his acting career included numerous walk-on parts as antisocial types and loners. And those parts would, of course, have required him to *dress up as a tramp.*

"James," she said. "The vagrant... Was it you?"

"At last," he snarled. "Took you long enough, didn't it? I'm an actor; and a good one."

"Not my idea of one," she said. "The only actors I've ever known, apart from you, have been good people. *You're* sick."

She swung round in disgust, ready to continue her flight, and ran into the arms of Natasha.

"I've taken care of Poppy," said Natasha, tightening her grip on Zoe's upper arm, just above the elbow. "Now I need *you*."

"What have you done to her?" screamed Zoe, twisting and squirming, but unable to escape Natasha's grasp.

"Stop struggling. It's hopeless. I've got the child. *She*'s nice and quiet. You'd do well to follow her example. It's all over, Zoe." Still holding Zoe's arm, she turned her torch on James, who was struggling to escape.

"Well done, James," she said. "But get out of that bog. You look dreadful."

James heaved himself out and came to stand beside Zoe and Natasha, covered with a thick coating of mud, and training a murderous glare upon Zoe. Zoe stared back at James. She was trembling as a result of her recent exchange with Natasha – who still held her fast.

Something hard struck her on the head. A black fog descended. She felt herself sinking following the shape of a spiral.

# CHAPTER THIRTY-SIX

Zoe opened her eyes. She lay on her back on a bitterly cold surface. A sharp pain stabbed her in the side. She blinked a few times. The darkness was relieved only by a very low light.

She began to explore her ribs with her fingers and they met a soft, smooth material, which felt like silk. Then she put her hand out again, to feel around her. Her fingers met stone. Her head throbbed. She tried to roll onto her other side, but couldn't summon the strength.

She worked her parched tongue around her mouth. After swallowing several times, taking two or three deep breaths, and balling her hands into tight fists, she managed to raise herself onto one elbow and look around. In front and above her was a tall candle-stand with tulip sconces, in which burned four tall candles.

She shot a desperate glance down at herself. Her own muddy and torn clothes had gone, and in their place she wore a long, silk dress. Her feet were bare, and icy cold. With a groan, she sat up. She stared around again, her heart pounding. She could barely make out dim shapes beyond the candle-stand. To the left, her hand met a flat, vertical timber surface. Breathing in again, she smelt a heavy fragrance: incense. She grimaced at the cloying sweetness of it.

Another candle burned in a stone dish on a table just to the right of where she lay. The flat timber surface to her left was the back of a pew. Elsewhere in the darkness, further candles burned. Twisting round, and looking up, she saw an arched window above her, deeply inset into the thickness of the wall. Another candle flame shone steadily on the window ledge and beyond it she could make out the leadlights. Wincing at the pain in her side, she turned again, and began to get to her feet.

"Awake, Zoe?"

She stood up, and found herself face-to-face with Natasha, who wore a similar dress to hers and over it a floor-length white satin cloak.

"Natasha!" she gasped. "What's going on? Why are we here?"

"They only hold services here once a month," replied Natasha. "Ideal. Sonya managed to get the keys."

"But why are we here?" Zoe repeated. "And why am I dressed like this?"

"Let me answer your second question first," smiled Natasha, "You wouldn't want to have stayed in those sweaty, torn clothes of yours, would you? And as to your first question, well, the answer is that tonight, we initiate you and Poppy. Now, relax, don't worry, everything will be perfect, so long as you obey me, of course."

"But I don't choose to obey you," cried Zoe. "I refuse to be 'initiated'. Remember, Natasha," she continued, urgently trying to contact something in Natasha that would respond to normal human decency and reason, "when you healed people, you always needed them to ask you first, didn't you?" She spread her hands out, palms uppermost.

Natasha laughed. "Yes, that's clever of you, Zoe, to remember. But I'm afraid, in the spiritual dimension things are far more complex than that. It was important that your guests believed they'd chosen freely. But in reality, I was reaching out to them with my own subtle will, making them want the very thing I knew would be perfect for them."

Zoe clapped both her hands to her head.

"No, Natasha, it won't work with me, I promise you. I do *not* choose to be 'initiated'. I have *not* asked to come here. And I reject whatever it is you plan to do. And where is Poppy?"

"Safe on the chancel steps. But Zoe, there's no need to reject me; you have nothing to fear. You and Poppy will both be initiated into a world so beautiful you could never have imagined it. Just remember. *All power has been given to me, in heaven and upon earth.*"

Zoe swallowed.

"What on earth makes you think those words apply to you?"

Natasha gave a light chuckle. "Zoe, you have a very rebellious spirit. But I must admit I like that in you; you're more of a challenge to me."

Zoe swiftly changed tactics. "Never mind me. What of Poppy? She's far too young to have agreed to anything."

"Of course," said Natasha. "We must make decisions for her. It happens with infant baptism all the time."

Zoe tried to push past, but Natasha remained immobile.

"Just now you said Poppy was safe. What does that mean? And why should I believe you? How can you play such a dangerous game with an innocent child, Natasha?"

"'Innocent', you say?" responded Natasha. "Who gave you the right to judge? Only I can do that. Once I've initiated you both, and you've sworn to follow me, then neither you nor Poppy need worry any more about whatever you've done in your lives. I'll assume responsibility for all the years to come."

Zoe longed to fight Natasha's bizarre claims, but a desperate sense of vulnerability and powerlessness rose in her, and the dryness in her mouth had worsened.

"Ultimately, of course," added Natasha, "I'll have the Celtic Knot studio. It will be ideal as a chapel and well-suited to my purposes."

Zoe tried to speak, but her voice broke up. "Can I have a glass of water?" she asked huskily.

"Sorry. No running water here, I'm afraid. This church is unmodernised."

Zoe nearly sobbed, but instead, forced out another question she'd been longing to ask.

"You say you want to 'collect' children; but how?"

Natasha gave Zoe a look of cool contempt.

"That's no concern of yours. All you need know is this: I'll rescue children from the life they would have lived, if not for my intervention. I have a lot of support in this. Disciples in many professions are working for me."

Zoe's face burned and her arms and legs tingled. The powerful incense in the atmosphere took hold of her, beginning to fog her mind and make her dizzy.

"No more questions," said Natasha.

"But…" said Zoe, fighting for clarity.

A key scraped in the church-door lock.

"Ah, here comes my assistant," said Natasha.

Behind Natasha, the heavy door creaked open, and the new arrival stepped in. The door closed and Sonya stood there, wearing a gown identical to Zoe's and Natasha's. Natasha swung to face her.

"Welcome, Sonya," she said.

"Ah, Zoe's awake. We can get on with the ceremony," said Sonya.

"I'll take part in no ceremony," cried Zoe. "Show me where Poppy is."

"Over there," said Natasha, turning back again, and pointing towards the chancel.

Zoe ran up the narrow aisle and stopped dead when she reached the chancel steps. Two tall candle-stands were placed in front of each choir-stall. Between them lay Poppy, quiet and still, on the crimson runner at the entrance to the chancel.

The child's eyes were closed. By the light of the candles, Zoe saw she too was dressed in white. Zoe's heart thundered against her ribs, which still ached from James's attack. She knelt down on the second chancel step and placed her hand on the little girl's chest, leaning in to put her ear to her lips. Poppy was breathing softly. Zoe had no doubt at all that her sleep was drug-induced. Still kneeling on the step, Zoe twisted round to face the two sisters once more. Neither had moved from their position at the west end of the church, between the medieval font and the votive light stand.

Zoe scrambled to her feet, keeping her eyes on Natasha and Sonya. Her head began to swim again. It seemed as if the observing part of her had detached and floated away from her body. And then she started to feel Natasha's psyche reaching out to her, across the length of the aisle; seeking to leach her free will from her. She fought against it. *God, help me*, she repeated beneath her breath.

Natasha's healings sprang again to her mind. Although Natasha went through the charade of waiting for people to ask, they were in reality bound by something much stronger than themselves, over which they had no control. Their main concern was the bodily pain which had previously held them in its grip; and when Natasha released them from it, through a power nobody understood, she won them, heart, mind and soul.

Zoe shot a desperate glance down at Poppy again. The child still lay on her back, fast asleep. Then Zoe looked up towards the altar. Another four-foot-tall candle-stand stood to its left. And beside this, Zoe saw a small table. On it had been placed a large plate, a jug and two goblets.

Zoe gasped. She recognised these items at once. The

special ceramic communion set! Even now, the high gloss of the cobalt-blue glaze glimmered in the candlelight. She spun to face the sisters again.

"You're a thief, Natasha," she cried.

Natasha laughed. "They're mine by right," she said. "I'll put them to much better use than you and Theo would have done."

Before Zoe could answer, she heard the heavy, iron latch of the south door clunk down, and the door opened once again. She froze. James entered, clean and well groomed, and wearing white robes. Sonya handed him the keys; he closed and locked the door, then deposited the keys in a pocket in the folds of his robes.

Zoe's stomach turned. This was like some creepy, perverse piece of theatre. But it was terrifyingly real. She cast a desperate glance towards Natasha again. The white satin of the healer's cloak gleamed as she stood close to the votive light stand, full of steadily-burning tea-lights. Sonya and James waited on her right-hand side.

"Soon you will be ready to be sworn to the service of the Divine Master," they said in unison.

Fighting tears of anger and fear, Zoe crouched down again to take Poppy's hand in hers. It felt limp and cool.

"Now James has arrived, we can begin," said Sonya. Zoe heard the swish of satin and silk as they processed up the aisle. She released the child's hand and jumped up quickly to face them.

"Never!" she shouted.

Only Natasha and Sonya had moved. James stood still, as if awaiting further instructions. Perhaps he was after all, despite all his behaviour in the previous weeks, merely a pawn in Natasha's game; but Zoe couldn't be sure.

Sonya halted at the foot of the chancel steps. Natasha

turned, walked across to the pulpit, and ascended the steps. Zoe's stomach clenched. God, she thought. Surely Natasha wasn't going to give some warped sermon to them all? Once at the top, Natasha turned to face her small audience, lifted her chin, held her arms out wide with uplifted hands, like an inspired preacher, and began: "I, alone, know the Truth. I alone can connect you with the world of Spirit to which you truly belong. I am the Divine Master."

Zoe listened in cold horror, her spine prickling with perspiration. James moved swiftly to join Sonya. Their eyes fixed on the healer, the two disciples both murmured their rapt agreement.

"Zoe, soon you and Poppy will be given your permanent entrance into that world," said Natasha.

Zoe's heart pounded. The pungency in the air weighed upon her spirits, quite as much as Natasha's words and actions. But, she told herself, she must remain alert; all her energies must be concentrated on guarding Poppy, and keeping her from harm.

"You'll both be wrapped in security," continued Natasha, "you'll have an enormous sense of liberation and freedom from the limitations of the body, an increased sense of knowledge and power, and a vast capacity to cultivate those things which you feel should be cultivated."

Ice cold tears escaped from the corners of Zoe's eyes and traced their way down her cheek. She clenched her fists, and with mind and body she fought against Natasha's words, yet at the same time she felt her spirit weakening, as the sound of Natasha's voice now began to entrance her together with the vision of her lovely face, her pale-gold flowing hair, and her slim arms uplifted in glimmering white silk.

"The only reality is spiritual," said Natasha. "The only real world is the spiritual world, and the real 'you' haunts, but is by no means identified with, the temple of clay which is called the body. There are two things: the darkness and the light. If you have negative feelings, you are poured into darkness. I call upon you now to let go of all that is negative. Surrender yourself to me. Know that I am the power that rules your fate. Cling to nothing else. You have nothing to defend."

The tingling sensation down her back rapidly spread around Zoe's ribs, and to every part of her body.

"Why should I surrender myself to you, Natasha?" she cried.

"Because," replied Natasha, "I have entered the Silence. Just as it's possible for the mind to move in and out of the flesh at birth, sleep and death, so do I move in and out of different forms at will. I alone can be trusted, Zoe. Follow my voice."

Zoe's head swirled again. Her stomach contracted. She knew the incense was a psychoactive drug. It was invading her mind. She began reciting the Lord's Prayer.

"Our Father in Heaven, Hallowed be Your Name…"

Natasha's voice broke in. "In a few moments, Zoe, I'll open the door for you, which is the opening to freedom."

New thoughts flashed across Zoe's mind. This was a village church; there'd be a community close by. She might try to attract attention from outside. A passer-by could see the candlelight through the windows, surely. But why should they not believe it was a small Christian group using the church?

Natasha descended the steps of the pulpit and moved to the top of the aisle, facing the altar. James and Sonya fell back, and stood, waiting, behind her. Zoe remained where she was, on the top chancel step, beside Poppy.

Zoe's voice shook as she continued the prayer.

"Your kingdom come, your will be done…"

Natasha smiled.

"That's right, Zoe," she said. "Keep praying. But while you

do, please come back down here, away from the chancel steps, and stand next to Sonya and James. I'll start with Poppy, and need you well away from her."

Zoe broke off from the prayer. "I stay right here, Natasha," she said. "You'll have to fight me if you want me to move. I won't let you touch this child."

Sonya moved forward, to stand beside Natasha. Zoe remained steady.

"If you defy Natasha," said Sonya, "you'll suffer for it. You can't stop this initiation. We start with Poppy then move on to you."

The pain in Zoe's ribs stung her fiercely. She gasped. Sonya sprang forward and tried to seize her. Zoe slipped aside just in time, away from Poppy, past the candle-stand and behind the choir stall.

"Thank you, Zoe," said Sonya. "Now stay where you are. Let Natasha get on with this."

Natasha moved forward and knelt down on the second chancel step in front of Poppy. Zoe seized a bible from the choir stall shelf and hurled it out into the chancel. As the book hit the floor Natasha looked up sharply. Sonya started to inch down the choir stall, reaching out for her. Zoe slid out the other end and went across to the altar.

"Move away from there, Zoe," commanded Natasha. "I want you behind me. Go and sit in the front pew until it's your turn."

Sonya had halted. The silence surged back from Natasha's voice, spreading out in waves around her. It pounded against Zoe's eardrums. Beyond the stone walls and the stained glass windows, the night was still. Everything seemed to be holding its breath, ready for Zoe's next move.

Despite the chill of the church, Zoe was now sweating profusely. The moisture stung her palms and she rubbed her hands down the side of her thighs. Her fingers slithered against the smooth surface of the silk. She felt the hard wooden edge of the altar pressing into her spine. Natasha rose to her feet and stepped past Poppy, up into the chancel.

"I will have you obey me, Zoe, without duress."

Zoe kept Natasha and Poppy in her direct line of vision. But to her right, she sensed Sonya biding her time, waiting her moment to spring. She couldn't stop her body from shivering.

Natasha stopped in the middle of the chancel.

"Zoe, come to me." Natasha's voice echoed up to the rafters and reverberated around the space.

Zoe fought an almost unbearable urge to rush forward into Natasha's arms. She felt the healer's power pulling her, reaching out to her like something tangible. With all her strength, she wrestled this impulse, forcing herself back against the altar, wishing she could reach behind her and grab the cross that stood there.

Though I walk through the valley of the shadow of death, I will fear no evil, she repeated to herself, as Theo had taught her.

Natasha gave a shriek. Zoe extended herself, arching her back, lifting her chin and thrusting her head back. She felt the sweat slither down her throat and breast, soaking the low neckline of her dress. Her teeth were chattering. She tried to clamp her lips together.

"I assure you, Zoe," said Natasha, "this night won't end until you obey me." The soft folds of her cloak swirled with her sudden movement towards Zoe, the candlelight transmitting the pale glimmer of the satin. "You've no idea how weak you are, Zoe," she went on. "I can stay as long as this takes; I can hold the night back, I can prevent the sun from rising, I can stop the day from breaking. But you can't. You're limited by your flesh. You're subject to time, to death and decay."

Zoe battled the tide of nausea that gripped her stomach. Tears continued to roll down her face.

"I am the Divine Master," said Natasha. "You cannot resist me."

Zoe drew a deep breath and forced herself to speak again, though she knew her quivering voice would give away her terror.

"Jesus is 'the Divine Master', not you," she cried. "And He's all about love. *You* are nothing but cruelty and wickedness."

"Not so," retorted Natasha. "You may see it like that right now, Zoe, because you're blind. But, in order to break that stubborn ego of yours, I must compel you to come in."

Sonya broke in. "Natasha, please. Let's get on with the initiation, right now."

Zoe's body ached, the chill in her bones and dryness of her mouth continued unabated, and her sore ribs throbbed painfully. She knew she could not hold out against Natasha much longer. Her strength was failing fast. She and Poppy must surely die.

Natasha turned and walked back to where Poppy slept. Then she faced Zoe again.

"I'll give you one last chance," she said. "Come down into the nave and sit in the front pew and await your turn, well away from Poppy."

Zoe shook her head desperately. James snapped. "She won't do it," he cried. "Sonya, grab her and force her to obey."

Sonya acted at once, and flew at Zoe, hands outstretched. As she grasped Zoe's shoulders, Zoe lunged forwards and bit her neck: something she'd never done before in her life to anybody, even as a small child; but desperate circumstances called for desperate measures.

Sonya screamed and sprang back, as if she was on a riverboat and a crocodile had leapt from the water and snapped its jaws in her face. Zoe hoped her tooth-marks were now reddening ferociously on Sonya's white neck, though she couldn't see that by the candlelight.

But despite her agony, Sonya renewed her attack, fastened onto Zoe's arm, and held it tight.

"You're a fierce little bitch, aren't you, Zoe? Now we see what you're really like! We'll soon bend that hard will of yours."

She clasped Zoe's arm while Zoe struggled and twisted. Close by, at the entrance to the chancel, Poppy began to stir.

"Leave the child alone," cried Zoe. "Do what you like to me, but set her free."

"No," snapped Sonya. "I'll have the child for myself."

Natasha stared at Sonya. "You've got that wrong," she said in a calm, authoritative voice. "This child will *not* be yours."

"What do you mean?" gasped Sonya.

"This is a sacrifice I'm asking of you," replied Natasha. "I'm more important than your dreams. You must leave all your earthly desires to follow me."

Zoe shuddered. A deep chill flowed towards her. Sonya tightened the grip on her arm, and she felt as if the blood was being drained out of it.

"Let go, Sonya," she begged.

Sonya ignored her. "You promised, Natasha!" she cried. "Give me the child!" Dragging Zoe behind her, she rushed towards Natasha and thrust her face close to her sister's.

"No," said Natasha, "you've already forfeited Poppy. Instead, you must show that you trust and believe in me."

James, who all this time had been standing at the top of the aisle, watching events between the three women, now sprang forward, panic on his face.

"Stop this, Sonya. Leave Natasha alone."

"No," screamed Sonya, letting go of Zoe and fastening onto Natasha's arm instead. "I've believed in you, Natasha. I've given my life to you. You cannot betray me now."

James reached for Sonya, about to speak; but was interrupted by a mobile ringtone.

Zoe froze.

It came from within his robe.

James stood transfixed.

Then he reacted quickly, fumbling for the phone.

In a flash Zoe snatched the phone from him. Before she could speak, James grabbed it back, then lost his grip. It slipped from his hand and slid under the choir stall.

"They'll never get Natasha! She'll fly!" he cried.

Sonya reached into a fold of her gown and drew out a knife. "If I can't have the child, no-one will."

"No, Sonya!" screamed Zoe. She dived forward, and fell on top of the child's body, beneath the descending knife.

CHAPTER THIRTY-SEVEN

Heavy blows fell upon the church door. The wood began to splinter, and gave way as a section of it crashed to the floor.

Zoe rolled off Poppy's body, expecting to be drenched by a fountain of blood. Raising her hand and reaching behind her, she explored her back with her fingers. No slippery wetness. She waited for the burning pain to kick in. Poppy was now trying to sit up. Zoe seized her in her arms.

A new voice shouted from the west end of the church.

"Taser! Taser! Taser!"

Zoe raised her head once again and peered down the aisle. She saw flashlights, then armed police officers converging on them.

Her mind went blank; her senses were dulled; and she felt emotionally numb. An uneasy calm possessed her; she felt no surprise or relief that rescue was near.

A female police officer was bending over her. "Are you both all right?" she asked in a warm, deeply concerned voice.

"Yes, thank you," said Zoe in an expressionless tone, as the police officer took Poppy from her; then another came forward and wrapped a blanket round her, helped her to her feet, and guided her across to the front pew.

"Get back. All of you."

Sonya's voice had rung out, harsh and shrill.

Suddenly, all capacity to feel emotion slammed back into

Zoe's body with full force. Her heart began hammering again and she broke out into a cold sweat once more.

Covered by the armed officers in the aisle, Sonya and James were locked together in the chancel, at the foot of the altar steps. With one arm Sonya held James fast around the waist, and with her free hand she pressed the edge of the knife blade against his throat.

A hush fell upon the officers behind Zoe and Poppy.

"Sonya, what are you doing?" cried Zoe.

"Move one step forward, any of you, and James here dies," said Sonya.

James was clearly resisting Sonya with all his strength, yet failing to break free. He gagged, and his eyes began to bulge. Zoe felt sick.

"You're a lying bastard, James!" snarled Sonya.

Then a low, calm voice interceded: the police negotiator.

"Listen to me, Sonya. Take it easy. Let go of the knife."

She didn't reply. Instead, she began to tighten the blade against James's throat. He strained against her, his head thrust back, making harsh guttural sounds that froze Zoe's blood. The negotiator moved slowly towards Sonya and James. Sonya kept her grip upon the knife handle, and James gave a thin high animal sound of terror.

"Give me the knife, Sonya," said the negotiator.

Then Zoe saw Natasha at the south side of the church. She had somehow escaped and stood poised upon the front pew, seeming to grow luminous; next, oblivious to the armed officers who were covering her, she began to spring across the backs of the pews. She swooped through to the west end of the church. Zoe expected one of the armed officers to taser her; but none did. As she passed burning candles, their light snapped out, then re-ignited again, and again. Yet neither gown nor cloak caught alight.

Zoe jumped to her feet and darted into the aisle, desperately trying to see what was going on at the west end of the church, which Natasha had now reached.

The sound of beating wings filled the space above their heads: the frantic flight of a trapped bird, batting itself against the walls in a panic. It alighted on a candle-stand, and Zoe glimpsed its black, glossy feathers and its long wedge-shaped tail. It launched itself at the vaulted roof, then lost height, and flew up the aisle above the heads of the rescue party. When it reached the chancel, it dive-bombed the police negotiator. He dodged, just before it could strike his shoulder. The bird wheeled, and soared back up into the roof-space, doing a somersault in mid-flight. Its deep reverberating croak echoed through the church. It perched on the tie beam, where it sat, watching and waiting.

"Keep your eyes on that bird," yelled one of the police officers. "It's dangerous. It's going to attack again."

At this, the raven took off once more, its wings stretched wide, head protruding forward, thick, pointed beak scything through the air. Without warning, and at lightning speed, it lost height, lunged at Zoe and made a low, raking strike to the back of her head. She screamed in agony as she felt blood gush from the wound. The bird struck her again and again, targeting her head and neck, as she threw her arms up, frantically trying to protect herself in a fruitless effort to beat the raven off, while three police officers swung batons at it with little effect.

The bird pecked and jabbed relentlessly, until, without warning, Zoe was free. She looked up in bewilderment, her heart thundering against her ribs, in time to see the bird make its retreat. It flew back down the length of the church, over the pews, straight to the south doorway and disappeared out into the night.

Meanwhile, the female police officer was pressing a pad against the back of Zoe's head in an attempt to staunch the bleeding. Stunned, Zoe looked around for Sonya and James.

During the bird's attack the situation had changed dramatically. Sonya was now handcuffed to two police officers. A third officer was sealing her blood-stained knife into an evidence bag. A fourth was addressing Sonya: "You do not have to say anything but it may harm your defence if you do not mention, when questioned, something which you later rely on in court. Anything you do say may be given in evidence."

Zoe looked for James. Another officer was wrapping a bandage round his throat. Despite the trauma of the last few minutes, he was making every effort to gasp out some kind of a statement.

"Take me if you like," he wheezed. "Lock up Sonya. You'll never get Natasha; never. She's flown. Only we, her true disciples, will ever know where she is."

His words drained away into choking, gurgling sounds. But his eyes still held a fanatical gleam. Gone was the charming persona of his occasional film roles – along with the role he'd played during his first few days at the Celtic Knot. Now Zoe could add two more roles to his gallery of characters: one, the vagrant who'd behaved so threateningly to her; and two, a demented cult follower, swearing allegiance to his master. She shuddered as the police officer continued tending her own wounds.

Since her capture, Sonya had, for her part, gone very quiet. The arresting party made their way up the aisle, taking James and Sonya out into the night. Zoe had no idea whether Natasha had yet been captured.

The female police officer finished bandaging her head. "Come on. Let's get you into a warm car and straight off to hospital. And don't worry about Poppy. She's safe and on her way to the hospital too."

"Thank you," said Zoe, as they left the church. "But... how did you find us? You arrived only just in time. It was a miracle."

"A miracle? Maybe," said the police officer. "How did we find the church? I think we must say that was a joint effort between your husband Theo and your friend Alice."

CHAPTER THIRTY-EIGHT

On the way to the hospital, though Zoe no longer felt emotionally numb, everything seemed strangely unreal to her.

Later that night, at the hospital, after her injuries had been treated and freshly dressed, and she'd been fed with painkillers and antibiotics and received a tetanus shot, she looked up as the door flew open and Theo ran in. He swept Zoe into a warm embrace, as she struggled to her feet.

"Thank God you're safe, Zoe," he said.

It was several minutes before she was able to ask, "And Alice? Where is she?"

"In another room nearby, with Leila. You'll see her very soon now. Zoe, I can't tell you how much we owe Alice. If not for her... what might have happened doesn't bear thinking about."

"And Poppy? Have they found her mother? Is she here?"

"No," said the female police officer. "We've had no chance to get to the bottom of that. We don't know who Poppy belongs to, or anything about her situation."

Zoe bit her lip as she gazed at her.

"But you certainly saved Poppy's life, Zoe. Your bravery was amazing. Like you and Alice she's had a thorough medical check and is getting the best possible care. By now you must feel very close to her, and we'll keep you fully informed."

"Thank you," said Zoe. Then Theo indicated the slim figure in leather jacket and jeans who'd appeared in the doorway, her brown eyes glowing.

"Alice," cried Zoe, as the two girls hugged. When they fell back, words spilled from Zoe. "If it hadn't been for you, God alone knows how this would all have ended up."

"Stop right there," said Alice. "It wasn't just me. It was Theo. He held the key to this."

Zoe swung round to Theo. "How…? When…? Please tell me. I must know right now."

Theo nodded at Alice. "Over to you, Alice."

"Long story," said Alice, coming to sit down in the chair next to Zoe. "But since you asked, I'll tell you. Several days ago – at the centre, before James abducted me – I had a creepy conversation with Natasha."

"Ah," said Zoe. "Was it that time you told me you'd spoken to her but refused to go into details?"

"Yeah, that's the one," said Alice. "Well, it was about 'The Scottish Play'. Sorry, I know I can say the name, because I'm not in a theatre, but still… Those Weird Sisters, I don't think they had anything on Natasha. Still. Let me get with the story. The subject came up because I mentioned the raven to her. I suppose I was feeling a bit provocative. I quoted that speech of the Lady's, from Act 1 Scene 5. *The raven himself is hoarse that croaks the fatal entrance of Duncan under my battlements. Come you spirits that tend on mortal thoughts,… fill me… top-full of direst cruelty. Make thick my blood, stop up… access… to remorse.* Shakespeare used the raven, of course, because in folklore it's an omen of death."

Zoe clasped her fingers together, and opened her eyes wide, desperate to concentrate, for the powerful painkillers had started kicking in; and she still couldn't banish from her mind the sound of flapping wings and that harsh, echoing croak, nor the repeated heavy blows to the back of her head and the sticky sensation of blood clogged in her hair.

"I should have known better than to bring up such a subject with Natasha," continued Alice. "Though as it turns out now, it was a good thing I did. She knew well how superstitious actors are – and that being an actor does lend itself to strange rituals."

Zoe shivered.

"Natasha remarked that entering the soul of Lady M must be like becoming a 'transfiguration medium'. She questioned me about the deconsecrated church we performed the play in. She noted we were playing on the sense of violation and sacrilege. It's true that during that production the altar end was ablaze with candles and the act of betrayal was bloodily shown on the altar.

"Natasha started speaking of churches she knows, twelfth and thirteenth century, built on former pagan sacred sites. Places, she said, where the power of the earth rises up, where our forebears felt that connection between this world and the underworld. She said she knew a church, St Oswald's, where a raven often circled the roof. It was particularly appropriate because St Oswald is associated with ravens. She added that she had a special connection with that church and felt the spirits calling from the ground."

Zoe nodded, her heart thumping against her chest.

"I got away from Natasha eventually," said Alice. "I didn't feel good about having had that conversation with her. I felt I shouldn't have talked to her about the demonic powers Lady M draws upon to achieve her desires. I felt I'd made a terrible mistake. So I didn't share it with you. Then, after James abducted me and dumped me in the mill with Poppy, remember I said I had a few visits from Natasha and James?"

"Yes."

"During Natasha's second visit, I demanded to know why she and James were keeping us there. Natasha said, 'Just think of Duncan, Alice; bloody betrayal on the altar.' That made my blood run cold. Then she added, 'Remember Oswald?

He's not far from here. His raven flies in the glass.' And she gave a name. It meant nothing to me. I just thought she was delusional. Then I forgot about it – until last night.

"Let me backtrack. After I jumped off the roof onto that tree, I got to the ground and ran like hell. Eventually I reached a road and flagged down a motorist. He called the police. They came to pick me up. I took them to the mill then they insisted I go to hospital to be checked out, while they searched the mill. I hoped to God they'd find you safe and that it wasn't too late. And I knew Carol had already contacted Theo to tell him I'd been found. Later, the police officer who was with me here, got the message that the mill was deserted, and they had no leads. I was petrified that Natasha had killed you both and dumped you somewhere. That was hell.

"Then suddenly words came into my mind. *Oswald... not far from here... his raven flies in the glass...bloody sacrifice on the altar.* At once I thought – church. St Oswald? I remembered the word Natasha had spoken, which meant nothing to me. I shared it with the police officer. It made no sense to her either. Then I said, 'Call Theo. He's a priest. He'll know.' She called him at once."

Theo took over the story. "And that was it, Zoe. I recognised the word, I'd been to that village, I knew the church and I'd led some services there a few years ago. I even knew it was built on a former pagan sacred site. I gave directions to the police. But it wasn't until half an hour ago I got the call I'd been praying for."

"Theo wasn't the only one thanking God you'd been found safe", added Alice, "and in St Oswald's Church."

Zoe tried to speak, but failed. She swallowed two or three times, then took hold of Alice's hand and held it tight.

"Natasha's very powerful," she said. "I don't know whether she'll ever be found."

None of them spoke for a minute. Zoe visualised Sonya's knife-blade, and the blood welling from James's throat.

Theo reached out and covered Zoe's other hand with his.

"Everything you told me about James and Natasha was true. I should have acted much sooner. I hardly believe either of you could forgive me."

Alice looked at Zoe.

Zoe leaned across and kissed Theo on the lips.

"Forgiveness granted. I love you and always will."

He held her tight.

"And as for me," said Alice wryly, looking at them both, "I forgive you too, Theo."

The other two broke apart, smiling, and drew Alice into their joint embrace.

CHAPTER THIRTY-NINE

During the car journey back to the centre the following afternoon, Theo shared news of Jessica.

"Right now – rather like you, Zoe, but for different reasons – she's suffering delayed shock. But before that, she did speak to the guests, cancelled the next few weeks' courses, and arranged to refund the full cost. And in a few hours' time the trustees will hold another emergency meeting. They'll have a major damage-limitation exercise on their hands to save the centre after this."

"Yes," said Zoe. "And Theo – are we still leaving? Or has everything changed now?"

"I can't answer that question," said Theo. "We'll have to speak to Jessica first."

SIX MONTHS LATER

Theo closed *The Guardian* and turned to Zoe, who sat behind the desk in the first-floor study.

"A very full account from their court reporter," he remarked.

"Yes," murmured Zoe, "though I'm still reeling from the sentence. I honestly hadn't expected them both to get life."

"The charges were pretty serious," said Theo.

Zoe nodded. "And something else has been bugging me," she said. "I can't stop wondering about Sonya. Despite all that happened, surely she *didn't* mean to kill Poppy, or me, or James?"

Theo drew a deep breath.

"I'm afraid the jury decided that she did; though it does seem unbelievable when she desperately wanted the child for herself."

Zoe sighed. "Natasha was never going to let Sonya's dream come true. And meanwhile, *she's* disappeared. James did say she'd *flown*. And I think she has... literally."

Theo gave her a quick look, but said nothing.

Zoe cast her eye over the news report again.

In Gloucester Crown Court today, James Willoughby, 48, and Sonya Morrigan, 35, were jailed for life after being convicted of child abduction, child abuse, assault with intent to cause grievous bodily harm, kidnapping and attempted murder.

Willoughby and Morrigan had denied the abduction of five-year-old Poppy but the jury returned guilty verdicts against them both. Mr Justice Hardcastle said they would both serve a minimum of 20 years.

The judge told them 'Your lust for control and power over others was greater than your love for this child and your concern for her best interests and welfare.'

Willoughby and Morrigan's story that they had legally adopted Poppy was ruled to be 'a tissue of lies'. The adoption services maintain that they knew nothing of Poppy or of any official adoption procedure. Five-year-old Poppy, the court heard, is the child of a psychiatric inpatient at Rookwood Private Psychiatric Hospital. Her mother suffers from paranoid schizophrenia made worse by her heroin addiction. Poppy's father is her mother's abusive former partner.

A number of staff at the psychiatric hospital have been charged with conspiring to aid the abduction of a child through false pretences.

In view of the severity of the offence, the judge overruled Morrigan's plea for special mitigating circumstances to be taken into account. The court heard that Morrigan had a child of her own when she was twenty. Her mental health has long been fragile and she had suffered a nervous breakdown in her teens. But then her partner, who was a soldier, went out to serve in Afghanistan and was killed, leaving her on her own with their young child. Morrigan went into deep depression. She maintained that her little girl kept saying, 'Where's my daddy?' Perhaps, if not for her mental fragility, Morrigan might have reacted differently. But, weakened by depression and grief, and to stop the little girl asking for her father, Morrigan strangled the child.

Morrigan was jailed for two years after the murder, and then released on grounds of diminished responsibility because of

*the state of her mental health at the time. Later she discovered
she had become infertile; most likely, it was believed, as a result
of her anti-psychotic medication. It was understood that she
tried every avenue, including donor programmes and official
adoption, but all failed. She had, however, refused to give up
looking for a child of her own.*

*The judge directed the jury not to be swayed by the
undeniably tragic background that Morrigan had disclosed.
The severity of her present crimes was so great that these
circumstances could not mitigate the sentence, and he directed
the jury to return a guilty verdict.*

*After the trial, Detective Superintendent Gavin Fanshawe
described the couple's behaviour as 'A vile and disgraceful act
against a vulnerable child whose welfare they subverted for the
sake of their own personal gratification'.*

*On sentencing, Mr Justice Hardcastle told the couple,
'Poppy has now been saved from you, but she is unlikely to
be able to avoid the legacy of this experience. There is only one
sentence that I can impose upon you and that is a sentence of
imprisonment for life'.*

Zoe closed the paper. She preferred not to read the parts that
referred to her and Alice, and to the Celtic Knot Centre.

"And not a word about Natasha," she said. "Despite all that
I tried to tell them about her, it's just as if she never existed."

Then she shivered; for Natasha had said *'I eliminate memories'.*

"I'm afraid," said Theo, "that for Sonya and James, the
outcome has been exactly as Alice warned us. Such is the
reward for those who give Natasha access to their souls. She's
escaped, leaving her victims to suffer the consequences."

"Like the end of *Macbeth*," murmured Zoe. "Alice told me
that Shakespeare has Queen Hecate appear, who triumphs over
Macbeth, having led him by deceit to *a dismal and a fatal end*."

Theo nodded. "Unless Natasha or her disciples surface again, she'll never be brought to justice, and we won't know her full story. However, one thing's clear: James brought Poppy here on the afternoon of Monday 15th September in the Cayenne. Poppy was kept in the goose house with Natasha. That was why they found it easy to keep her hidden: even, I'm ashamed to say, when I visited the goose house to see Natasha."

Zoe shivered.

"However," went on Theo, "the fact that Alice was receiving Poppy's psychic cries for help unnerved James. That settled it for both of them. Alice had to be got rid of. And then, Zoe, there was you. I'm afraid you became a target because Natasha, for some reason, saw you as an ideal recruit for her sect. And she was using her sister Sonya, who was well placed to exploit your dreams of being a film star."

Zoe bit her lip and said nothing.

"But in the end her plans failed," said Theo.

"Even though James supported and encouraged her all along the way."

"Yes," said Theo. "He's certainly a devoted disciple. I admit he took me in as much as anyone."

Zoe sighed. "But I'm glad that Poppy's safe now," she said, "with kind, loving foster-carers. And in time, if both sides are happy with the arrangement, they can opt to make it permanent."

TWO MONTHS LATER

Theo set his half pint of Windrush Ale down on the table beside Zoe's gin and tonic, and put his arm around her as they snuggled up together before a cheerful fire on a small sofa in the lounge bar of the Lygon Arms, in Broadway.

Jessica had given them both a well-deserved two-week holiday before they returned once more to their former duties at the centre. They hadn't chosen to go far. Neither had any interest in sightseeing, only in relaxing and enjoying each other's company with no work duties to worry about.

"You know," said Zoe, "even though St Oswald's has now been reconsecrated, I still feel I couldn't step into it again without remembering what happened to me, and to little Poppy there. Natasha was very close to succeeding with me. It would have been so easy to surrender to her."

"Yes," murmured Theo.

Zoe went on. "I still don't truly understand how Natasha did those 'healings'. She claimed that she 'eliminates people's memories' of their disease."

Theo spread his hands. "I can't explain it either. But we now know *why*, of course."

Zoe squeezed his hand. "Yes. As Alice said, she gave them 'a sweet reward' in return for access to their souls. James, Sonya and several other disciples are now paying a heavy price for their allegiance to her, while she herself has flown. As for our former guests, it seems that Natasha – wherever she is right now – has let go of her claim on them for the time being."

She and Theo had made a number of phone calls, following up on the guests who'd been 'healed' by Natasha. One had rebooked his day surgery for cataracts which Natasha had supposedly banished; another now found his prolapsed disc was giving as much pain as before Natasha miraculously corrected it, and was shortly to see his neurosurgeon; and a third guest, who'd believed himself to have been cured of cancer by Natasha, now needed a new course of chemotherapy.

Zoe and Theo had heard similar stories from several other former guests too. They also sadly claimed that it was impossible to contact Natasha, who 'seemed to have disappeared from the face of the earth'.

One of them added something that chilled Zoe:

"And yet… it's odd, but I can't seem to remember her distinctly at all. It feels like a bird in a room, beating its wings against the glass, desperately trying to break free. Soon she'll fly and there'll be no memory of her left."

"But as to Sonya," went on Theo, "– well, I feel that sometimes, people who've had pain inflicted on them go on to inflict it on others. We humans, however solid and real, are 'elemental'. We can turn to ice, to steam, to water. We can evaporate, or we can boil. Does that make sense to you?"

"Yes. But if we're all so changeable, what or who can we hang on to, and trust?"

Theo held Zoe tight, as if he believed she'd act out his words right there and then, by evaporating.

"For you and me," said Theo, "the answer is to make sure we always have 'three in our marriage'."

She sat up straight. "Three? What do you mean, Theo?"

He broke into laughter. "I mean us and the one person who never changes."

Zoe smiled, and cuddled up to Theo on the sofa.

"The rest of us – we change," he continued; "sometimes liquid; sometimes ice; sometimes steam; never the same."

Zoe nodded.

"And for an actor," went on Theo, "that elemental nature is harnessed and put at the service of their gift – as in Alice's case."

"Yes," said Zoe, her eyes sparkling. "I'm so happy she got that part. I can't wait to see her in the first episode next week."

"Neither can I. And remember, Zoe, she isn't the only one with a special gift of 'sensitivity'. What about your own vision of Poppy, before you ever met her?"

Zoe nodded. Then she sat up. "Theo. You never told me *your* ghost story."

"No, I didn't, did I?"

"Tell it to me now."

"OK. You know where I served my curacy, in East Acton, west London," said Theo. "One evening, not long after I'd first joined the church team, I was in a meeting in the vestry with the vicar and his secretary. The meeting finished and I opened the door. We walked out and were met by a group of ghostly monks. My companions were close behind me. We all three saw the hooded figures fade and disappear before our eyes."

He paused. Zoe watched him.

"I learned there'd been several reports, extending over a period of thirty years, all coming from independent sources, which reported sightings of these monks," said Theo. "A short while after my own experience, a sceptical investigator came to the church, to spend the night there and prove the paranormal tales wrong. He'd settled himself down in a pew on the left-hand side of the nave. After a while he dozed. Then he found himself wide awake. And there walking towards him was a procession of six or eight ghostly monks. Heads bowed, they made their way up towards the altar. One stood apart from the rest. Then he heard a quiet voice.

"*'Near here, five hundred years ago, stood a monastery, and we were the occupants. This is our past. This is our future.'*

"When they reached the altar the monks knelt. The spell was broken and they vanished. A few days later he returned with a professional photographer. They saw nothing. But on numerous other occasions, both before our own sighting, and after this event, ghostly monks were seen."

"And do you believe they're spirits of the dead?" asked Zoe.

"No. My guess is that energy lingers in a place where there's been deep emotional trauma. People often pick up an atmosphere in our house. Spirits lie hidden in the timbers and in the stones, as Alice said, as actors feel about the 'relic wall' at the Royal Shakespeare Theatre. We must acknowledge them: and live alongside them."

"I agree. Spirits lie hidden; which reminds me, I've got news for you."

He seized her hand. "What do you mean, Zoe?"

"I mean, I'm pregnant, Theo! We're going to have a baby."

Radiance broke out on Theo's face. He swept Zoe into his arms. The back of her head throbbed, where the raven had attacked her. Even though the physical wounds had healed, sometimes the pain did flare up without warning, especially when Theo held her close. But when she looked into Theo's eyes again her pain vanished, for she saw his eyes had filled with tears of joy.

"This baby will belong to us alone," murmured Zoe, "and never to Natasha."

ACKNOWLEDGEMENTS

The majority of the ghost encounters in *A Passionate Spirit* are based upon real stories. In particular I would like to acknowledge the following:

Peter Ackroyd for his book *The English Ghost: Spectres Through Time* (Chatto & Windus, 2010).

Paul Adams, Eddie Brazil & Peter Underwood for their book *Shadows in the Nave: A Guide to the Haunted Churches of England* (The History Press, 2011).

My sister, Julia Gardner, who first recounted her paranormal experience whilst babysitting in a French villa several years ago.

I wish to thank the following people who gave guidance, editorial feedback and encouragement at many different stages of this journey: Ann Andrews, Gaby Calvert, Vanessa Comer, Alison and Sarah Hull, Helen Lambell, Victoria Lee, Coral Pavitt, Mike Priaulx, Dave Rawcliffe, Abigail Robinson, Freda Skillman, David Smith and Kim Watson.

Many thanks are due to those who helped me with research: Stewart McGill, Director and Founder of Playbox Theatre; members of the Anglican clergy John Alderman, Ellie

Clack, Sharon Jones and Nat Reuss; retured police officer Andy Mitchell; and Missing Persons Co-ordinator for the Gloucestershire Constabulary, Christine Pfister.

AUTHOR'S NOTE

The initial idea for Natasha and her sect arose from a real-life New Age sect known as The Family which began in Australia in the 1960s.

The Family was led by Anne Hamilton-Byrne, who taught an eclectic mixture of Christianity and Hinduism with other Eastern and Western religions on the principle that spiritual truths are universal.

The group began benignly enough as a religious and philosophical discussion group led by Anne at *Santiniketan*, the home of Dr Raynor Johnson at Ferny Creek on the eastern outskirts of Melbourne. The group consisted of middle-class professionals; a quarter of whom were nurses and other medical personnel.

During the late 1960s and the 1970s, Newhaven Hospital in Kew, Australia, was a private psychiatric hospital owned and managed by one of Anne's followers; many of its staff and attending psychiatrists were also members of her group. Many patients at Newhaven were treated with the hallucinogenic drug LSD. The hospital was used to recruit potential new members from among the patients, and also to administer LSD to members under the direction of the Santiniketan psychiatrists Dr John Mackay and Dr Howard Whitaker. The hospital was closed down by 1992, and the building was later reopened as a nursing home with no connections to its previous owner or uses.

Anne acquired fourteen infants and young children

between about 1968 and 1975. Some were the natural children of members of The Family; others had been obtained through irregular adoptions arranged by lawyers, doctors and social workers within the group who could bypass the normal processes. The children's identities were changed using false birth certificates or deed poll, all being given the surname 'Hamilton-Byrne' and dressed alike even to the extent of their hair being dyed uniformly blonde.

The children were kept in seclusion and home-schooled at a rural property on Lake Eildon in Victoria. There they were indoctrinated with spiritual teachings which were a syncretism of Christianity, Zen, Hinduism, shamanism and an uncritical adoration of Anne. They were given photos of Anne to put on their altars to worship. They were told that she was their biological mother, and knew the other adults in the group as 'aunties' and 'uncles'. They were denied almost all access to the outside world, and subjected to a discipline that included frequent, severe beatings – often for little or no reason – and starvation diets.

The children were frequently dosed with psychiatric drugs. On reaching adolescence they were compelled to undergo an initiation involving LSD: while under the influence of the drug the child would be left in a dark room, alone, apart from visits by Anne or one of the psychiatrists from the group.

The group had an inner circle who justified their actions by their claim to be reincarnations of the apostles of Jesus. The basis of The Family's philosophy was that Anne was the reincarnation of Jesus Christ, who they said was a great master who came down to Earth, in the same category as Buddha and Krishna.

It was Anne's intention that the children would continue her sect after the Earth was consumed by a holocaust caused by a meteor or asteroid. They would be the inheritors of the

Earth. She originally planned to collect up to twenty-eight children.

Details of the abusive treatment of the children later emerged in an account of their captivity by one of the children, Sarah Hamilton-Byrne, in her book *Unseen Unheard Unknown* published by Penguin in 1995.

Sarah was expelled by Anne in 1987 because of arguing and rebellious behaviour. With the support of a private investigator and others, she played an instrumental role in bringing The Family to the attention of the Victorian police. As a result, a raid took place at the property on Friday, 14 August 1987, and all children were removed from the premises.

One of the children, says Sarah in her book, *probably around 12 years of age... was the size of a 5-year-old... suffering from... psychosocial short stature... a condition of failed growth which occurs in children who have been so psychologically or physically harrassed during their development that they fail to produce the growth hormone required.*

Sarah later went on to study medicine and become a qualified doctor. She also learned that she had been adopted, and eventually met her biological mother.

After the raid in 1987, Anne and her husband, William, remained outside Australia for the next six years. Anne was never brought to justice for child abuse, as the children were so severely traumatised by their experience that for some time they were unable to give evidence in court. *Most of the abuse was under statutory limitation,* writes Sarah in her book, *which meant that charges could not be laid because a certain period of time had elapsed after they had occurred.*

The only charges that were ever brought against Anne and her husband were for financial misdemeanours, and conspiracy to defraud and to commit perjury by falsely registering the births of three unrelated children as their own triplets. They pleaded guilty to the lesser charge of making a false declaration and were fined $5,000 each.

One of the children sued her in 2007 for alleged psychiatric and psychological illnesses. She alleged that she received 'cruel and inhuman treatment' from Hamilton-Byrne and her servants, including beatings, being locked in a freezing shed overnight and being forced to take medications. She also alleged that she was given insufficient food. Her payout was estimated to be $250,000.

As at April 2015, Anne was reported to be in the dementia care wing at a nursing home in suburban Melbourne *where a handful of acolytes still cling to the belief that she is a living god and visit her regularly while behind the scenes her once plentiful assets or properties are being sold, transferred or given away. Despite this her estate is estimated to be $20m.*

(**The Family 'Living God' Fades to Grey, Estate Remains**, article by Chris Johnston, 17 May 2014 in *The Age, Melbourne, Australia;* and **Notorious Cult 'Lodge' in Legal Battle,** article by Chris Johnston, 7 April 2015 in *The Sydney Morning Herald.*)

Please see the author's blog post on this subject: http://scskillman. com/2012/07/27/mystical-experiences-and-glimpses-of-eternity-mini-series-part-2-the-curious-case-of-the-kindly-professor-and-the-cunning-cult-leader/

DID YOU ENJOY THIS BOOK?

If so, why not write a review and recommend
it to other readers?

For more from SC Skillman, visit

WWW.SCSKILLMAN.CO.UK

and

WWW.SCSKILLMAN.COM

Keep up with the latest writing news at

WWW.FACEBOOK.COM/
SCSKILLMANAUTHOR

SC Skillman on Twitter

@SCSKILLMAN

ABOUT THE AUTHOR

SC Skillman studied English Literature at Lancaster University. She has previously worked within a BBC radio production office and later spent four years in Australia. She now lives in Warwickshire with her husband David, their son Jamie and daughter Abigail.